A Life's Full Summer

A Life's
Full Summer

ANDRÉE MARTINERIE

A Helen and Kurt Wolff Book
Harcourt Brace Jovanovich, Inc.
New York

First American edition

ISBN 0–15–151900–5

Library of Congress Catalog Card Number: 76–124835

Printed in the United States of America

Originally published in France under the title L'Eté d'une Vie

To the memory of my mother,
and to my dear ones

I

The curtains were drawn, and in the room's yellow twilight the candles crowded on top of the cake lit up the faces turned towards Marc as he uncorked a bottle of champagne. Cécile and the children watched silently, their smiles a little anxious, but the operation was skilfully performed. For a moment Marc held the bottle upright and smoking in his hand before pouring out the wine for his wife, his elder daughter, his younger daughter, his son, and lastly for himself. Then, looking at Cécile affectionately, he solemnly raised his glass and said, 'Many happy returns, darling.' Laura, the younger girl, burst out laughing and was the first to echo him: 'Many happy returns, Maminette'; then they all repeated it several times, clinked glasses and drank; their laughter and their kisses mingled, and they all blew on the candles to help Cécile, who was getting nowhere fast.

Laura drew back the heavy curtains and once again the sun shone in on satin, velvet, upholstery, glass, the day-old dust on the polished furniture, the crumpled newspapers, the cigarette-ash on the coffee-tables and all the untidiness of a Sunday morning at home.

Nathalie had put a fat parcel with a red rose on it by Cécile's plate. Laura stood there, waiting. But Cécile took her time, smelling the flower, hefting the parcel, struggling with the knots, reverently parting the tissue-paper, sniffing at the contents, delaying the discovery of what she knew must be a handbag. She had scarcely uttered a most con-

7

vincing cry of surprise and delight when Laura said, 'If you don't like it you can change it, you know. I told the shop.'

'The saleswoman in the shop,' muttered Stéphane. Laura made a face at him.

'It's lovely, lovely,' Cécile was saying. 'I'd never dreamt of such a lovely bag.' She lifted it on the palms of her hands. 'It's exactly the colour of my new shoes.'

'I told Laura to take one to match it,' said Nathalie.

'Did you guess it might be a bag?' Laura asked.

'If you've got any reservations about it'—Stéphane stuck to his point—'it can be changed, as she says.'

'It's a splendid bag,' said Marc.

She looked at them all, her three big children sitting round the table with her husband at the head. Stéphane's eyes had taken on an anxious, doubtful look, a look he had had even in his kindergarten days, when he unfolded his fat little hand to show the present he had made at school for Christmas or Mother's Day—a tiny plaited basket, a plasticine salt-cellar or a poem: for the child never thought his gifts worth giving, and he dreaded present-giving occasions.

Next to him, Nathalie, still immature despite being twenty-two; she had drunk a good deal of wine at lunch but had not managed to lose her pallor. Between mouthfuls she drank as she smoked—nervously, in little sips, her thoughts elsewhere, picking at her food without knowing what was on her plate, her whole being reaching out—not without a certain brassiness—beyond this family feast towards the real feasts and delights of her own life.

Laura, with her sooty eyelids, her white cheeks and her wonderfully innocent expression, looked like a sweet-natured clown. She was a great reader of illustrated magazines and had a passion for accessories, so it was she

8

who had undertaken the buying of the present. She was still solemn, the pretty bow of her mouth tensed, awaiting vindication of her choice.

Marc sat smoking between his two daughters, full-faced, thick-haired, happy.

They were sitting round this table in the places which had been theirs for years—ever since the children had been able to sit up: Cécile herself nearest the door, to be close to the kitchen, opposite Marc and between the two youngest, Stéphane and Laura. They had escaped so many dangers and were destined to face so many more, but once again they were all there, her own flesh and blood, there for her birthday.

But the candles pulled from the cake, their rose-shaped holders chocolate-stained, now lying extinguished and jumbled on a plate, those candles whose number, no matter how great, was always less than the actual number of years they celebrated, cried out that the moment was already past, that this birthday had already joined the host of former birthdays, that this air of continuity was deceptive, that family rituals were no more than a pitiful dam set up by frail hands against an ocean, that time was hastening towards dispersal and death, and that sooner or later this family, like all other families, would fall apart.

Cécile was still holding her children's present above the table, like the Blessed Sacrament, and it was to her husband that she turned for help and refuge; but Marc only smiled kindly at her and said:

'Aren't you going to open the bag and look inside?'

She guessed from their air of detachment that Marc's surprise would be hidden somewhere in an inside pocket; but she said again, 'I think it's lovely,' meaning 'Never mind: practicality comes after pleasure.' And she played with the catch, a little self-assured gilt knot—'Delicate,' she said, 'as delicate as the flourish after a splendid name'—before embarking on an exploration interspersed with ecstatic remarks, and deliberately avoiding a zip-fastener. When she finally pronounced the bag to be as useful as it was elegant, had asserted that it was the perfect bag, exactly the kind she liked, only more beautiful, more fashionable and more magnificent than she could ever have dreamt of, even lovelier inside than out, she shut it again.

Laura protested at once. 'But you haven't looked all through!'

So, teasing them, she went back to her slow exploration. 'Oh, I hadn't noticed this pocket . . . Oh, there's an envelope inside . . . an envelope addressed to me . . .'

Marc blew out his cheeks and turned his head from side to side, gazing upwards, elaborately unconcerned.

'You can be so maddening,' Laura said.

At this Cécile opened the envelope and, keeping her daughter at arm's length as she tried to lean over to read the note, she smiled at Marc and folded the paper. 'Thank you, darling,' she said. 'Thank you, children. What a splendid birthday. Thanks to you I shall be the most elegant woman in Paris this spring.' Then she kissed them again, one after the other, right round the table. Eyes closed, she immersed herself in the family flesh: the corner of Marc's mouth, gentle and bristly; Laura's neck, with the childishness and weakness nestling under her fine round cheeks; the two furrows in Stéphane's forehead that her caress smoothed out for a moment; then her kiss slid questing over Nathalie's smooth, reserved face.

All three children were behaving as though they were ten years old. 'What has Papa given you? Tell us,' they clamoured. 'What has he given you? Can we read it?'

'Shall we let them read it?' asked Cécile.

Marc grunted.

Laura had snatched the paper; now she read out pompously, 'With my best wishes to the esteemed and estimable forty-year-old. This is a voucher for half a spring suit.'

There was an immediate outcry. '*Half* a suit! The skinflint! He's not exactly generous.'

'Pretty good for a civil servant,' said Marc, with unruffled good-humour. 'I have several women to dress, and you're all very stylish.'

Noble, stern father, impish children, virtuous but coquettish mother: they were going through their old act.

'What about the other half? Who's going to pay for that?'

'If I work fast,' said Cécile, 'I may have finished my translation by the autumn.'

'You mean you won't be able to afford the suit right away?' asked Stéphane.

Immediately she wanted to kiss him again, although she was advised to treat him as a man: she wanted to rock him in her arms, this poor darling who always took everything so seriously.

'Of course I can afford it,' she said. 'Don't worry. I shall certainly treat myself to the other half of my suit. You wouldn't want your mother to be badly dressed, with such a lovely bag.'

'I hesitated for ages between two models,' Laura said. 'There was another that was like this—look, I'll draw it for you. A more classical style, with two gussets. Personally, I think this one is younger—more fun. The other one was the sort of bag you choose for yourself. This one's with it.' Laura pursed her lips in a patronizing kiss to the empty air for the indifferent taste of a mother who really rather liked being teased.

'A with-it bag is just the thing for a woman of forty,' said Cécile.

Marc looked at the sky and then at his watch. 'The

champagne's getting warm,' he said. 'What about this cake: are we going to eat it?'

But they no longer wanted food, drink or anything else, and Nathalie, pulling a face which meant her eyes were bigger than her stomach, asked, 'May I leave it?'

They left the birthday champagne at the bottom of their crystal goblets and the remains of the cake on their plates with the pattern of pale flowers. Cécile looked at the bunch in the centre of hers. 'These plates always remind me of Thursdays at my grandmother's when I was a little girl. She used to have all her grandchildren to the house every Thursday. We either had floating islands for tea or chocolate blancmange, one one week, one the other, invariably. When the flowers showed at the bottom of my plate it was dreadful, for then I knew the party was over.'

'You never tell us about your childhood, nor about the time when you were young,' said Nathalie with a sudden intense eagerness. 'Why not?'

Cécile looked quickly away and said, 'I'm no good at "I remember".' There was something very like hostility or a legitimate defensive reaction in her terse reply.

'How old were you when the war started?' asked Laura.

'Seventeen.'

'That's why.'

'How do you mean, that's why?'

'You were happy before, and then all of a sudden . . .'

'No,' said Cécile. 'No, that's not it.' She grew confused, smiling vaguely. 'It's more that in a sort of way the past seems to me still present, or else it's utterly lost. I don't know. I find it hard to talk about.'

They had escaped so many dangers and were fated to scatter; but once again, those who at this moment belonged to her were all here round the table for her birthday—the birthday of an ageing woman. Already she saw them as in a photograph, a souvenir of the chance events that had kept them together and safe for so long, a picture of happiness and also of distress; she saw the companion from whom sooner or later, in one way or another, she would be sundered; she saw these grown children who would presently leave her. It is rather that I no longer believe sufficiently in existence, and that nothing, neither past nor present, seems to me quite real any longer, she thought. Yet in fact it was she who was unobtrusively leaving them and drifting towards that enchanting time when her own meant nothing to her, a time deeper than memories, as imperative as the future, a vast uneventful expanse in which she had floated receptively, her heart and senses wide open, as though in the love of God—the time that had been before them and would be after them.

'I must go and do some work,' Stéphane announced.

'Right now?' asked Marc. 'Why not go out for a bit? It's a lovely day.' From where they sat they could see a great patch of blue sky.

'I must work the whole afternoon.'

'Get some fresh air first,' Cécile urged. 'At least go for an hour's walk in the Bois.'

'Much fun that would be on a day like this!'

'Then go somewhere else. How about the town? Paris is lovely on summer Sundays. Couldn't you telephone Raymond?'

'Raymond's in the country.'

'Leave him alone,' said Marc. 'It's only a month to the exam.'

'If we had a place in the country,' said Nathalie, 'we could go and prepare for exams there. We could work out of doors. It would be a lot nicer than being shut up in a bedroom in Paris.' She said *Paris* as she might have said *hell*. For some time now the town had filled her with loathing.

13

'What do you expect me to buy a place in the country with?' asked Marc.

'I've no idea, but everybody has one.'

'What you call everybody,' said Marc.

'No. People much less well-off than we are have one—the girl who does my hair, for instance.'

'I hadn't reckoned with your hairdresser.'

'It's perfectly true,' Laura said. 'You two don't know how to manage properly. Everyone has a place in the country. All you have to do is to sell your land.'

The old argument was going to start again. The old objections would be raised—the difficulty of finding a spot both quiet and accessible for the weekend; the problem of heating in winter, with its attendant solutions—gas, fuel oil, butane, propane, radiators, solid fuel, immersion heater, emptying the pipes; the question of domestic help; the question of taxes. And she, Cécile, would say that she could already picture the encampment on Sunday mornings, with beds everywhere, twenty of the children's friends in a five-roomed house (for naturally they would never be able to afford a big country house and servants), queues outside the bathroom, and of course all the work left for her. And no money, debts more likely, the day the children got married or some emergency happened. Then would come the arguments designed to sweep away all these objections: agonising reappraisals, promises. But in the end Marc and Cécile would conclude that keeping up two houses on a civil servant's pay would be difficult, without private means. Once again they would wonder how in the world others managed; they would observe that other people drove themselves to death to amass possessions, whereas they were much freer as they were; nevertheless, they would be irritable, dissatisfied with themselves and with the children, for it was perfectly true that they were bad managers and that their fastidious dislike of material problems was partly due to mental laziness. And it was only too true that the children were spoilt and that, grown up as they were, they could not be relied upon to give a helping hand.

Yet the parents, too, hankered after a house in the country, as they hankered after life with a capital L, love, the song of birds, continuity, time recaptured, solitude, grandchildren and friends with whom they might at last share their bread, their days and their nights. They had several mental pictures of this kind of happiness, picked up while travelling the roads of the Ile-de-France, Burgundy, Normandy or Provence; thumbing through magazines; visiting friends; or looking at other people's photographs. The photographs showed an enchanting ruin behind a clump of willows; a thatched cottage at the edge of a pond; a big southern-style peasant's house surrounded by cypresses; a squat farmhouse at the far end of a farmyard, its grey stone-tiled roof scarcely higher than its high walls; the privacy of a garden in the shadow of the church; wrought-iron outer gates; palm trees stroking flat roofs; dazzling landscapes. These mental pictures were so powerful and their appeal so varied and seductive that the argument promptly went off on another track. They would give up the idea of the week-end cottage in exchange for a holiday house in the real country, farther away from Paris. But in that case, they would object, we should be forced to go there for holidays —no more travelling, no more abroad, no more sea. Yes, these things would still be possible because they could let the house and the rent would pay for holidays staying at an hotel; they could . . .

'Please,' Cécile said, 'let's not go through all that again on my birthday. It's all been said a hundred times before and you know quite well that for the moment we don't want to have a house in the country.'

'I suppose you'll come round to it when we've all left home?' Laura said nastily.

Perhaps; when the children had all left home, when the grown-ups, the old people, could really benefit. When the place would be pleasure and nothing else; when the money they earned would be enough for their needs; when they could ignore time and meals; be free and alone, harmoniously attuned to each other, stretched out in the sun amid the general immobility, with nobody demanding attention. Or when this flat was so quiet that the desire for communal life could reassert itself; when life acquired that marvellous to-and-fro that one dreamed of, alternating from numbers to seclusion, from nearness to withdrawal, from noise to quietness; when time, instead of buffeting them, had been mastered. And when she, Cécile, would no longer be the only woman in this family.

'I'll make the coffee, shall I?' Nathalie offered. 'How many cups?'

And Cécile felt herself too well obeyed, sentenced without debate, torn from the comfort of sitting with her elbows on the table, cheated, yes, cheated: just like Laura, who asked sharply, 'You mean you know how to make coffee?'

'In the new coffee-machine?'

'In the new coffee-machine.'

How superior Nathalie could be sometimes. Nevertheless, Cécile suspected her of using the new coffee-machine according to a peculiar and dangerous method of her own—she would shortly have a chance of displaying her ability to cope. She was not so very far from the odious state of being grown-up. It would soon be her turn to show what she was capable of. She would have a dream house, a dream life; she would join a model community; she would rediscover everything on earth.

'Turn the gas down. The flame catches the bottom of the coffee-pot.'

'I'll watch it.'

How white and fragile Nathalie was! She touched your heart even as she vexed you. If they wanted, if they really wanted, they *could* buy that place in the country. The whole thing depended primarily on Cécile. Oh, the things these children wanted.

Cécile folded the tissue-paper that had enveloped her bag and put it back in the box; then, with her present on her lap, she sat down next to Laura by the low table, opposite Marc, who was already stretched out in his armchair.

'I'm going to work,' Stéphane said again.

'Wouldn't you like a cup of coffee?'

'No.'

She looked at the door through which her son had disappeared. 'Poor child,' she said. 'He's not happy.'

'No one is happy when he is studying for a big exam,' Marc said cheerfully.

'He knows he's not up to the standard.'

At odd, unexpected moments you noticed that leg of his: indeed, you saw nothing else. The ravage inflicted upon childhood stabbed your heart anew. Yet it amounted to nothing—a very slight withering, scarcely a hint of a limp. For a boy, it meant nothing. How often had they said, 'For a boy it means nothing. What luck it didn't happen to one of the girls!'

'Maybe not this year,' said Marc. 'But next year he'll get through.'

'Do you really think he'll have the heart to tackle it a third time?'

'Of course he will,' said Marc.

Laura was lolling in one corner of the sofa with a disappointed look on her still unformed face. Cécile returned to her handbag. 'Do you like it?' Laura asked immediately. 'Do you really and truly like it?'

'Of course I do,' Cécile said. She sniffed the hand-sewn beige leather, lighter and softer inside. 'How nice it smells. It smells like children's new shoes . . .'

Was it Cécile who had drawn Laura's head on to her shoulder or Laura who had laid it there? Cécile rested her cheek against her daughter's hair. With one hand she stroked the bag and with the other the baby-soft skin by the ear of this adolescent who was a fully developed woman. But her caresses, though they had continued, had imperceptibly adapted themselves to Laura's growth. The child she had held to her breast, so small with legs drawn up that Cécile's two hands could nearly contain her, now took her mother into the shelter of her own body. In vain, Cécile tried to feel like a little old woman in her younger daughter's arms; Laura was still a child to her. She was still at the stage of being held in her lap.

Nathalie came back with the coffee. Cécile sat up straight, embarrassed and therefore smiling all the more at Nathalie. 'Thank you, darling,' she said. 'Your coffee smells lovely.'

When Nathalie was pleased, instead of smiling she lit up from within. The glow appeared, then vanished, just as though someone had pressed a button.

'I really can make coffee, you see,' she said.

'Who's coming with me to Margency?' asked Marc.

'Not me,' said Nathalie.

'Nor me, either,' said Cécile, who had gently disentangled herself from Laura, 'unless you really want me to.'

Marc's eyes were saying the words he did not utter: 'Do come, since it's your birthday. Be kind and come, darling; be nice to me for your birthday and let's spend the day together, with our old friends.'

She had been getting this Sunday lunch ready since the day before. It was she who had chosen the wines and the cheese, she who had cooked the *canard à l'orange*, her best dish and the symbol of family celebration, she who had taken the best glasses and china out of the cupboard. She had been busy since the day before so that, with everything ready, every detail settled beforehand, their love could burst into flower; and indeed there had been a moment when all their eyes shone in the candlelight, when Marc uncorked the champagne and their faces seemed fixed like reflections in the same water; when they gave her their presents there had been a moment . . .

'I'll come, I'd love to go to Margency,' said Laura. She had spent yesterday afternoon at the hairdresser's and preparing for the dance that night—preparations in which make-up played a large part. She had slept until past noon.

'Haven't you any work to do?' asked Cécile.

'Not really.'

She never had work to do. It seemed likely that her school year would end in failure. But Marc loathed being alone, even for half an hour's drive.

The drawing-room windows overlooked a sports ground. You could see the red surface and white lines of tennis-courts and glimpse through the lime trees' branches the athletic movements of players with elegant legs. Such movements and colours belonged to a happiness that had once been very dear to Cécile, and she had only to catch sight of the swing of a short pleated skirt to miss it bitterly.

They would play; they would stretch out in the sun on the lawn; they would repeat their familiar jokes; they would sing in chorus, in twos, in threes; they would eat Véronique's famous pear tart; and then, thoroughly content, they would separate in the soft darkness. What could be better?

'If you don't keep it up,' Marc said, 'you'll never be able to get back on form. At our age, you mustn't stop.'

At our age you mustn't stop. At our age you must; you must, at our age; at our age you mustn't. He did not stop. How did he manage to work eight hours a day in an office, write articles, read the papers and magazines, scholarly works and novels, and still play tennis?

Marc said he felt no lessening of his powers. And anyhow the others weren't stopping. Admittedly cancer, accidents and heart attacks had begun to strike here and there among the forty- and fifty-year-olds who were their friends. But it was still blind chance, without much relation to age. The stuff of life was still resilient; it closed over the holes. And all of them went on, some wearing a truss, some on a diet, some taking pills, some filled with despair and some ever young; they all went trotting on towards physical decay and death.

'I wonder how I could ever find the time to play tennis nowadays,' Cécile said.

'But you used to find it when you had much more to do at home.'

'That's true. I just don't know what has taken the place of everything I used to do then.'

She was the only one to quit before time, not because she did not find it fun or no longer liked it, but because she was now more tempted by the thought of some kind of rest she could not define, some kind of task, rearrangement, analysis, synthesis, something not unallied to the upheaval of adolescence, but without either its rich variety or its confusion. It was a clear, urgent call towards another life, a life of which she knew nothing except that it was hedged about with death; in much the same way as the future, when she was young, had promised her nothing but love and babies. To go on with what she had been doing for nearly twenty-five years, to go on without ever calling it into question, to go on with it as long as possible—that victory which most people rejoiced in perpetuating to the very end was something she dreaded to such an extent that sometimes, among her own people, among those she loved best, she felt like a wild beast at bay, instinctively fighting for survival. They never guessed it; and why, and by what right, should she tell them? In what words? She could never have explained this feeling of decay she had, nor this awareness of a new threshold, new demands. After all, she was only their mother, their housewife in the home. What talents had she displayed? What did she want? Her claims were vague and without justification.

Nonsense, she thought, perhaps it is merely that I am growing old; some fresh graspingness or a deficiency, a weariness?

Until quite recently an elasticity of spirit had allowed an instant and perpetual passage from one plane to another. One might be weeping, howling for days and nights on end, and then a rain of love would pour down upon the earth. A prismatic halo surrounded activities, other people, oneself, shimmering like an ingenuous promise of still more life. And the future was infinitely valuable. Until quite recently love, play and work were wholly love, play and work, and wholly necessary; but bound up with a certain expectation. There was no boundary between one's life and *life* itself. The other world was part and parcel of this one. All you had to do was to stay quiet for a few moments, even if only on a seat in the Métro, and something unknown, something deeply cherished, another love, a dream, a longing, a promise, began to caress you, to become articulate, to inhabit you, haunt you. High above her children's heads the young mother sailed along in her own heaven. But now the call was a silent one. It had become urgent and imperative. Work was merely work and play was merely play. Life no longer had a dream as its lining. It was interspersed with death: and even loved ones were taking the place of something unknown which was more desired than they.

'Come on,' said Marc again, 'come with me.' He looked at her affectionately. 'Come and play. Don't act the old lady.'

That was what they said about her. Remarks made affectionately behind her back, with a knowing air. They hinted that she could not reconcile herself to growing old. But how could anyone be reconciled to it? 'Poor Cécile,' they said. 'She is still charming and she is spoiling her last good years with this obsession. She's taking it very badly.' But didn't they carry on about their age? 'You're as old as you are: you're as old as your arteries, as your heart, as your tastes: you're as old as you look. You can't always be twenty. Make way for the young. Besides, when one has children . . .' They'd got it all wrong. They would not leave her alone to cope with her age as she chose. How could she say that it was actually her age that she wanted to think about, her autumn, her sunset, that evening blaze and that dawn whose call was so strong that it could be compared only with the call of love? How could she say that what she was listening to was the call of love itself? Out of affection the family had resolved to stop her birthdays at forty. Today's was actually her forty-fourth.

She let herself be a party to the game, to the nonsense, for it was easier and indeed kinder. She was as modest, as embarrassed as an adolescent used to be, and as defenceless; she said nothing, not even to Marc. Yet the rapidly changing tally of her years no longer mattered, except in so far as it continually reduced the number left to her, which seemed to her to be the years of freedom, glimpsed at last. The fear of losing her charm, which had somewhat marred her youth, had left her with youth itself. Old age seemed no less horrifying than before, but curiously enough, the closer she came to it, the more eager she was to grasp the present and the less she thought about it. Beauty dropped from her like a disguise that she had worn with vulnerable delight, knowing from the first time that it was an illusion, and a frail one. A dawn was breaking in which she saw herself with nothing left to guard but essentials, and ready for some fulfilment.

Yet in that very moment fear gave her a hundred arms to stroke, hold, retain her last child, her Laura.

'Your coffee was excellent, Nathalie,' she said, putting her cup back on the tray.

'If you go to Margency, Mama,' said Nathalie, 'you won't see Jo.'

'Jo?'

'You know all about him.'

All she knew was that, whatever happened, this afternoon was not going to belong to her.

'It was you who asked to meet him. But if you want to go to Margency, Mama, go by all means: it doesn't matter.'

'Tell me again, who is this Jo?'

'The pianist; you know perfectly well.'

'Jo what?'

'Jo Giniewsky, Jenesky, something like that.'

'They're unbelievable, these youngsters,' Marc said. 'It only needs a missed appointment and they've lost each other for ever. How are you going to look up the phone number of someone whose name you don't know?'

'I know where Jo lives,' said Nathalie. 'And he isn't on the phone. So his name doesn't matter.' She said it haughtily, with the expression she had assumed since her earliest childhood whenever she felt—and she felt it often—that family existence was desecrating her private life.

Cécile had certainly never asked to meet Jo. She would

not have dared. It was Nathalie who wanted this meeting. And impulses of this kind were rare with her.

'Is he a foreigner?' asked Marc.

'No,' said Nathalie. 'At least I don't really know. But he speaks French like you or me.'

'The name sounds Jewish.'

'Possibly.'

'I don't see why you should reply in that tone of voice,' said Marc. 'There was nothing offensive about my question.'

'What does it matter if he's a foreigner, or a Jew, or both?'

'There are occasions when it might be important.'

The maddening look on Nathalie's face had sometimes provoked exasperated slaps in her childhood. Now it was her parents whose ears were calmly boxed. 'My poor dear parents, marriage is the only thing you can think of.'

Laura got up quietly and left the room.

'I suppose it's better to hear that than to be deaf,' Cécile said evenly, 'though I sometimes wonder whether I wouldn't rather be deaf than hear certain things . . . To say marriage is the only thing we think of. We, who at this very moment . . .' She shook her head.

They had every reason to be wary of Nathalie's entanglements after those they had seen already. Far from urging marriage, they had up to now been opposed to it.

'I still don't know who's coming with me to Margency,' Marc said, showing his wish to change the subject so obviously that no one answered him. After a while he added sleepily, 'At all events, I'm going in half an hour. Let those who love me follow me.' And with his most benign expression he settled down for a nap.

Whenever there was a risk of unpleasantness, Marc preferred not to hear. Nothing would keep him from sleeping or from going to play tennis. Young or not so young, he had always done just what he wanted to do. His was an easy part to play. If Nathalie only knew how tiresome it was to be perpetually holding back, looking ahead, saving and mending. But it was the children who clipped one's wings with their unoriginal stupidities, their unreal brilliance, their unreal love-affairs and their unreal crises.

Let everyone go where he wanted to, and with whatever companion he chose. All that she, Cécile, wanted was peace, one afternoon's peace in her bedroom, for her birthday. 'Yes, Marc, do go to Margency; but go without me. Yes, Stéphane, do work all day and whatever you do, don't get any fresh air. Yes, Nathalie, by all means fling yourself into Jo's arms without even knowing his name. Yes, Laura, have as much fun as you can; after all, you'll never have to earn your own living, or will you? But I'm going to read this afternoon, I'm going to rest, I'm going to have a wonderful time. I'm through, thank God, with all those things that worry you and that are no business of mine, as you keep telling me.' The two women of the house, the two opponents were alone together, face to face in the untidy room; and their ankles, their hands, their eyes and the colour of their hair were the same.

But the daughter had a hard look on her face and the mother seemed tired and bewildered.

'You wouldn't like me to introduce Jo to you, I suppose?'

Why of course Nathalie had already asked her. She had asked in an offhand, casual way, but a light had come into her face. She had lowered her eyelids at once and her glance had fled sideways, like a quick animal in the undergrowth. She had had the look of a doe when she asked if she might bring him.

'I don't really want to go to Margency all that much,' Cécile said. 'So if you like, I could stay and see your Jo.'

'As you wish,' said Nathalie.

'It's not *as I wish*. I said *if you like*: I could have a cup of tea with you both.'

Nathalie was obviously remembering that it was her mother's birthday and settling for peace. 'I'll call you just when it's ready to pour out,' she said. 'Then you can have a rest first.'

Sometimes Nathalie was thoughtful like this: sometimes she did stir her wings. Then she would leave you, dissatisfied with yourself.

She carried the coffee tray out and Cécile was left alone, next to Marc, who was sleeping in his armchair with a gentle steam-engine noise. What did she, Cécile, sitting in this pretty sunlit room upholstered in jade-green chintz, really know about life? What advice could she still give? What experience could she hand out? What did she know about the advantages of reason and the benefits of folly? She knew nothing. She was afraid, that was all. From now on she wanted to be left alone and no longer to have that feeling of being perpetually pulled by the arm, by the leg, by the heart, of being at one and the same time powerless, cast off yet still responsible. All that she had had to say, those few things of which she was certain, she had said already. And these children were so grown-up, as everybody was always telling her: 'At twenty-two your daughter no longer needs looking after. You're an adult at twenty-two. She knows more about things than you do.'

Fine, fine.

But Nathalie was still at school; she would not have her interpreter's diploma before autumn even if all went well. Nathalie was pale; Nathalie was delicate. Sometimes she was hare-brained. 'My poor mother, marriage is the only thing you can think of.' In fact, marriage was the only thing Nathalie could think of. If a young man had some slight connection with music or the theatre, or with writing, she imagined she was in the company of a genius. She was so naive. 'That's her look-out,' people said. And the psychologists, psychiatrists, sociologists, journalists, queens of correspondence columns, advice-mongers who were all quite free from doubt with their little humane, pacifying, understanding, professional and minimizing smiles, did not tell the whole truth. There was that recent report on girls—unmarried girls: 'Michèle is twenty-one; she has a nine-month-old boy; she is studying science at the university. She has had the courage not to marry her child's father and to return to her life as a single girl with her parents, who are bringing up the baby.' She was asked if she loved her family. 'I love those who love me,' replied Michèle proudly. No one mentioned whether the parents were well housed, whether they had enough room, whether they were in good health, whether they had help, whether they had money, whether they were happy. No one asked the parents' views on anything. But then, had women now over forty ever been asked their views? But if Nathalie had a child by this Jo, this pianist, who would look after it? People would not think Nathalie grown-up enough then. They would drop their little smiles and take on moralizing airs to preach—at Cécile, of course. 'You certainly let her run pretty free,' they would say. 'But these days it's no longer a tragedy.' They would say, 'Bring the baby up.' As if there were any need to say it. 'It will give you a great deal of satisfaction.' What did they mean with their 'you'? Someone who had already been doing it for twenty-two years, who was no longer the age for it and who would rather die than begin again!

She counted: she knew three for certain among Nathalie's friends who had had abortions; there was even another, a mini-skirted schoolfriend of Laura's, who had had hers on a kitchen table. She had told the whole class about it. Laura had been physically sick. But now she was fascinated by this girl.

Four of them had been pregnant when they married. Everything has changed, they said. Girls are free. You only have children when you want them. But it was quite obvious that love was still a matter of life and death.

Nathalie gave herself airs. She said, 'What does it matter?' She liked it to be understood that she lived as the spirit moved her and in the immediate present with all that fine freedom that came so naturally to Belmondo and Macha Meryl and Anna Karenina. But the slightest hurt made her turn pale, and her face puckered up like a baby's the moment any trap threatened to close upon her.

To her surprise, Cécile found she was formulating good wishes for the success of the 'total defence', as the television called it, though saying with the same breath that nothing of the kind existed yet. Total defence, atomic war. And she reflected that, nevertheless, she was glad this pill had come too late for her; she preferred having lived otherwise, with that element of danger that gave love its tragic dimension and that had earned her the treasure of Laura, not wanted but not refused either, like so many babies, after all— Laura, whom she would never have chosen to bring into the world if she had had a 'total defence' at her disposal. And could you really choose to give anyone life, when you had any knowledge of what life really was?

She reflected that her daughters seemed rather revolted than otherwise by this promised freedom, this banquet. They said people talked too much about it, that love was going to end by frightening or disgusting them. They wanted the inspired, romantic impulse, trust in the man, the pair alone together and the acceptance of their fate. They said it was the older women who were so enthusiastic about contraception. A sort of verbal love-making. But

28

Nathalie also claimed the utmost freedom. There was certainly cause for alarm. If Nathalie had a child, she would trample over it rather than not go just where she wanted to go.

The ideas went on turning in Cécile's slightly wine-befuddled head.

'Women of my generation, will your motherhood and your responsibilities never end? Will the journalists, the writers and all the gossips who establish the moral code never once look in your direction? It is terrible to think that; you never manage to be at the age when people pay attention to you—you are always too young or too old. When you were children you were literally small fry. When you were twenty, there was the war: let's say no more about that. You only just missed being juvenile delinquents, but you did miss. As young wives you were automatically dedicated to the maintenance of the race and your highly-principled men began to move about the world again without you.

'But your babies, your children, your young people—oh, what treasures! You were told often enough how much you owed them and how they called for all the care you could provide. And now here we are, and there is no end, especially for your daughters. They are the ones who matter now. The best thing society has been able to devise to ensure the utmost development of these young women who are used to taking and giving nothing in return, who are now the age that you were when you brought them into the world, is the institution of grandmothers. It has just been rediscovered that adults too have their needs; but only young adults, not those of your age. Never those of your age. That scrap of inner freedom which you have preserved with so much labour, that lifebelt in the sea of responsibilities into which all these irresponsible creatures have flung you, that last hope, that ultimate poetry, that need—behold them all threatened, besieged once more by washing and cleaning, by whinings and snivellings, by the necessity of giving orders, by grazed knees and grubby fingers, and nightmares, and tidying, always tidying, because you still have to bring up your grandchildren. They explain to you that your daughters need this, and perhaps the grandchildren too, for, without you, they might find themselves quite cast adrift.'

Those Polish friends the other day had said how in their country too grandmothers were returning to work in young households so as to allow the wives to have a job, to train and to enjoy their husbands. They said that this cheering sociological fact was called the grandmothers' renaissance. It was certainly good for the country's economy. And apparently the grandmothers were delighted at finding that they were still of some use. How Cécile dreaded that particular renaissance! What a splendid article she could write on the subject; or what a talk she could give to an audience of dissatisfied middle-aged women, complete with touching reminiscences which would be thoroughly appreciated by those who were twenty in the war and thirty during the 'fifties: the humour she could put in, and the sly digs she could make! It was already there in her head.

But Marc's quiet snoring, as soothing as a woman's lap, the stillness, the kindness of the objects around her, and the blue sky calmed her mind. She looked at the peaceful room, the window softly lit behind its white net curtain. What had happened? What had Nathalie done? What had she said?

It needed only a word or a look to touch off these harangues, these inward, disconnected ramblings, just as though the child presented some threat; it needed only a word or a look from Nathalie for her mother to feel wounded in a familiar yet indefinable way.

Cécile was ashamed. She turned back to that little girl who one day had asked her, 'I suppose you wouldn't like me to introduce Jo to you, Mama?'

The desire to write her article or give her talk left her. It was these wretched articles, lectures, ill-considered speeches, this pseudo-sociology and pseudo-psychology, these dubious investigations, these films that worked up fear and aggression, these were what gave each generation a stereotyped picture of the others, persuaded Nathalie that her mother was a woman of limited experience who wanted to oppress her, and gave Cécile the feeling that she was threatened by all these young people who were encouraged to make every sort of demand before they were capable of undertaking any responsibility. The hell with that commonplace way of thinking.

Once again Cécile envisaged herself quite free, wandering with Marc through gardens and cities, those opulent friends of one's later days. She saw herself alone for hours on end, set free by age, open at last to the ineffable, to the pointless, the surreal, to everything that had always been brushed aside, postponed, never listened to, because of the pressure of everyday life and because of the conserving, preserving role that those who hand on life are morally obliged to assume. Now it was over, or nearly. Her time of motherhood was drawing to its close. An open, clear-cut life was unfolding, one in which she was going to move about, as free as a man.

On this, her forty-fourth birthday, Cécile had the feeling that the tide of life was on the rise. She believed in the value of the sequence of events, instincts and duties that had carried her along so far; but she also believed in the nobility of the way of life and freedom that was to come after them. She believed in the adventure of the third age and in the setting-free of vital energy that had for too long been taken up with the preservation of the species. It seemed to her that middle age was the time in which the promise of adolescence was fulfilled. The children's call for freedom was echoed by their mother's. 'The time of love is about to begin,' Cécile said to herself, and she saw this time as one of regal impunity and of an exhilarating lack of responsibility.

Marc stretched and saw her sitting opposite him, not dressed to go out. 'Well, I'm off,' he said. 'You really won't come?'

'I can't,' she said. 'The one time Nathalie wants to introduce a young man to us.'

'It can't be very important,' said Marc, and he hesitated before adding, 'Does she still see Alain?'

'Oh, Alain!' Cécile spread her hands.

Marc wrinkled his brow, as though straining towards a lost horizon and its stability. 'Personally, I liked Alain.'

'So did I. But perhaps it's too early to be using the past tense. Oh, by the way,' she said unexpectedly, 'Nathalie's portrait fell down in the night. The string had broken.'

'Is it damaged?'

'No. Luckily it was caught and wedged between the chest-of-drawers and the wall. I didn't know what on earth had happened. I heard a sudden noise, like a door being flung open. I called out "Who's there?" and when no one answered I got up and saw the picture.'

'Well, so long as it's not damaged . . .'

'No.'

She said it hesitantly, trying to formulate some other idea, trying to comfort herself, but she gave it up. She was well aware that fate did not despise obvious symbols of this kind. The tragic events of her life had often—often, or always?—been preceded by some startling portent, such as the cripple Stéphane had pointed at the day before he

32

became one himself, as though . . . But Marc said all such signs were invented, perceived only after the event.

'Only the wall was scraped,' Cécile added.

'You aren't coming, then?'

'No. I'd like to see this Jo.'

'Didn't Laura say she would come with me?'

'Yes,' said Cécile.

'Is she ready?' He looked at his wife reproachfully. What had she been up to while he was dozing? He called loudly, 'Laura! Laura!'

But Laura did not answer. In her room, where Cécile found her, the record player was going full blast.

She was ready. She was wearing a sweater that showed her navel, Bermuda shorts that (unlike her skirts) came almost to her knees, socks and brand-new two-colour shoes. A cyclist's outfit. With her head thrown back and a haggard, tragic expression, she was dancing, making slow, cabalistic gestures towards the sky. For a few moments after Cécile's arrival she kept it up, a Laura such as her mother had never seen. Then she stopped and gave Cécile a baby-faced smile.

'Your father's just going, Laura. Are you ready?' Cécile's eyes had already settled on her daughter's feet. 'You're not going to wear those new shoes for running about the fields?'

'I haven't any old ones left,' said Laura. Her eyes grew fierce again: she was trembling.

'What do you mean, you haven't any left?'

'All my old shoes are completely ruined.'

Cécile opened her mouth again, but said nothing. She looked into the cupboard. It was true: the old shoes were completely ruined. Battered, corrugated, turned-up, torn, smelly. The shoe-trees, no longer matching, lay in a heap.

33

It was not feet these girls possessed, but steam-rollers. Yet to see them out of doors, all neat and demure . . .

'Oh do switch off that racket,' said Cécile. 'Your father's waiting for you. Find your tennis shoes—anything. You might be able to play too.'

Laura did not like games. She thought she was too big already, and she was afraid of putting on muscle, which would make her legs look like a man's. 'You needn't think I'm going to play tennis,' she said. 'Fat chance anyone's going to want to play with me.'

'Where are your tennis shoes?'

'Who do you expect me to play with?'

'Turn off that record, *please*.'

The machine gave a short groan. 'Someone's pinched them,' Laura said.

Marc appeared in the doorway. 'Is she coming?'

'Yes,' said Cécile. 'Yes, she's coming.'

'Why say it like that?' asked Marc. 'I've got to go, haven't I?'

'I should like her to take her tennis shoes,' said Cécile, 'and they have disappeared. If she wears those new shoes all over the place at Margency . . .'

'She's fine as she is,' Marc interrupted. 'Come on, Laura, or it won't be worth going.'

'Oh,' moaned Cécile. But still she would not give in. 'Where were your tennis shoes stolen?'

'At school, of course. Everything gets pinched there.' Marc burst out laughing.

'The Giraudons will lend me espadrilles, don't worry, Maminette,' said Laura, kissing her mother.

'Of course they will,' Marc said.

'And what happened to all the rest of your gym things and your track suit?'

34

'Stolen too,' Laura said.

Marc kissed Cécile.

Shoes one hundred francs, track suit fifty, sandals ten: ruin. They ought to give Laura a set allowance for all her expenses, as they had done for Nathalie, and let her manage for herself. But it hadn't worked with Nathalie.

'Goodbye, darling,' said Marc. 'Don't worry.'

It was all very well for Marc. He did not trouble about these details. He floated above it all. He made game of her and the children took advantage of it. But when it came to wringing money out of him . . .

'Please don't drive too fast. They said on the TV . . .'

But the telephone rang and Laura had already snatched up the receiver. In the curt new voice she had adopted for answering boys she said, 'This is Laura.' Then, covering the mouthpiece with one hand, she turned to her parents. 'It's Didier,' she whispered. 'He wants to know if I can go to the cinema with him.' She was suddenly all eyes, blazing with delight. Marc shrugged and Cécile made her usual doubtful, consenting gesture, her hands apart. It would have required great cruelty to refuse. 'You don't mind, Papa?' Laura whispered.

Papa, who knew what he wanted and was well aware that nobody was going with him, was already on his way to the front door, saying, 'I'm going to make the most of the sunshine.'

And while Laura, resuming her telephone voice, said, 'All right, I'll be there,' he departed by himself, followed and kissed on the landing by Cécile, who watched him reappearing on each landing, smaller and smaller, more and more distant, more and more beloved.

She stayed leaning over the banisters for a few seconds after she had heard the outer door of the building shut, with the feeling, the foreboding, the recollection that that was how people left you for ever, sometimes. And if she had not been afraid of appearing quite insane she would have run after Marc to tell him to wait and that never mind she had decided to come with him.

Laura had already changed her shorts for a skirt and her socks for wide-meshed white net stockings. All the drawers and doors in her room were open. The shorts and socks lay in a heap on the floor. She was putting on the jacket of a dazzlingly new suit.

'Are you off already?' asked Cécile.

'We're going to the two o'clock performance.'

'But it's half past already.'

'The main feature doesn't begin until half past.'

'But you won't get there before three. Where is it?'

'Oh, I don't know, Maminette,' groaned Laura.

'What film is it?'

'I don't know.'

'Ring Didier back and ask him. I don't like this.'

'Oh, Mama, Didier's already waiting for me. He said he'd go down and wait for me at the bottom of the stairs.' In her smart suit, all ready to go, her eyes ringed with mascara, Laura was on the edge of tears. All right, all right. 'Don't look like that, Maminette. You know Didier. You don't have to worry.'

'But I don't want you to see just any old film,' Cécile continued weakly.

'No, of course you don't.'

As they kissed the daughter felt her mother's love, her pain, her distress at always having to be a wet-blanket, and that she was at the end of her tether; and Cécile knew that Laura knew, did not blame her for it and even pitied her for having to play such a role.

The bedroom was a shambles. But observations on tidiness would have to wait for another time. 'Have fun.'

'Yes.' Laura gave a feeble smile. 'I hope he'll have waited for me.'

'He will,' Cécile said. 'Of course he will.'

Laura took the elevator down, which gave her time to give her mother another kiss, a hearty smack that wiped out the anxieties, scruples, blemishes, and restored everything to rights.

'Brrr . . .' Cécile shivered, closing the door of the flat. Stéphane and Nathalie were busy in their rooms, as usual. There was no sound anywhere. For a moment, as she stood in the hall, she felt like a tree putting its leaves straight after a storm.

She refrained from going and tidying Laura's bedroom and closed the door firmly. But in the dining-room she came up against the table, still covered with dirty dishes. She cleared it. The kitchen was chaos too. She could have asked Stéphane and Nathalie to help. But they were not much use and they would have said, 'Well, that's just fine! We were working, and now we get roped in to do the washing-up while Laura goes to the cinema . . .' Besides, she would rather have peace than help.

The kitchen was the quietest room in the flat, the only one that opened on to the courtyard. Two months ago you saw nothing but lovely trees from the window. For a long while Cécile had dreamt of moving the kitchen and making this her own room. Standing in front of the sink with her rubber-gloved hands churning the crockery in the dirty water, she was at once out of doors, among the birdsong, and in that bed which would be put there some day, looking out at the sky and the greenery, that solitary dreamer's bed in which her life would draw to its close.

The building that was going up made the idea less attractive, but there were still two fine horse-chestnuts, and on the right the house did not yet hide the sky and perhaps never would, for the nearest sections, already roofed, were only one storey—probably garages.

Holding them up to the window, Cécile looked through the heavy cut-glass goblets. She could feel the facets under the dishcloth. Gently, ranged according to size, she set them on a tray, just not touching one another. They covered the whole surface. She put them away in the cupboard, the biggest at the back, then the medium-sized, and then the little ones. Next to them, the champagne flutes. The glasses filled the whole shelf. They were very nearly touching, but not quite. She loved them.

The old china was difficult to wash and needed several rinsings. Side by side on the draining-board stood the white and gold plates, with their scalloped edges. The lid of the vegetable-tureen had little protuberances, as though the man who made it had caressed it. The coffee-pot, with its long neck, wasp waist, fragile spout and air of an elegant young woman of 1900, called for particular care. Cécile put the silver back in its cases, back in its bed of green or crimson velvet, the teaspoons and the ivory- or pearl-handled knives with their silver blades.

Perched on a stool, she slowly took down the piles of plates, the big dishes and the sauce-boats that were never used; she stepped down, set them on the table, climbed on to the stool again loaded with another pile of plates, dishes and sauce-boats. She put everything back into the cupboards according to her own private system. It was beautiful china, though it did not match; it was inherited, brought out of family attics; for long unvalued, and all the more unmatched for that very reason. But in the last few years the value of what remained had increased and Cécile now kept it for family celebrations. She insisted upon washing and arranging these things herself. The only person she would willingly share it with was her mother, when her mother visited Paris. On these occasions, as the two women stood, one by the sink and the other by the cupboard, their movements took on the same rhythm, hands stretching out, arms reaching up in a ritual. And from this ritual a harmony developed between them and they felt elated.

When the telephone rang Cécile started so violently that the china rattled. But no one called her. So much the better.

There were still plenty of the more unpleasant things to clean—the casseroles, stove, oven, saucepans. Maria would see to them tomorrow morning. It needed a certain effort of will not to finish the task of restoring order and cleanliness, for all at once Cécile noticed dirty marks everywhere between the kitchen and the dining-room, round the door-knobs, on the walls, on the windows and on the carpet. She picked up a wet cloth, soap and a dry duster, then put them down again. No, she would not do it. She would resist that well-known momentum which led her, especially when she was tired, to want the place clean and to go on and on without stopping.

But in the very moment of making this effort of will a dissatisfaction, an old sore, began nagging at her. It was less than a year since the kitchen, the hall and the dining-room had been redecorated. It was the girls who had wanted that jade green for the dining-room, that not really washable paper for the hall and the light-coloured carpet. Oh, they had made promises by the dozen—at the time. All gone with the wind. They did not choose to use the doorknobs; they walked barefoot out of the bathroom; they ate chocolate while watching the television. They would not take the slightest trouble to save her work and irritation. They thought themselves free and bohemian because of their untidiness, but they were turning her into a stupid housewife who thought of nothing but chores, mending and money, and was no longer capable of thinking of anything else when she saw all this dirt everywhere. Yet they were not ill-natured.

'Martha, Martha,' she said to herself, 'thou art careful and troubled about many things: but one thing is needful.'

But they were not camping out, nor living in luxury; they were not even living in a bohemian manner. Someone had to keep busy in this flat—everything got so dirty and ugly so soon. In the old days her mother used to say, 'Our home is not so splendid that it can afford not to be clean.'

Cécile resented the Marys, those strong-minded, selfish women, those aristocrats who flourished on the labour of others. From her room Nathalie could perfectly well hear her moving about at this moment. But she would never come and offer to help. It was even possible that the noise of the washing-up irritated her, as the noise of the saucepans and dishes had once vexed Cécile when her mother clattered them in the kitchen next to the little dining-room where she and her brother—the children of those days, the students —were having lunch with their father, the dreamer, the philosopher, helping themselves, arguing, heedlessly gulping down the food which her mother had cooked. Sometimes she would complain from the kitchen, 'Wait for me: I can't hear what you're saying.' They would break off for a moment, but then the ideas and the words would sweep them along. Maman would come back with a dish, having lost the thread of the conversation: she would be silent, and would sit silent, sulking, brooding. They would be cross with her for being a Martha.

Cécile suddenly remembered how one day, when they

came back from school, her mother greeted them with a strange sort of smile. 'My dears, I don't know what's gone wrong, but lunch is not ready. Dear God, what will Papa say?' They had comforted her with a compassion beyond their years. Cécile remembered that childish pity very clearly. 'It doesn't matter, Maman; we'll have a sandwich. Papa won't mind.' Papa had not minded.

Yet in those days grown-ups still knew how to stop. Even the women. Even her mother. They sat down in their favourite armchairs, they read, they smoked, they did nothing, they dozed. Their need for silence lay upon the house. Even the youngest children were fenced in by respect and boredom. If there was a ring at the outer gate no one answered it. Sometimes this would last whole Sundays on end. Oh, if she could only be spared this Jo . . .

Cécile had reached her den. Two of the walls were lined with books, the third taken up by a window and the fourth opened on to the drawing-room. Once the drawing-room door was closed the noises of the flat and even the sound of the telephone bell no longer reached this room. On the other hand it was filled with the roar of the city—the stream of cars in the avenue, the trucks thundering along the near-by boulevard, the voices of people and the vibration of the Métro. And Cécile loved this town that swirled about her refuge.

The den was not a real bedroom. It was only a recess, and it was so narrow that there was no space in it for any furniture apart from Cécile's couch. To get in or out one had to go through the drawing- and dining-room because the drawing-room doors on either side of the fireplace had had to be replaced by bookshelves when the library—that is to say, the present den—could no longer hold all their books. Cécile had once been rather proud of this display of culture, but now she would willingly have made a judicious

41

selection so that the books Marc particularly cherished could go into his room and those which she had never had the time to read or re-read into hers. The others only served to block up the doorways, gather dust and cause mental distress. For they would not be read; they would never all be read. One day she would have to sort them out and give the drawing-room back at least a second door. After that they would have to redecorate again.

This might look like quite a big flat, but in fact it was too small for the number of people in it and their way of life. As the needs of the family changed, its five and a half rooms were continually altering, taking on different shapes and functions without ever reaching their true, restful crystallization.

'I ought to have a study,' Marc had said one day. 'I can't go on working in the drawing-room with all the bustle there is in it nowadays. I need a room of my own, where I can shut the door.'

The library? There was scarcely room for a table and a chair. How could he spread out all his papers? One of the girls' rooms? That would be possible if they both moved into the one Stéphane had and Stéphane went into the little room behind. But the girls would be very cramped in there, and where would they do their homework? They would do it on the dining-room table like countless other children. But in fact Cécile and Marc were both perfectly well aware that the study could only be installed in their own bedroom.

It was Cécile who had the courage to put it into words. 'We must turn our room into a study for you. It's thoroughly shut away and quiet, and very easily cleaned. You'll be fine in there.'

'Do you think there's room, with the bed?'

'No, not with the double bed. It would have to be changed for a single one. I'll go somewhere else.'

'Where?' he asked ingenuously.

So in due time, almost unnoticed, separations which had seemed unthinkable came about. Cécile had already thought it out. 'I'll go in the library. I believe there's room for a small couch in the library.'

'But would you like it in there, tucked away?'

'Yes, I think I should, for a few years. Of course, it's not the final answer. When one of the children leaves us I'll take over that room. And when the girls have gone we'll both settle in at the back.'

They smiled kindly at each other. Twenty years, thousands of nights. Twenty years, thousands of nights, breath and bodies mingled, thrown together, intertwined, a hand, a side, a foot, warmth, enwrapped all night through, thousands of nights. 'I can't sleep without you,' Marc used to say. Days and nights ran into one another. Waking up, getting up, going back to bed again, embraces, weariness, little sleeps, beds unmade, children climbing over one. Kisses, loving words, nibbling. Marc's arms round them all, one, two, three small children and Cécile, right across the big bed. The children would escape from Marc's arms, hide under the sheets, creep beneath the blankets. No one could tell whose arm he was nipping. All confused flesh, laughter, wriggling. They carried the children away, they made love; each satisfied, each unsatisfied; sparing nothing. At the end of twenty years they smiled at each other, accomplices in their separation.

Marc used to go to sleep first, almost as soon as he was in bed. She read for a long while. He moaned at her turning of the pages and because she did not put the light out. His moaning got on Cécile's nerves and delayed her dropping off. She would close her book long before she felt sleepy. Hours went by. At last she would fall asleep. But Marc would suddenly turn in bed: he had a habit of waking up at five o'clock. He did not like to put his light on. She lay mute and unstirring so as not to wake up entirely. Marc no longer used to say, 'Are you asleep? I'm not.' With somewhat equivocal care he got out of bed, quietly enough not to be accused of waking her but not so quietly that she could be wholly ignorant of his sad state and of how considerate he was being. Groping, he would find his cigarettes, his paper. He bumped into an armchair, swearing under his breath. He left the field of sleep to Cécile. Through the open doorway the light from the drawing-room diminished the darkness, making its way beneath Cécile's eyelids. Marc took a great while to come back. She looked at the alarm-clock and found that she had slept only three hours. She called to Marc, 'You'll catch cold out there.' The night was ruined and the next day would drag heavily along looking forward to bed. How dreary for both of them, those sour morning hours when each worked out what had to be done before the evening, when each found the energy for the effort lacking and each told the other.

The big double bed had gone off into storage. If one of the children married or if they bought a house in the country they might want it again. Every quarter they paid the repository a small fee for it.

As soon as it had gone the handsome square proportions of what had been their room became apparent. They redid the walls with a paper of a masculine pattern and colour and laid a tobacco-coloured carpeting on the floor, to match the curtains. Their savings and the second-hand shops provided an armchair, a filing cabinet and a Directoire desk. A planisphere covered the wall above the desk, and the TV set stood on the left. The little radio and the telephone were within hearing and hand's reach on the adjustable bedside table that could be tilted for working in bed. The lighting was excellent and well distributed. What hint of austerity

44

all this might have possessed was offset by a pretty Chinese rug, a record player and its records. At first Cécile had started putting a carafe of water and a glass on the table every night; but quite soon she stopped bothering.

The creation of this study had given Marc a pleasure similar to that of his success in the Audit Office long ago. For a while he took himself terribly seriously, going back to his desk as soon as he had finished reading *Le Monde*, and in four months he completed his book on Louvois—a book that had been dragging on for years. But now he spent more of his evenings watching television than sitting at his desk. The papers spread out on it remained open at the same page, their motion suspended, rather like the open mouth of that rectangle cut out of the arm of the sofa that was meant to fit into the first shelf of the wall bookcase they had planned to take Marc's books—a bookcase which, after five years, had still not been installed because of lack of money and energy. The absence of the bookcase in Marc's study despite the provision for it, like the torn upholstery of the handsome Louis XV armchairs in the drawing-room, the half-empty display cabinet in the dining-room, the rickety chairs and shabby beds in the children's rooms, and the many bare places on the walls and the worn old paintwork of the rooms at the back, revealed the relative poverty and carelessness of the flat's owners: but it bore witness also to a certain dynamism and a stubborn progression towards the future.

Moving as quietly and unobtrusively as a girl, Cécile had reached her den. The little alarm clock on a low shelf, next to an old casket that held handkerchiefs, pills and earplugs, said that she still had about an hour before Jo arrived. As the den was so very small its furnishing had been complete once the couch was fitted in and a few cushions thrown upon it. Although it was inconvenient in many ways, and she knew it was only temporary, Cécile loved it. Here there was no untidiness—no gaping, unfilled holes. Here objects no longer harassed her. Even the children respected this place. Here, in the flat's blind alley, Cécile found her freedom.

The den was also a bower of roses. They seemed to be everywhere. It was an Austrian friend who had sent them, a man she would certainly not recognize if she passed him in the street today. Yet Dr Erich von Fahrheim, who sent her roses every year in May, for her birthday, must surely have come to Paris now and then during the twenty years since they had met. But no doubt it was wise of him not to appear. What would they have to say to each other, he and she?

The man in civilian clothes, the only one among the uniforms and the soldiers' families, must have been about her present age or more (or maybe less, for in those days what did she know of the difference between forty, fifty and sixty?). He had bowed to her in the corridor of the hotel—a most luxurious hotel, and one that she would never have been able to afford if those had not been the days of the French occupation of Austria. She was there after an illness and after the prolonged degradation of her country, and she was bewildered at being in such a place and at playing such a part: surprised, she had replied to his greeting with a vague smile at the grey face, grey in spite of the sun and the snow—a face that bore the well-known traces of hardship and humiliation. The man had explained: 'I thought I might allow myself to bow, because of yesterday.' 'Yesterday?' 'Because of our meeting yesterday, in the ski-lift.' The ski-lift? She gazed at him uncomprehendingly. 'Oh,' he said—and she never forgot the sudden desolation in that face nor the feeling that she had failed to answer some call—'so it was only on my side, then?'

And so as to be forgiven, so that it might be said that it might have been on her side too—indeed, it was on her side—she had sat down beside him for a moment, under the gaze of the French soldiers and their families.

He did not speak French as well as she had thought to begin with. He lived in Salzburg. In the course of his life he had seen seventy-three performances of *Der Rosenkavalier*. He would be coming back next weekend. She would no longer be there. They had exchanged addresses and he had asked when her birthday was, and then they had parted and had never seen each other again.

Next May the roses appeared. They had gone on appearing for twenty years, just as they had this morning for her forty-fourth birthday—roses which were no longer really meant for Cécile, which had perhaps never really been meant for her, the gift of an unknown to an unknown, a message of harmony, an affectionate reminder that life runs on two planes and that, however limited and transitory it may be, our existence does traverse another world.

Cécile reflected that both she and the elderly man were travelling towards that blank day, that day of mourning as imaginary as their love, towards that year when the roses would not come—unless, indeed, it were she who was not there to receive them—towards the inescapable and ignominious failure inherent in every living thing. The flowers, pledges of unchanging sentiment, stood for the rapid beat of passing time. They were the symbols of human faithfulness: they were also part of a holy rite, and as such, as valid as singing or dancing.

Cécile looked at them. They were still in bud. But a few fragile, transparent petals were already unfolding from the firm, swollen hearts in a breathtakingly lovely movement towards full bloom. Cécile arranged the cushions on the couch, lay down and put a rug over her knees. And she began to sink immediately, as though drawn down by a heavy weight.

She closed her eyes and she was at once floating in the rumbling quietness of a Paris Sunday as though in a womb. It occurred to her that she had not looked at the roses with sufficient attention, had not listened carefully enough to their crimson voice; but she had not the energy to open her eyes again. Pictures and words floated through her head, swelling with the noise of a motor in the street and exploding somewhere within her chest. Once more the heavy weight pulled her down. Heavy and relaxed at last, she felt herself anchored to the couch by the whole weight of her body, her back, her shoulders; it was delightful. She was asleep, but she was aware that she was sleeping; she could discern marvels just as, from far off, one perceives a landscape where happiness seems to dwell; she was swimming, she was drawing closer, she was gliding over phosphorescent waves . . .

Knock, knock, knock on her door.

She stayed shut, struggling to attain her wonder.

Knock, knock, knock.

It would have needed only another second.

'Yes?' she said.

'Tea's ready, Mama,' said Nathalie.

Her back, her shoulders were still fast asleep. She looked at the time. 'But he's early,' she said.

'Yes,' said Nathalie. 'We thought we'd go to the cinema at six.'

She had closed her eyes again: she wanted to make the most of the sleep still lingering in her body. One minute of diving down, just one minute to catch the key word, the essence of it all.

But now she could hear the gentle sound of spoons and cups in the next room. She forced herself awake. Nothing remained to her of the happiness she had glimpsed but the ill-temper and confused regret of having been dragged away.

She got up and saw how untidy everything was. She folded the rug, put back the cushions: she was doomed to be reduced to these perpetual tiny battles. Was it possible that she had slept for close on an hour? This was it: now she would have to see Jo. As soon as she had a moment to herself she dropped off like an old woman. She had to move about in order to stay awake. She would never read books, she would never understand anything, she would never even know what it was that she was yearning for.

Now she could hear quiet voices on the far side of the door. She did her hair and saw herself in the glass, pale, tired. When she leant over the mirror like this two hollows appeared in her cheeks, criss-cross wrinkles under her eyes and lines along her nose. The first invariable impression, the dominant aspect, was ugliness, decay, fatigue. She was cross and tired, it was in that state that she was going to encounter these young people who could so readily do without her, these embodiments of a youth whose capers she knew so well, and had known for so long. When she leant over her mirror like this, as in love one leans over another face . . . She raised her head. She pulled at her skirt and her pullover and drew a deep breath. Jo, Alain, and all the others.

For a moment she stood by the door before opening it, not to overhear what was being said the other side but to gather courage, for all of a sudden her heart was racing. All of a sudden she was afraid of Jo.

They were sitting side by side on the sofa and they fell silent as she came in: but their talk had been so quiet that it was as though they had merely moved, open-mouthed, from one silence to another. Cécile had the impression that the children had been sitting there a great while, motionless and dumb, gazing at her as she stood transfixed in the doorway, before they smiled and stood up.

'This is Jo, Mama . . . my mother.'

He was wearing a sweater and an open-necked shirt and he sat down again with a curiously familiar grace.

'Lemon? Milk?'

She observed that Nathalie, acting as hostess, was showing a new self-assurance.

'A slice of cake, Jo? It's the remains of Mama's birthday cake. We had her birthday party today.'

'Really? Many happy returns, madame.'

And all at once life had become as soft as a nest and at the same moment it opened—an opening so well known, so long-lost, so beloved—opened like a wound.

'Thank you.'

Cécile smiled. Nathalie saw that she liked Jo; that her mother liked him more than she had ever seen her like any young man.

Good Lord, how he reminded her of Emmanuel!

The old lump was strangling the words in Cécile's throat. Had she ever thought of anything worth saying to Emmanuel?

'And how old are you?' she asked.

'Twenty-seven.'

It had been the first question she had asked when they met in the Place du Palais-Royal, at the exit of the Métro on that freezing winter's day. Well, they had been much younger then than these two here.

What was it about this young man that reminded her of Emmanuel? He was darker, more thickset, and his eyes were bolder. He looked you straight in the eye. The resemblance lay in a certain grace, something of a high-bred animal, an intensity, an air of loneliness, or rather of having been singled out. Their appearance alone was enough to make one remember that life was short, beautiful and tragic. Their appearance alone made one love youth.

But there was no need to search for what to say to Jo. He asked nothing better than to talk and put you at your ease. He lay back in the sofa, crossing and uncrossing his legs—splendid legs, probably, under those twisted trousers. What a difference: and what restfulness!

Jo knew that he did not look his age. Nevertheless, he had been born in a concentration camp. Yes, indeed. It was to music that he and his mother owed their survival. She used to play the piano for the Germans. Although he was so young in those days he could remember something of them. But he preferred not to. He would rather . . . He laughed.

He was about to leave for Belgium and Holland with his quartet. After that they were going to Japan. He had just signed his contract.

These young men whom she thought of as warriors with a sabre at their side, young sabres, they were all said to have this air of health and self-assurance. Jo had grown up in the harsh dryness, in the sun, beside that sea for which Emmanuel also used to make her long. And now suddenly the truth burst upon Cécile. This sense of silence, mystery, flight did not originate in them. Their tragedy was not wholly imaginary. They might indeed have been healed of their palsy. At this moment, thanks to Jo, the truth burst out. Emmanuel was a Jew; that was all. He was a Jew in 1941, that was all. That was their tragedy.

Jo's head was thrown back. He was laughing silently, privately, looking as though inwardly he were even more amused, his open mouth showing magnificent teeth. Emmanuel used to laugh like that sometimes. But with restraint, secretly.

'Will you go back to Israel, Jo?' Nathalie asked in a little-girl voice.

'Lord, no. I can't breathe there. If you knew how religious they all are, how bigoted! Besides, there's no future for a musician in Israel.'

'Do you think you'll stay in France?' asked Cécile.

'I should like to. Mama is very happy to be back. She only went to live in Israel because of me, you know—she was afraid all that business might begin again some day. Mama is French. My father was Polish, but he had emigrated to France. France is our country.'

'Do you speak Hebrew, Jo?'

'Of course.'

'Will you teach me Hebrew?'

Nathalie had dressed with a care that contrasted with Jo's sloppiness. She was a harmony in blue and orange, from top to toe. With her hair demurely drawn back, but puffed out and tied with a velvet ribbon and one curl carelessly brought forward on to her neck, carefully made up, her complexion suddenly perfect, she had never looked more like a daughter of the French bourgeoisie. Yet her modest beauty went exceedingly well with the young man's bohemian grace.

Jo noticed Cécile's pleasure in her daughter. 'She looks pretty with her hair like that, doesn't she, madame?' He had a singing voice, but harsh: even his voice reminded her of another's.

'Yes, it suits her.'

Life sang like a nest; it was as harsh as an incurable wound.

Cécile and Jo looked at Nathalie, pretty Nathalie. And in the same glance Cécile saw the back of Jo's neck with its bushy hair in need of cutting, and the movement she had never made towards that well-known neck, the caress held back for so long, stirred again in her unmoving hand.

'Shall we go, then, Nathalie?' He wrinkled his nose.

She was on her feet already. 'Let's go.' With a pretty motion of her slim arms, kept these many years for other people, Nathalie embraced her mother. And Cécile kissed the warm cheek that her child was at last holding out. When she shook Jo's hand there was a momentary hesitation, as though they too were going to embrace.

'Don't forget your key, Nathalie.'

Nathalie had very pretty legs, well-shaped knees, rounded hips; and Jo was rather taller, rather broader than she, and even more supple. He held her by the elbow, lifting her from step to step, making her dance. They were a floor down already.

Cécile did not lean over to see them reappear. Upright and motionless on the landing with her head high and her face hidden in her hands, she stood fate-struck, as it were, until she heard from below the sound of the front door slamming.

Then, quickly, she darted in, hurried to the dining-room window, and saw them again. She watched from the balcony, as once Emmanuel's mother had watched, saw the children cross the road side by side, and she thought them beautiful.

As though she were used to it, Nathalie got into a little car cheerfully parked on a pedestrian crossing, while Jo felt for the key in his pocket with one hand and with the other plucked the parking ticket from the windscreen. When the car drove off Cécile still tried to follow them. But the car had slid into the file of those already returning from the country, a little red creature running anonymously towards God knew what, through the broad Sunday streets.

Cécile closed the window. 'She looks pretty with her

53

hair like that, doesn't she, madame?' The room was empty: it still reverberated with fate's great bang on the drum.

Cécile concentrated on the cups and the teaspoons. She gathered them up and carried them into the kitchen. And now she was standing there with her arms dangling, in front of the window, opposite the two chestnut-trees that had been spared by the clearance and the demolition. They were in flower and they were calling out something splendid, something unbearable towards the sky above the building-site.

She could still see Jo and Nathalie walking hand in hand through the broad Sunday streets, through the black and magnificent streets of the days of the German occupation, dragging chains. 'It is impossible to live,' cried Emmanuel.

But Nathalie and Jo were dragging nothing. They were driving about the town. The lines of street-lamps were lit for them. It was holiday. The reflection of Paris gleamed in the river. They were dancing. And the voice of this child sprung from the concentration camps cried that it was possible, possible, possible to live; that indeed it was the only thing possible.

She dried the cups, put them away. The sky behind the building site was beginning to redden. She went back to her burrow and stayed there a long while without turning on the light, given over to the exquisite, the incurable wound that once upon a time Emmanuel had opened in her—had inflicted when first she set eyes upon him.

But when someone else knocked at her door she sat up abruptly and switched on the lamp. It was Stéphane. He saw that she was upset. 'Sorry,' he said. 'Were you asleep?'

'I was daydreaming,' she said. 'And you're hungry, aren't you, my poor pet? It's time for your dinner.'

'It's not so much that I'm hungry, but that Unesco film

on the third world is coming on in a moment. You said you would watch it with me.'

'Oh no!' she said.

He was backing away already, his shoulders drooping. He spent the whole afternoon working, alone with his inadequacy, and she had been as oblivious of him as if he had never existed.

'Yes, of course,' she said. 'I'll come and watch this film with you.' And thoughts of her other child, her Laura, came back to her too. 'By the way, do you know whether Laura has come back?'

'Did she go out?' Stéphane never knew what was going on.

'Yes, she went to the cinema with Didier . . .'

'Good for her. Well, are you coming to see this film?'

Both girls were cheerfully gadding about with their young men. Perhaps youth had no tragedy other than poverty, war, prohibitions, monsters.

'She looks pretty with her hair like that, doesn't she, madame?' All that was needed was a trifling remark like that for life to be possible—indeed, to show that it had already begun. But perhaps something else was already lost by such a remark; an indefinable something; a purity; not a virgin's cold purity, but the furious purity of total love. Perhaps there was no resemblance between Emmanuel and Jo beyond the purely physical, perhaps that pleasant ease was merely smoothness; perhaps Cécile was dreaming.

'The film's starting, Mama,' called Stéphane.

They saw Brazilian children setting off almost before it was light in search of their day's food. In India they saw holy cows wandering vaguely about among the bodies of people who had died of hunger; they saw illiterate, blind, deformed people; flies, great swollen bellies, skeleton legs; they saw mothers whose black eyes were devoid even of despair, quietly waiting for the last breath of the child dying in their arms. And in conclusion, there was the smiling face of a little Vietnamese girl propped up on crutches, one leg cut off so short that not even a stump was visible beneath her skirt.

The blonde announcer then introduced a variety programme and sat there with a fixed smile, waiting to disappear: her place was taken by a singer with no voice, a young man whose expression was one of extreme suffering.

Stéphane got up and turned off the television. 'That was a very well made film,' he said gravely. Cécile remained sitting there. Stéphane looked at her and added, 'It is not enough to see things with a Christian conscience.'

Without elaborating, Stéphane, the one who knew the remedies, was going towards the door and back to his work, offering the world's hunger the sacrifice of his dinner and leaving his mother to her uneasy conscience. 'You know enough to teach those children how to read, don't you?' she struck back at him.

He turned round. 'When you speak like that you are still seeing things only from the charity angle. But I am thinking about it,' he said. Then he went out.

She saw the nape of his neck with its over-long hair too fine to be so long; the well-cut suit of the young bourgeois with its vented jacket; his leg . . .

She followed him. 'Look,' she said gently, 'don't worry so much about this exam. There's plenty of work in the world today for young people.'

He had closed the door of his room behind him. She opened it again. He was already bent over a book and he did not even look up when she stood beside him. 'Would you like something to eat?'

'Don't bother.'

But she knew he was perpetually hungry. She could

provide food; she could at least do that for him. 'Just a little cold meat and salad. Without leaving your book. I'll bring the tray here.'

He looked at her then, and she saw his hunted eyes.

She went back to the kitchen. Oil, vinegar, mustard, salt, pepper, the dressing thick, as he liked it: a little garlic in the bowl. A good slice of duck's breast. And some oranges. Knife and fork on the tray. The napkin in its envelope with an S. What was left of the claret. And the last of the cake.

She pushed a dictionary aside. 'Can I put the tray here?' She sat down next to him. She and Stéphane were not going to hurt each other. While he ate, Stéphane kept his eyes fixed on a Latin text crowded with handwritten notes:

Grandior hic uero si iam seniorque queratur

atque obitum lamentetur miser amplius aequo,

non merito inclamet magis et uoce increpet acri?

Between mouthfuls he pencilled in a fresh note, still ignoring her.

The year before he had been in love with a Chilean girl. But how could this schoolboy prevent Marta from going back to her own country? For weeks on end he had had this wild look of loneliness and this stubborn way of working on and on.

Aufer, abhinc, lacrimas, balatro et compesce querelas . . .

She sensed here a self-assured greatness, advice that could be communicated, questions asked solely to elicit decisive answers. 'And to think I no longer know any Greek, or Latin, or anything,' she said.

'Culture is what's left when you've forgotten it all,' grunted Stéphane.

'My poor boy, I'm no longer anything but an ignorant woman.' It was a long while since she had seen the post bring any letters from Chile. There was a kind of glow

57

around his forehead, as there was about Jo's, as there had been about Emmanuel's. Even if Jo had limped a trifle. Even if Emmanuel had had no legs at all . . . 'Nathalie has gone out with her Jo,' she said.

'Oh?' he said. 'So that's it . . .'

'Do you know this Jo?'

'No,' said Stéphane.

'I have a feeling that this time it might be serious.' She saw the flash in his eyes, and the shyness.

'You don't say!' he said.

In her time at the Sorbonne she had known boys like her Stéphane. Talented, but not talented enough, and in subjects where it was necessary to be very talented indeed. She had looked on them with an unpitying eye in those days. She had not thought much of plodders of that kind.

Now, she felt she might be her son's sister, both of them tormented by a longing for the ideal and yet forced to follow the common paths at first, to prove to themselves and others that they could start like everybody else, bringing their yearning for the absolute to the tasks of everyday, yet bogged down, powerless, in those very tasks.

She added inappropriately as she left him, 'This Jo seems full of confidence, for all that he's a musician . . .'

She drew the double curtains and sat down in the drawing-room at the little writing-desk covered with letters, bills, requests, unread magazines and papers. The coming week was full of dinners and appointments; the publisher was asking for her translation by the end of the month. She had better make the most of Sunday to sort these papers and write a few letters.

'You who have stayed young enough to believe in fairy tales, help us with your gift, with your belief, to lighten the last days of those who no longer expect anything from a world that has forgotten them.' A little old lady, being kissed

58

by a young man, smiled with all her wrinkles at a bunch of flowers upon a white tablecloth. She sent a cheque.

'He is thirteen and he has never seen the sea. A day at the Villa Chante-Brise costs ten francs.' A sad child at the door of a slum dwelling was asking to join a laughing, naked band playing among the waves once the page was turned. She sent a cheque.

The SPA's magazine told heartbreaking stories of dogs and asked for donations for the society's work during the holiday season. She sent a cheque and noted that she had only six hundred francs left in the bank.

She leafed through the latest parish magazine. Stéphane accused her of still being influenced by religion, but she was no longer a practising Catholic—indeed, she no longer paid much attention to these things; nevertheless, she admired the parish priest's activity, his zeal, his sense of social duty and his open mind. She took in the magazine and she was astonished at the evolution of the Catholics.

'The Kingdom of God is impossible,' said the curé, 'without a full development of the human person. The Kingdom of God is impossible so long as two-thirds of mankind have not enough to eat and so long as the nations go on spending the money they do on armaments. How many of the Christians in our parish are committed to politics, to direct civic or social action? It is at the level of the City Council, the trade union or the professional today that this commitment begins.'

Yet Stéphane said, 'It is not enough to see things with a Christian conscience.'

She turned the page. 'Total reorganization of the faith.' That was a bit much. 'You who will soon be getting married . . .' Soon? In a month, in a year? An odd echo: Sagan, no doubt, rather than Racine. 'Do you know what young married couples tell us again and again? The young

59

marrieds say, "If we had not attended those evening meetings for the engaged, how much we should have lacked in building up our home! But more than that, it seems to us that our love has been deepened and enriched as a result. Of course it was enormously useful to have a better knowledge of the differing psychologies of men and women, and to know more precisely some of the problems which might arise in our physical union, and a score of other points that worried us. But what was infinitely more valuable was to sense the meaning of successful love through the words, smiles, hesitations and general approach of the young married couples who talked to us." ' The article ended: 'Do not hesitate to come to these evening meetings arranged by young married couples.'

'You don't say!' as Stéphane said.

The words 'married couple' ran through Cécile's head for a moment as once more she saw Jo and Nathalie dancing their way down the stairs. A curious expression; a sad one.

Another article, called *Life Ascending*, fortunately did not see fit to give 'old people approaching eternity' any advice other than to pray. In spite of everything, they were apparently still promised a Kingdom of God, with or without 'full development of the human person'.

The *Parents' Journal* was also brimming with advice. Helping a child in the lowest class practically amounted to a full-time job. Yet the writer of an essay she had read a little while ago on woman's position allowed four years, everything included, for the having and bringing up of each child. Cécile, thank heavens, was no longer concerned with anything beyond reform of the graduation examination; and that was complicated enough, in all conscience.

There were still two books and a thesis sent by the friends who had written them which Marc was leaving her to look through. She gave up hope of getting everything dealt with and abandoned the heap of handwritten and printed paper.

The only time Emmanuel had taken her to his house, had she seen anyone except his mother? Was there one or several of those numerous brothers and sisters he told her about sometimes, but told her about in such a way that the family appeared mythical, frightening, so that she felt herself unworthy of them as of everything else? What had Emmanuel's mother said to her? What was she like? Cécile could remember nothing of this sole meeting except for a corridor, a dining-room table with her on one side and a woman on the other, and black-eyed adolescents: and even now she could not positively assert that this woman, corridor, table and young people had not been part of a dream. 'Mama watched us leave. They did not dine, you know. They were quite incapable of doing anything, after we had gone,' Emmanuel had said.

She, too, was incapable of doing anything, this evening.

Emmanuel's letters were kept in the little cupboard at the foot of her bed. She looked at the brown-paper parcel with *To be destroyed* written on it: a solid object casually planted among vases, statuettes and albums. She took it and opened it. The top letters were in their envelopes. From the first there leapt out her maiden name (that treasure) and her curious address of those days—Rue des Bons-Enfants, Paris 1er—written in black ink in that beautiful, unrelenting hand that had addressed nothing more to her for twenty-three years.

The blue stamp showed a stiff Marianne with a red one-franc surcharge over her. The perfectly clear postmark showed the date: 24 February 1941. Rubber stamps on either side said 'Give to the National Assistance Campaign: winter relief.'

Sheets of paper covered with the same writing showed

in the untidy pile, and that was enough for her instantly to feel flayed, transported back to those days which were at one and the same time those of the war and those of her youth, the only days that had been granted her for the making of her life, the days of oppression and of the greatest freedom she had ever known.

She took the first letter out of its envelope and at once she was overwhelmed by the immense weariness of those days, when she felt herself overcome at the mere unfolding of the three or four sheets, thick with black ink, which for some months had reached her almost every day, often by special delivery, written without a space, almost without a correction, words underlined with a powerful stroke.

'I had sworn to myself that I would wait: I cannot do so. I cannot do anything—not even read. I have waited until half past twelve at night to begin doing the only thing that it is still possible for me to do, although I did not want to admit it to myself—to speak to *you*, even if only through this wretched medium of writing. When I left you this afternoon I boasted to myself that there would be several days of waiting. A few hours and it has already grown unbearable. I do not know whether I am not in greater danger than you in what is beginning here. But I know that I cannot *not* go on with it, any more than in that summer shower.'

One stormy day in German-occupied Paris she had coasted down the Champs-Elysées on her bicycle. From the Etoile to the Concorde one had only to let oneself go to glide down the sloping avenue in the rain. The whole length of the Champs-Elysées she freewheeled towards Emmanuel. Home again, naked in her dressing-gown, she had written to him with an entirely new feeling of happiness and freedom, as though they had at last been able to belong to each other; indeed, as though they belonged to each other already. Would she ever again ride a bicycle through a thunderstorm in a town, even though it would not be towards anyone? It was such a simple thing, yet it was very unlikely that she would ever do it again.

And yet they had not loved each other. Do you let a loved one go away? It was worship rather than love which linked them, and each was racked at the notion of being no more than an outward appearance, a transparency.

'I am incapable of holding fast to any person or thing and saying that I should like to stay there. I could not do it without a total inner bankruptcy that would be tantamount to suicide.' Who could? 'But you are the one to whom I have often wanted to pour it all out, to cry all the unuttered, pointless cries and bewail my fate in being a man and in being set upon this earth. No one is more fitted than you to hear.'

Hidden away in her den, the letter in her hands, the packet heavy on her knees, Cécile raised her head and moaned softly. 'I ask only to see your face again. Nothing beyond that. I am not easily roused, I swear it, and no mere beauty of face could inflame me to this degree.'

But what else was it? Did men leap out of the Métro these days to catch up with her? Yet it was only her face that had changed. Who would waste a second glance on her today? When she was in the street with her daughters she saw men eyeing them. And she remembered how glorious it was to be beautiful.

Each had refused to be the instrument of love's dissolution, he by shying away from marriage, she by fleeing from him. Yet he had pursued her to the very last moment.

'It bursts on you like a bolt from the blue that it is impossible to live.'

Noon, no, it was not a noon but rather a daybreak, a trembling dawn, filled with scents, promises and foul bloodstained terror: and she was a sick child who had got up too early in the hope of seeing wonders.

Sometimes the only thing they had been able to do to comfort each other was to hold hands. But she knew that if she were to let herself go an inch he would get her with child before she even knew what was happening to her. And this child was his hold on her, this child for which the desire had come upon them so quickly and clearly that, chaste though they were, it already existed for them; it was also through this child that he had pursued her up to the very last moment. Was it really possible that he had written those words on an interzone card and ┆ ┆t life should still have gone on as though nothing had hap┆ ┆┆┆ Could it be that even so she had really loved Marc? Could it be that he had written that to her when she was r ┆┆┆ving Marc?

'I have only one desire left, and that is to put my head on your shoulder and hear you tell me that our child will not be born.'

But it would have killed me, she reflected. And she did not know whether it would have been the censure, the secret unhappiness they dragged about with them, their poverty, or the inescapable death of those couples who try to live an absolute love.

And now the longing for that child was with her again, bursting out like fireworks at a fête. At last it was possible. She saw herself leaving her flat and walking through the streets to Emmanuel's old address. Today everything was still possible—or was possible at last. What did she risk—now? Emmanuel opened the door: they stood there for a moment, she on the landing, he in the flat: they recognized each other and he understood why she had come. At last the promise of their youth was kept. It had taken all these years.

'She looks pretty with her hair like that, doesn't she,

64

madame?' Gracious heavens, perhaps this very evening the child of her youth was being joyfully conceived without her.

Another idea occurred to her. Was Emmanuel Polish, perhaps? Why not? One who had escaped to France? What had she known about him? Not even that he was a Jew. And Jo was his son. Jo and Nathalie, their happy children, were doing what they had not managed to do: they were living out their love.

Envelopes; dates; words. 26 February 1941, 1 March 1941, March 1941, March 1941, April 1941, April 1941, April 1941, April 1941, April 1941. Every day, or very nearly, for months on end, he had written to her. 'Need', 'desire', 'esse...' 'life', 'life', 'death', 'forgiveness'. One day she would plunge into this black river; one day she would try at last to fathom this tragedy. One day she would embark on the search for this love.

'Even beyond that point which it is unbearable to imagine without wishing for my death or yours, I know that we shall always be in harmony, holders of the same secret of which we know nothing, or almost nothing, except that we hold it in the face of one and all, and that everywhere, always, in all circumstances, we shall be able to smile at one another as I am now smiling at you, Cécile.'

Perhaps all that we needed was to go swimming together in the ocean, she reflected. Would an affair like this, with its attraction and rejection, still be possible today? And if this love (but was it love?) had at least been lived out in the time of its present, that is to say in today's past, would the memory of it be stronger? However strong the voice of the flesh, it was not its renewable joys and distresses that rang loudest in one's memory. It was only in the fleeting instant that the flesh seemed paramount. Perhaps if that love had been lived, consummated, as they say . . .

She closed the packet of letters, retied the string and

crossed out the words *To be destroyed*. In their place she wrote *For my daughters*. One day she would dive as deeply as anyone could into this past which was not really a past nor really a memory, for it was not a question of any man other than Marc, in competition with Marc; rather was it a completely different life that she had perhaps kept safe by not living it. At twenty she had married for ever this handwriting, more hers than her own, that had never been used to write anything but 'we shall never be able to live without each other, and we shall never be able to live together.'

In the glass she looked at the face time had given her, the face she would present to Emmanuel today if she could manage to smile at him 'as I am now smiling at you, Cécile', having come to tell him that she had kept that secret they knew nothing about. She saw her forehead wrinkled in the lines of a familiar expression of waiting, inquiry, astonishment; she saw her half-open mouth, her pale, forsaken look. But it was not this defeat she wished to record. Apart from her looks, which could only deteriorate, had she in fact kept the secret? And had Emmanuel? Could he still smile at her? Would he want to? What do the words one writes at twenty amount to? 'Yet life cannot be merely sap alone,' she thought. But what else was it? What was it that was rising in her this evening but a transfusion of sap from Nathalie?

'She looks pretty with her hair like that, doesn't she, madame?' They were taking love at once, as it opened; without fear, without delay, without even respect. Oh, let them do what they want. What do I know about it, anyhow?

'Mama, Mama!' Laura burst into the den. 'I've been looking for you everywhere. Why didn't you answer? What's up? Are you cross?' She saw the tied-up packet on the bed and gazed at her mother, seeing—as Cécile well

66

knew—a face she did not care for. It was a face worked by the present and the past, a face from which the blood had ebbed; it had that look of understanding nothing about anything; it was the face she would have presented to Emmanuel this evening, her truest face, and Laura did not like it. 'Didier and I went and had a drink after the cinema. We've been talking. I've brought Didier back. There's plenty of . . . What is it? Are you cross?'

'Not a bit. I was quite sure . . .'

'Were you worried because I was late? Are you annoyed with me?'

Darling.

'Not at all. There's nothing wrong—I wasn't worried—I was quite sure . . .' She was coming back to Laura; she smiled; and in a voice whose falseness she herself could hear she said, 'Well, did you have fun, both of you?' She had a way of saying 'Have fun' when Laura was off to a dance with a boy and kissed her goodbye on the landing; and then of saying when she came back, 'And did you have fun?' as though she were talking to a baby; this habit irritated Laura. 'I mean, did you spend a pleasant afternoon? Was it a good film?'

'Come on in, Didier,' called Laura.

Didier appeared in the den, which was just big enough to hold all three of them. 'Good evening, madame.'

'Good evening, Didier.'

He was rather smaller than Laura, though he was older. 'Was it a good film?'

'Terrific,' Laura said.

'I thought it was ridiculous.' Didier laughed. 'Laura wept. Everyone was looking at her as we came out.'

Laura's voice trembled with fury and tears. She took up all the room; suddenly she was alone there in the den. 'You don't understand. It's a desperate, hopeless film. You didn't understand anything about it. That fellow would have liked . . . He can't make a success of anything, he messes up everything, he's in love . . . It's fine . . . And then even his death, even his death, he messes that up too. Oh!' She was still crying. Her face was stained with tears. It had suddenly burst upon Laura that it was impossible to live. She was stifling between this fool Didier and her mother whose thoughts were miles away. She got out. 'Idiot,' she cried.

Cécile caught up with her.

Darling, darling, darling.

'But what film did you see, Laura, pet?'

Cécile was with her. Laura wept in her arms; Laura hid her head on her shoulder. 'Oh, I know I'm being silly, but Didier makes me so mad.'

It was *Pierrot-le-Fou* that they had seen.

'What did you think of it, Mama?'

What had she thought of it . . . what had she thought of the stabbings, the savagery, the leaping about, of beauty disembowelled? What had she thought of it . . . The film had hurt her, like the sun in her eyes, like a factory siren ripping a holiday sky, like a horrible mess, like tragedy piled on tragedy, like those dreams in which one cannot make out the words. The film had shattered her.

She said weakly, 'But . . . but . . . I thought it was restricted.'

Didier looked guilty, and Laura, recovering her poise, rose to the occasion. 'It wasn't Didier's fault. He wanted us to see something else, but by then it was too late, so I said, let's go and see *Pierrot-le-Fou* instead.'

Cécile had not really seen *Pierrot-le-Fou*. Marc had kept her waiting. They had been tired and cross. Once they reached their seats, all they wanted to do was rest. Instead, all that activity, brutality, agony, all that redness, all that dancing, that life bursting open, all that chaos broke over them. Marc sighed. As they left the cinema they glanced at one another. 'Oof . . .'

Cécile looked at her child, at Laura, who, twenty-five years later, surrounded by security and comfort, was shrieking out the same cry that Emmanuel had uttered, close to death and in misery. She would have to see this film again. Laura had not got it wrong. 'This fellow wanted to love: it's fine, he's in love . . . he can't make a success of anything; even his death, even his death, he messes that up too!'

'We'll go back and see that film together, if you like, Laura,' said Cécile, with no more logic than before. 'I don't think I can have seen it properly. But have you had anything to eat?'

'No,' said Laura, 'but there's plenty in the . . .'

'I'll go and see what I can find for you.'

'Don't bother,' said Laura. 'We'll forage.'

No doubt they would! Cécile made a skilful move to rescue what was left in the refrigerator. 'Look, darlings, I hadn't thought in terms of a real dinner this evening. But there's bread and cheese and fruit. And there's a drop of soup left too.'

'No, no soup,' said Laura. 'But there's some duck, isn't there?'

Tomorrow she would have to begin shopping and cooking all over again. Hunting for a shop that was open on Monday.

'Don't you want us to eat the duck?' Laura demanded obtusely.

'Of course I do. I just hadn't thought of it. Eat the duck by all means.'

'And the cake. There must be some cake left.'

'No,' said Cécile firmly. 'We finished the cake with Jo and Nathalie.'

'Good work!' said Laura.

'Don't bother . . . trouble . . . not hungry,' protested the polite Didier, who had sensed a certain agitation around the refrigerator. But Cécile was not going to play the skinflint this evening. This evening was a celebration. Eat, eat by all means, my dears. Nathalie is in love and Laura is weeping over love as a dog howls at the moon, as a dog howls at death. Eat, eat, my dears: this is a celebration. You are not twenty years old for ever.

'You must have some of my mother's duck,' Laura said. 'She cooked it herself—it's her speciality. *Canard à l'orange*, we had it for her birthday.' She seized a saucepan. The one which always caught, of course. 'Shall I warm it up in this?'

'It's just as good cold, you know.'

'Oh no! Warmed up's better.'

'Then use the casserole.'

Log fires, moonlit nights, life, death and wild tearing love. The flat too small, the money short, no maid, a strong sense of order, and monsters of children with cannibals' appetites and manners fit for a barbecue.

'Holders of this secret of which we know nothing . . .' If he could only see her, busily economizing and thinking about tomorrow's shopping among the saucepans and the Louis XV furniture.

One day, just for fun, she and Emmanuel had taken the first train pulling out which happened to be going to Chauvery. Just for fun, that day they had eaten their whole month's bread ration at one go.

Eat all the duck, my dears, eat every bit.

'Don't make too much noise,' said Cécile, 'Stéphane's working.'

She sat down in the drawing-room. She thought of Emmanuel's mother and his brothers and sisters; they were really poor, and according to him they had remained there the whole evening, as though turned to stone by the sight of them. She envied that destitution.

Gradually all around her the outside world extended its frontiers and at the same time closed in upon itself. Cars were travelling fast along the avenue. The hangings, furniture, flowers and bookbindings took on an exquisite beauty, even the cigar box, the most trifling sheet of paper, the door handles, the mouldings, they all harmonized with that swishing of the cars on the asphalt, that breathing of the night outside and that strangely cold yet sensuous voice that came from a great way off, a dream voice perhaps, and sang, 'An exact point beneath the tropic, either of Capricorn or of Cancer,' and that cried 'Under the sun precisely' when Laura opened the door and thrust her long neck, her huge eyes and her confidential air into the room.

'Did you see Jo?'

'Yes.'

'So what's he like?'

'Good-looking.'

'Really good-looking?'

'I think so.'

'Tall?'

'No: average, rather.'

Laura made a face. 'But taller than Nathalie?'

'Oh yes. Certainly.'

'Dark or fair?'

'Dark: hair almost black.'

Laura made another face. 'Can't you describe him a bit better than that?'

'I really don't know any more,' said Cécile.

'Then he can't be all that extraordinary,' said Laura.

'Yes, he is extraordinary.'

'Who's he like, for instance?'

'Nobody, really. Except perhaps . . .'

'Perhaps who?'

'Perhaps . . .'

'Someone you . . . ?'

'Oh, never mind, sweetheart: I don't know. There's nothing to tell you. Besides, he was only here for half an hour.'

'Half an hour that didn't put you in a very good mood,' said Laura.

'And what about you?' said Cécile gently. 'Did *Pierrot-le-Fou* put *you* in a very good mood?'

'Oh well . . .'

'It's just the same, love.'

And the way she said it made Laura start crying again; and now Cécile was crying too with her great big girl in her arms. And at the same time they were laughing. 'What idiots we are, really; what idiots we are,' while out there the voice began protesting again, 'Under the sun pre-cisely.'

'Close the door, Laura, sweet—suppose Didier were to come in! Oh my darling, my darling.' Like two lost, drowned creatures, laughing, weeping, they clung to each other. 'What idiots we are, really, what idiots. Suppose Didier were to come in! Go on, go back to him.'

'Do you think they'll get married?' Laura asked.

'I don't know . . . They'll do what they like—what they can.'

'But what about Alain?'

'Oh, Alain . . .'

And now they were weeping over Alain and young love lost; but gently, without laughing any more, and they calmed down.

'In any case it never really got going with Alain . . . They wouldn't have been happy. There's nothing to be sorry about. Go on, darling, do; go back to Didier. I'm going to bed. Try and stay out at the back for a while so that I can get to the bathroom and along the corridor without being seen. Go on, love.'

Cécile was in bed. Marc had not yet come home. He must have dined at Margency. She hoped he had not drunk too much. He did, sometimes. The girls there amused Marc. They suited his longing for new beginnings, his dream of another sort of life. Perhaps he would bring one or more of them back in the car this evening. It did not matter to her, or hardly at all. But what about him? Could one ever tell? Love: had they ever really known it? Time was running out: had she known love? Love is always somewhere else. And then a young man like Jo appears, takes your daughter by the arm and you say to yourself: love is there, how crazy can you get. Life together kills love, everyone knows that; and yet life together is also one of love's mysteries.

Eyes closed, eyes open, you know no more than you did at twenty: you go on towards separation, towards horror, with your eyes sometimes open, sometimes shut; you go steadily towards that time when you will have to live without ever again uttering that cry no God can wring from you: you are bound for the desert, torment, old age or death; old age *and* death. How will you, how can you, bear it?

She did not want to go to sleep before Marc came back. Sometimes Marc drank too much and then he drove badly. She took one of the many books she had promised herself to read before she died.

'When these eager longings to serve God come over me I sometimes long to undergo penances, but I cannot do so, because of the weakness of my body. Yet they would ease my mind; and indeed the few I do perform are a comfort to me and a delight. If I were free to yield to such longings, I should undoubtedly commit excesses.

73

'On other occasions I find it most painful to have to enter into communication with anyone whatsoever; my tribulation is so great that it causes me to shed copious tears. My sole desire at such times is solitude; admittedly I do not always busy myself with prayer or study when in solitude, solitude is in itself a consolation to me.

'At other times I feel a most lively distress at being compelled to eat and sleep, particularly when I perceive that I am no more able to do without these things than anyone else. I do them to obey God, and I offer my sacrifice to Him.

'It always seems to me that time is too short and that I have not enough for prayer. I should never be weary of solitude. I unceasingly long for the leisure to devote myself to reading, for I have greatly loved it. Nevertheless, I read very little, for scarcely do I take up a book than I enter into a religious contemplation in which I find great happiness: thus my reading turns into prayer. Yet this is rare, because of my occupations; though they are good in themselves, they do not give me the ease of mind that I should find in reading. That is why I perpetually long to have more time; and it seems to me that everything loses its savour when I perceive that I accomplish neither what I desire nor what I long for . . .

'*I should never be weary of solitude . . . I unceasingly long for the leisure to devote myself to reading . . . I enter into a religious contemplation in which I find great happiness . . . I perpetually long to have more time . . . to have more time . . . I accomplish neither what I desire nor what I long for.*'

Cécile was dropping off. She closed the book. She closed her eyes. Even without God and without faith there existed a promised happiness which life and human beings did not mar. This promise made one long not to miss the experience of growing old . . . Cécile was going to sleep.

No, she was not going to sleep. Suddenly she was awake. She saw Jo in all his glory, just as she had vainly tried to rediscover him ever since the moment when he had left the flat. Nothing can take the place of love. You go through the motions of drowning, that's all. Life is sap and nothing more. Old age is a torment and nothing more. She would not tell Marc about Jo unless he asked her. The children should be left alone. It was *their* miracle. Time would show whether for them it was a matter of living together.

She heard the drawing-room door open and Marc's hesitant footsteps outside the door of the den. He came in, although she had put out the light and was pretending to be asleep.

'Are you asleep?' he asked gently.

'Not quite. Did you have a good time?'

'Did you?' he asked in the voice of someone who has had bad news.

'Yes.' She switched on the lamp.

He was sitting on her bed, looking at her with a strange sad light in his eyes. 'You know, it's too awful. Françoise was operated on yesterday. A mastectomy. I knew nothing about it, did you?'

Françoise used to skip around the tennis-courts, wanton, naked under her sweater.

'No, I didn't know anything about it either. Was it cancer?'

'Yes.'

Françoise was—how old? Thirty-seven, thirty-eight?

'They hope it'll be completely successful,' Marc went on. 'The doctor says there's a very good chance that it will. The Giraudons saw Yves. The terrible thing is that Françoise hasn't been told she's had a major operation.'

'But can they mutilate a woman like that without telling her?'

'It seems they can't know what they're going to find until they operate: the doctor asked Yves for his authorization.' And as Cécile said nothing more, Marc added, 'Perhaps I shouldn't have told you this evening.'

'Yes you should,' she said. 'Did you play all the same?'

'Yes, we played.' He kissed her. 'Sleep well.' But he stayed there, his face in shadow above her, and she with her head on the pillow, lit by the lamp. 'If you like,' he said, 'I'll come in with you for a while.'

'All right,' she said. 'Would you see whether Didier has gone and whether Laura is in bed? She ought to go to sleep now.'

'The others aren't in?'

'Stéphane is. He's working. Nathalie's gone to the cinema with her friend.'

'All right, I'll go and see if Laura's in bed.'

As she waited for him she thought of Françoise and of the horror she would feel from now on for that body which had given her so much pleasure. She thought of Françoise and Yves, who were younger than they. She wondered whether a man's love, say Marc's or Yves's, could ever rediscover desire. She wondered whether she would ever consent to such a mutilation.

Marc came back and they lay tightly pressed: their bodies had grown older together and each knew the other through and through, as weak and wretched as those of babies, yet still able to attract each other, to desire each other, or rather to desire and attain by means of each other their sole and brittle certainty, their pleasure and their moment's delight.

Presently they began to doze off together, without anything more being said, cramped on Cécile's narrow couch, as close to each other as possible. They were falling asleep, gliding between splendour and horror, life and death,

76

mutilation and final decay, still spared, spared for so long, so short a time.

From time to time Marc twitched. Perhaps he was dreaming of a tennis stroke; or perhaps it was only the relaxation of their shared repose. The twitch would wake Cécile momentarily, just long enough for her to be aware of their heavy torpor, of the well-being that came to her from this bathed, muscular body, her husband's body, from this shared flesh which gradually, impelled by Marc's twitchings, sank a little more deeply into sleep each time, until they were so soothed at last that desire would once more return to them.

2

'So you liked Jo?' This time Nathalie's eyes did not slide away; they were new eyes; they looked straight into her mother's.

'Yes,' Cécile said.

'I knew it. I could see it at once.'

They were in the dining-room, Cécile still in her dressing-gown, interrupted in her usual morning tidying up, and Nathalie just up, but wide awake, pink with expectation.

'What's more, he liked you, too. He thought you were very beautiful.' She said it generously, like a grown woman, and it was the mother who behaved like a girl, glowing, smiling, pushing back a lock of her uncombed morning hair; she opened her mouth to say something, but all she could manage was a look so youthful, so naked, so loving that Nathalie leant towards her and Cécile's hands reached out eagerly. But Nathalie merely sat down at the table where her breakfast was waiting.

'The toast is cold. Would you like me to make some more?'

'No, don't bother, thank you, Mama.'

This last word, which Nathalie hardly ever used now except as a challenge, was like a caress too. Cécile drew up a chair and sat down by her daughter, as she often did when one of the children was breakfasting alone. She could see perfectly well that Nathalie was waiting for her to speak. But what could she say? She fingered the teapot, the kettle;

she pushed the sugar and the marmalade nearer. Finally she asked, 'Did Laura tell you I liked him?'

'No,' said Nathalie. 'I haven't seen Laura since yesterday. I only had to look at you.' She daydreamed a moment, blushed, sipped her tea. 'He's good-looking, don't you think?'

'Yes,' said Cécile. 'I do.' And seeing that this morning Nathalie accepted her as a ratifying authority she added, 'He is . . . filled with light.'

Nathalie showed both surprise and gratitude at these words coming from her mother. Then her face clouded; she poured out another cup, took a sip, pushed aside her plate, the toast, marmalade and butter until she had a clear space, and said, 'And do you think I'm beautiful enough for him?'

Nathalie beautiful? Nathalie filled with light? What woman was beautiful? Who did not feel herself to be an empty shell, a void, at the moment when she was called upon to be everything?

Nathalie as a child in her dressing-gown with a cup of chocolate, Nathalie pale, Nathalie cross, Nathalie charming, long-legged, triumphant, Nathalie known so intimately, bandaged, taken care of, strengthened, comforted, set on her feet again for these twenty-two years past—was Nathalie beautiful enough for total love?

'Of course you're beautiful enough. You mustn't even think about it. These are questions you must never ask yourself. You are beautiful enough, Nathalie dear, don't worry—you're beautiful enough for anyone.'

'And nice enough?'

'Nice enough for anything.'

Run, Nathalie, run on, as though you were running through a summer shower.

'I think he'll be a great pianist,' Nathalie said.

'Have you heard him play?'

'Yes, several times. But he's already beginning to be known, you know. He has given recitals in the *Maisons de la Culture*, and he gave the first performance of a Schönberg concerto at the *Domaine musical*. He's had very good notices. He has bookings for the whole year.'

The press releases were all there already; they had only to be handed on. Like all set pieces, they were revolting.

'Did you talk to Papa?' asked Nathalie.

'About Jo? No. Papa didn't ask me anything so I didn't say anything either. Why should we?'

Nathalie was taken aback. 'Oh, but in any case Papa . . .' she said, in the same tone as she had announced, 'My dear parents, marriage is all you ever think of.'

The tenderness of last night still lingered in Cécile. 'Well, what about Papa?' she asked gently.

'If a boy doesn't wear a tie . . .' Nathalie gave a little smile and, surprisingly, her eyes caught and held her mother's. Cécile had the feeling that her daughter, spurring like mad, was galloping her off into a complicity that she did not altogether care for.

'Oh no,' she said, getting up. 'Oh no,' she said again. 'Papa came home late. We talked about other things. That's all.' She saw her daughter as from a great way off, childlike, astonished at no longer having to tug at her chains, frightened of her freedom, not daring to stand on her own feet, a fragile being among the antique and reproduction furniture in this penurious and middle-class flat, too middle-class or too penurious, who was seeking further reassurance, or at least the usual obstacles.

If only I had as much freedom at your age, Nathalie—if only there had been no war—if only my mother had given me her blessing . . .

And at that moment Cécile made a gesture that had long

been impossible. Shyly she stroked her daughter's head and rested her hand on her hair for a moment. But Nathalie's little round warm skull remained harshly unyielding. So Cécile withdrew her hand; and in spite of everything launched forth.

'Look, you know everything Papa and I might say to you as well as we do. You know our lectures by heart, and I don't think there's much point in giving them any more. You've got to do your own living from now on. It's up to you to know what you want and what you're capable of. You have the luck to be young in a world where you're not blamed or threatened, where Jews are no longer sent to be killed, where you can travel, where you don't have to have children if you don't want them, where in fact you can do exactly as you please.'

She felt she was talking to the empty air, as a hungry man might tell a wealthy neurotic how lucky he was to be able to eat every day. And as she went on giving her lecture she had the feeling that she was talking nonsense and committing a crime against beauty.

'That's perfectly normal,' Nathalie said.

'For someone like me who was twenty during the war it seems perfectly wonderful.'

The look of a hostile child reappeared on Nathalie's face. 'But you always want people to take their cue from you,' she said. 'To listen to you, anyone would think that if you didn't run the risk of being killed everything else you risked was positive luxury.'

'In one way,' Cécile said slowly, 'it *is* luxury.' And she added, 'But it is true that this luxury is one that nothing and nobody will ever be able to cure us of. That's what makes life so difficult.'

'Do you think we'll be able to live together?' asked Nathalie.

'Is it on the cards?'

'It's been on them from the start.'

'Naturally,' Cécile said. 'But can't you behave as though it weren't and not think about it yet? You've always said you wanted to live only in the present. Only yesterday you blamed us for not thinking of anything but marriage.'

Nathalie seized on this. 'I'm not necessarily thinking of marriage.'

Fine, thought Cécile, nor am I. But she said nothing. If Emmanuel had had life opening before him, if he had been as gay and happy as Jo, if he had wanted her without marriage, and if she could have had her mother's blessing into the bargain . . . But go on, Nathalie, go on. Don't let fear of love prey on you. You won't actually die of it.

And now here was her little girl, her intrepid tight-rope-walker, looking like someone who had no head for heights.

Men of that kind ask for everything, and at once. And then off they go. *I am incapable of holding fast to any person or thing, of holding fast and saying that that is where I want to stay.* They blaze like a forest fire. And then, men of that kind are poor: they kill us with overwork. Whether they go or stay, whether it is peace or war, they kill us.

'What did you think of Alain?' Nathalie asked.

'I liked Alain very much. I do like him very much. It's impossible not to. To me, Alain is perfect. What do you expect me to say?' Cécile moved away from her daughter, and said again, 'It's up to you, my child.'

Now a pale light flashed in Nathalie's eyes; she too stood up all of a sudden and fell upon her mother. 'But Mother,' she said, and it was as though she had shouted it at the top of her voice, 'if I were to marry Alain, I should have *your* kind of life!'

'Who's asking you to marry Alain?' said Cécile in a toneless voice that she herself found surprising, for she felt nothing.

But Nathalie had gone, leaving her deflated; and Cécile began clearing away. She stacked the cups and saucers, put the pots of jam and honey on the tray. Then she put the tray on the marble-topped chest-of-drawers they used as a sideboard.

Her life, her humdrum life, this flat that was too small, this avenue, this city, these things, this family, no outbursts, no great upheavals, no passions that showed: you might think it abnegation. But was it really as horrifying as all that?

Cécile stood gazing at her hands as they lay on the chest-of-drawers, then slowly, first with the one and then with the other, she began patting the marble. Her face lengthened, her mouth opened a little, her eyes took on their puzzled, abandoned look. In any case, she thought, I should still be forty-four today.

Maria came into the dining-room, saw her and hesitated. 'I come fetch tray,' she said. 'Mademoiselle Nathalie don't want I make her bed. Says I bother.'

'You make her bed,' Cécile said roughly. 'I'll take the tray out.'

Little wretch, spoilt child who says anything she chooses. When she's in her garret with her Jo she'll see whether it's a bother to have her bed made for her. She'll see what life is like, and whether it's a cake you can eat in one go.

'Oh, madame, I daren't.' The Spanish servant stood there, with her powerful arms, her kind, animal strength.

'All right, take the tray out and do the washing-up first,' Cécile said.

The maid went back into the kitchen. Now, in a habitual attitude, though one a little out of place in her and her surroundings, Cécile stood in the middle of the room, hands on hips, staring into space, like a peasant woman.

83

The woman who had had her chance of life wandered for ever through the dark streets of the Occupation with a youth paler than herself, so intertwined that when, sometimes, despite their intertwining they had to rest, they would stop at a café and reach out their hands to each other over the table, like a bridge across the world. Was it not these wandering shades that she had been trying to placate with all her attentiveness, her love and her punctual running of the household these last three-and-twenty years?

But it would have killed me, she thought. And the child we should have had would have died too. It was beyond our strength. It was another age. It was impossible. Nathalie is cruel.

The children were grown up; she was practically an old woman. It was over, or almost. In any event she would have been bringing the children up all these years. And children, whether you had them by one man or by another, were always the same. In any event she would be forty-four today.

She went on tidying the family ark. She emptied the ashtrays. She watered the potted plants and the geraniums on the balcony; she nipped off the faded leaves and freshened up her birthday roses. During the night most of them had opened and the fullness of their bloom proclaimed their dissolution. Every year it was the same disappointment. Scarcely had the flowers reached their full beauty the day after the party than they began to die. Cécile did not even dare take them out of their vase for fear of making their petals drop. All she could do was give them more water and stand those whose stalks had softened and which might therefore mummify as buds in a deep jug.

These tasks gave her pleasure, as they did every morning; they calmed her spirit. Beds properly made, cushions plumped up, curtains neatly looped back, the newspapers sorted, letters put away, papers destroyed, ashtrays emptied —these were her daily exercises, the rhythm that led her to the immobility of objects and their grace.

Lord, she reflected, what a pitch one would have had to live at with Emmanuel! Anyhow, did we really love each other?

In the drawing-room she came across the portrait of Nathalie as a child where it was propped up on the chest-of-drawers.

'I must change this string,' she said to herself. She did so. She hung the picture again, stood back to see whether it was square, straightened it and looked at it once more. It was a very pretty portrait, the work of Strahimir, a Jugoslav painter they knew. Everyone said that this picture of an enchanting eight-year-old with auburn hair and light green eyes, against a background of pale green sky, was a very pretty portrait. But Cécile had never liked it, for although the painter delighted in his model, he had chosen the expression she liked least in her daughter—that secretive, harsh look, that air of saying, 'I'm going to outdo the lot of you,' but of saying it with no pleasure, more as though it were a sulky threat, her expression darkly introspective. It was a frightening expression and one that Nathalie had not lost. It was the face she used to wear not so long ago when she came back from children's parties with a secret light in her eyes and the marks of tears.

'Did you have fun?'
'Yes.'
'Were there a lot of people?'
'Not so many.'
'What did you play?'
'Games.'
'Don't you think Madame So-and-So very pretty?'
'I didn't notice.'

'But you had a good time?'

'Yes.'

And off she would go to her room to weep, exactly as she had gone just now. Leaving her mother feeling clumsy, full of guilt.

At meals Nathalie used to give a twist to some general subject that had a bearing on her own particular trouble, cleverly asking her father questions that he could deal with and her mother those she thought her more qualified to answer—those concerned with human relationships, for example. 'Mother, what would you think of a little girl who . . . ?' Cécile did her utmost to be objective, but as these enquiries were singularly transparent she sometimes mingled moral teaching with her information: morality that Nathalie took without batting an eyelid but always with that expression which said, 'Go on . . . I . . . I've got my own ideas about that.' And Cécile would hear herself spouting hypocrisy. She would have liked to hold her tongue, but Nathalie's face egged her on. At night, when she made her rounds to kiss the children goodnight, take their books away from them and put out their lights, she would hear Nathalie's door close. She opened it. It was dark in the room. Nathalie would pretend to be asleep. Cécile knew that she would switch on the light and start reading again as soon as her back was turned, but in the end she gave in. Her daughter was stronger than she. She had also, unfortunately, given up kissing Nathalie goodnight and the custom had proved impossible to reinstate. Even today.

Is it my fault? Cécile asked herself yet again. Do I really not give her enough?

What Nathalie wanted of her was a very great deal, something which would exhaust the last of her remaining strength. 'But I should have *your* kind of life!' If she were to say what her daughter wanted her to say, then she would certainly risk leading a dreary existence to the end of her days.

Yet they had both been at that point where their hearts quickened with joy. And it had all gone sour so quickly. Let her do what she wants, thought Cécile, so long as she leaves me in peace. Let her do what she wants, since that is what she has been asking for all this time.

Speeches came into her mind. 'My life may seem dull to you, but I did opt for it. We chose our responsibilities freely. We were actually a good deal more adventurous than you are. Your father had no job. We were living under a false name. We were cold and hungry. But we didn't need an all-risks insurance to live together and bring children into the world. In fact, we were less bourgeois than you, my poor children. Our relationship has lasted and we are still in love after twenty-three years. What do you really know about my life, Nathalie? What do you know about our life, our life as a couple; what do you know about this mystery, this passion? What do you know about our courage?'

Or again: 'It is because I loved you that I have led this life you think so petty, because of my maternal love that welled up in me as quickly as my milk. It was because you were there right away, there between us, so helpless that from the start it was impossible for either of us to leave you, whom no one else would have loved as we did. Do you imagine that I should have troubled to marry if it had not been to have children? I should have led the life of an adventuress, which is not one life but a thousand, not one man, but a thousand. What do you really know about my life, Nathalie?'

She was perfectly well aware of what she had been supposed to say. 'Yes, he will be a great pianist. You will be famous and beautiful. You will have a marvellous life.

We'll help you. And if you have a child I'll help you bring it up. I'll look after it while you go on tours with Jo. I'll help you, I'll help you.'

Or else she should have sat by her daughter's side and weighed everything up—religion, nationality, money. And Nathalie could have said all this griping was irrelevant and these things unimportant, could have said proudly, 'I'm not thinking of marriage.'

She heard her daughter calling from outside. 'I'm off. I shan't be in for dinner tonight.'

Cécile felt a stab of pity and went to join her. 'Nor for lunch, either?'

'No. You know very well I never lunch on Mondays.' Nathalie was now displaying her fine withdrawn expression.

'Will you be back late?'

'I don't think so, not very late. Goodbye.'

She was already on the stairs. Cécile called her back. 'Come back. Come back a moment.'

Nathalie stopped, turned, looked at her, came back. Cécile pulled her daughter into the hall. 'Listen,' she said. 'If you don't love Alain, for heaven's sake don't marry him. Don't do that. That's all I can tell you. Choose love.'

The two women stood for a moment in the dimness, face to face, motionless. Then Nathalie opened the door again and left without a word.

Going from one room to another, Cécile felt a tenderness swelling within herself, a happiness, a sort of pain, something indefinable, alive, both very old and youthful, full of the past, of promise and of detachment.

'Life is a savour,' she said to herself, just as the evening before she had said 'it is sap,' and then, a little earlier, 'it is a private adventure.' And these definitions, these words that hummed inside her as she went from room to room, made her spirits rise higher and higher. She saw the

88

furniture, the flowers, with all the movement of their leaves and their stems, their transparency and their brilliance, the bronze cherub kneeling on a coffee table, the pattern of the big drawing-room carpet. It was among these things that she had lived: the same objects might have made her feel sick—they had done so and would do so again.

'But I should have *your* kind of life!' Nathalie had got it wrong. You dream. You are not reduced to being merely what you do or to your outward appearance. And then she loved Marc. And he loved her too, in spite of all those girls. Quietly, conjugally, privately, they made a pair whose union was indissoluble. Marc was not an Alain.

The lilies of the field; the fowls of the air. Nathalie's and Jo's child, as beautiful as the lilies of the field. They would help them. They would sell the land. If they could get the building permit it might easily fetch two hundred thousand francs. To be divided into three, of course. It could not all be given to Nathalie. Oh, they would have enough to set themselves up and give a concert. Perhaps Jo would succeed. Some did, after all; at least sufficiently to earn a living.

Now Cécile was putting away all the things that lay about in the girls' rooms: petticoats, panties, money, papers, purses, handbags, stuffed animals. Nathalie had been nibbling biscuits; their crumbs were scattered over her desk next to the empty wrapping, on top of which she had carefully placed the browned core of an apple. Her untidiness was obstinate and systematic, whereas Laura's was prodigious, interrupted from time to time by massive clearing-up operations.

It was true that Cécile had spent her life simply in looking after a hundred and fifty square yards of space in Paris, and in feeding, tending and taking care of three children and one man. But once the children were there, what else could you do? Nathalie will see in her turn what it is like, if she has children . . .

'Thou shalt leave thy father and thy mother.' Leave us, children, leave us by all means: splendid. 'Thou shalt leave thy children.' In thy middle age, with what thou hast left of strength and freedom, thou shalt look the world in the face and thou shalt at last go off on the adventure of thyself. For the young are right: a life limited to the care of a few beings and a few objects, a life which does not extend beyond the family, is not enough; it is not a life.

The laundry woman rang at the door. Cécile gave her the sheets and tablecloths that she kept for her: the rest of the washing was done in a laundromat. She still had three hours before Laura came back from the lycée near by, which she did very regularly every day at a quarter past twelve. If the children had not eaten the remains of that duck last night, she would not have had to go out. The Spanish maid was a treasure because she never said anything, not knowing enough French; but for the same reason it was impossible to ask her to do anything other than routine chores. In any case, during her daily five hours in the flat Maria did not have time enough for everything.

Cécile looked to see what was left in the refrigerator: one duck bone, a few prunes and some stewed fruit, a few sausages, salad and cheese. If it had been only she and Laura . . . But Marc was one of the few remaining men in Paris who came home for lunch every day: there was no canteen at the Audit Office, restaurants were too expensive, and besides, he thoroughly enjoyed lunching at home because of his nap. Cécile smiled as she remembered a saying of Marc's to the effect that the only wise course was to eat and make love in one's own home. On Mondays Stéphane came home at one o'clock. Since lunch had to be made anyhow, it did not add to her work, and one could be certain that he had a proper meal.

Cécile reached the shopping centre, a traffic-filled street with sidewalks so narrow and cluttered that it was almost impossible to move. Butchers', grocers' and delicatessen shops stood side by side, together with shoe-shops and boutiques; even antique shops were beginning to appear here and there.

Girls stood in front of the windows in little groups, pointing at the models. They said 'hideous', 'sweet', 'great'. Particularly before the shoe-shops. They were lovely, with their bare thighs or their trousers tight over bottoms scarcely rounder than a boy's; indeed, from a little way off they looked like flowers, tropical creepers, does. When one came nearer it was apparent that many of them were not pretty or would not be for much longer, that some of them had shrews' faces and others middle-aged knees. These girls who swarmed along the pavements on Monday mornings in the fat, comfortable parts of the town were frightening; they had no shopping bags, no books, nothing but identical fashionable handbags dangling on their arms.

Sometimes women pushed against these girls' legs with their perambulators or their loaded shopping bags. Rude words were exchanged, there was a certain amount of stir, and then the groups coalesced again. All these girls—big, strapping wenches and little insect-thin ones—would end up by getting the things they were looking at: they would get those shoes (square-toed this year, and studded with gold and silver); they would get these silver stockings, silver dresses, silver bags.

The very abundance of what was available to wear, eat, put in one's home, was somehow nauseating. Yet Cécile too gazed at the shoes, the suits, the knick-knacks, the antique furniture and the jewels and the pâté royal and the Parma ham and the tropical fruit. She too wanted the lot.

The children from the near-by lycée were coming up the boulevard in groups with piles of textbooks and exercise books done up in a strap under their arms. They looked to Cécile very much the same as her own schoolmates; and when she met them like this, in knots, a few exquisite, some pretty and most of them lumpish and commonplace, she remembered what a friend had said to her. 'I've been teaching more than twenty years now, and as I see these girls go by, forty per class every year, I say to myself that all this fuss they make about the young today is so much nonsense. What I see is always the same average run, with two or three children who stand out in one direction or another, either for good or bad; but broadly speaking, it's always the same average run.'

There were crowds of boys at the gate of the lycée, some leaning on their mopeds, others at the wheel of their little cars, others standing and smoking. When the girl they were waiting for came out they kissed without the least bashfulness and went off together towards the Bois. Sometimes two or three couples would go off like this together, fondling one another, with a hint of exhibitionism. What had been the exception in Cécile's schooldays had become the rule; the girls who had been censured then were now legion—they had won. Once again Cécile thought resentfully of her headmistress, who used to hunt down innocent love-affairs even in the street; and of the fashions of her young days.

How pretty these jerkins were, these short skirts, acid colours and filly's legs. At last the delight of being female and of being young was bursting forth. Indeed, it was bursting forth rather too vigorously. For an instant, because of clothes and hair, Cécile thought one of those girls going off so lovingly towards the Bois was Laura, and her heart missed a beat.

'But in the end,' said her school-teacher friend, 'it's always three little twirls and then they're off. They have only one idea in their heads—to get married.'

Cécile called at the bank and saw the twenty-year-old girl clerks with commonplace features, bent over their papers. When they opened a cupboard for a file it revealed huge postcards showing snowy peaks, green forests and bright blue sea pinned up behind the doors.

Cécile went into a pharmacy. Waiting at the counter was a grey-haired woman with a hard, careworn face, carrying a heavy shopping basket. It was Viviane, a childhood friend. They now lived in the same part of Paris and met at rare intervals, sometimes in the street, when they had both run out to do a bit of shopping (in which case they were neither well dressed nor well groomed). On these occasions they were not too eager to recognize each other. Cécile was on the point of walking out of the shop, but Viviane had looked up and greeted her unsmilingly.

'I hope no one's ill at home,' said Cécile.

'Oh no, only my grandmother. Or not her so much as me.'

'Oh, is your grandmother still with you?' Cécile asked.

'And how. She's ninety-three. And as you know, the little house we live in belongs to her. She fractured the neck of her femur three years ago, but she got over that without any trouble at all. And she leads me such a dance. Deaf as a post—demanding. Now I'm the one who's ill. I can't cope any more. I've come to buy myself a tonic. Oh, these old people will be the death of us.' The talk had diverted her attention, her papers were in a mess, and Viviane's haunted look returned. When she had sorted out her papers she came back to Cécile. 'You know my son is married, of course. He had a little girl in January. Well, my daughter-in-law left her with me for a whole month while she went off to India with Michel. Did we ever dream of parading about the world with our husbands when our children were little? No fear! From the moment I was forced to stay at home because of my grandmother . . . And how are things with you? No one married?'

'Pretty well,' said Cécile. 'No one married.'

'Make the most of what you have left,' said Viviane and hurried out, anxious not to miss the green light which she could see from the shop and which would let her cross the street. Thin, leaning forward, carrying her basket, she was already walking fast along the opposite sidewalk. She looks like an old working-class woman, Cécile thought.

Viviane's husband was a distinguished scholar, a member of the Institut.

Cécile passed the tennis-courts, and here too the majority of the people running about were women, fairly old women for the most part, their joints already creaking, women who had earned the right to have fun from the morning on and who were chasing after the balls with as much zeal as though their lives depended on it. Cécile understood them particularly well. She had almost been one of their number.

Apart from a few commercial travellers and some workmen and house-painters on buildings, apart from a few old men and schoolboys, the streets and the open air were a feminine preserve. The men were all shut up. It would need an uncommonly sharp intelligence to say which were the slaves. Nowhere, thought Cécile, as she watched people intently and meditated while doing her shopping, nowhere do you see anything but slaves.

She went home carrying her bag in a hurry to get to work on her translation; she had no idea why she inflicted this task upon herself—a difficult task and one that brought in

94

precious little money. But she had grown used to living in an atmosphere of mild crisis, a private, inner harassment which always represented for her a higher occupation over and above what she was actually doing, and from which she was kept back by whatever she had in hand at the moment. These translations meant at least a few hours every day taken out of what might be called a housewife's existence. Yet these hours of work also took place in the house—the housewife's abode; she had no illusions about their intellectual scope, but when she did think about them she saw them as so many windows looking out.

Translation was an alibi, a way of escape from gossiping telephone-calls in the morning and from the daily round: it gave her status. It also gave her her little label—she was 'a translator'. When she was sitting there at her table, typing, or when she said 'Can't you see I am working?' it had much more effect than if she had said 'Can't you see I am dreaming?' or 'Can't you see I am thinking?' or 'Can't you see I am reading?' And she was far more respected than if she had been busy stirring a sauce. Later, when the children had gone and no one needed the small amount of money she earned this way, she would profit by the rhythm she had won, by this alternation from trivial talk to silence, from housewifery to self-discipline, from sociability to solitude. She would turn these translations into something better. Granted her life was commonplace; but how free it was, compared with so many others! And it promised to be freer still.

The book that Cécile was now working on was an autobiography, of course, the autobiography of a twenty-three-year-old beatnik, the offspring of a family of poor musicians who had come to England as refugees. The publisher's blurb said that this young man had abandoned his training and had flung his parents' sacrifices to the winds. They, the poor simpletons, judging by the promise he had shown, had dreamt of seeing him one day upon the concert platform in evening dress. Feeling within him a higher vocation, he had let his hair grow and had set off to travel the world with a guitar. He described the banks of the Seine, the hand-out soup behind Saint-Séverin, Trastevere, the Plaza where the waiters from the eating-houses used to give him leftovers at about three in the morning (one day he cut his foot on a piece of broken glass), and various police stations. The photograph showed a thin evangelical face framed in dreary curls.

As soon as the text set about trying to express ideas (and unfortunately it often did) it lost itself in a rambling obscurity whose darkness was certainly not that of genius. And yet among the rubbish, the high-falutin' assertions and the hatred, the writing carried with it dreams, feelings and intuitions, as touching as youth, as touching as the longing for a finer world.

Cécile had decided to translate the words almost literally, leaving the sense to look after itself. Sometimes the result was rather beautiful.

As for the songs, they were filled with worthy sentiments and had all the simplicity that was lacking in the prose. They celebrated peace on earth, coloured friends, children's tears. Laura, who was something of a connoisseur of these things, said that in addition to the rhythm the author's great originality lay in hitting upon such brilliant things as 'I Just Make Love With You', which had earned him his greatest success. Cécile liked the songs. When they became well known in France it still seemed to her that her translation of them was the best. She scanned the verses, marking the beat on her desk: she sang them. Doing this put her on top of her form. Sometimes she made up other songs and other tunes that ran on and on in her head, songs that she hummed when she was driving alone; they blended with the speed and with the landscape and they gave her the feeling that she was still young and full of potentialities.

She was particularly pleased with one of her efforts, whose first lines went:

> We have been Kings, you and I,
> For a couple of months,
> We who were nothing much,
> Keep that in your heart, Marlene.

Now the sun was lighting up the three windows of the drawing-room. In this fine weather the traffic in the avenue seemed happy. Cécile hummed, saying to herself, 'My life's nothing much, of course; it's a little middle-class life; I'll never ride over the Pampas; I'll never have a Rolls, nor a yacht, nor a marvellous flat, nor even a maid; I'll never go dancing again, I'll never walk barefoot on the hot pavement any more, I'll never die of love for anyone and no one will ever die of love for me; I shan't be a saint, or look after lepers, or lead a revolution; I shan't be the mistress of a genius; I shan't discover anything; I shan't write poetry; and the Gospel spews out the lukewarm, and the most amazing thing on earth, according to Trotsky, is growing old, and I'm quite old already and wounded all over, battered and scarred, and I don't know what I am blamed for, whether it is for not having had enough fun or for having had too much, or both together; there are hidden duties all round me that I don't perform because I'm not equal to them, and yet at this moment I'm happy—I can't help it. Anyhow, what do other people of my age do? Nothing much, either. They dream. These fine biographies are all just so much literature; in the long run even the most genuine artists come to look like third-rate barnstormers, and according to everything I see or read or hear, the young people in our country are not exactly famous for altruism, and they are not heroes either; but Nathalie is in love and how well I understand her!'

And then at a quarter past twelve on the dot Laura opened the door with a pretence of shyness and pursed her lips to make the sound of a kiss into the air. Laura came home with her long arms, her warm voice, her white stockings and her dark glasses, and already it was time to get lunch ready and to kiss Laura and there was the cooking and the table to be laid and Papa who would not be long now and 'You've forgotten to buy the bread again, Laura; you know perfectly well that you're supposed to bring it back every day since you go right by the bakery and I've got too much to carry already. How many times do I have to tell you? You might at least do that—it's all I ask of you.' And Laura said, 'All right, all right, I'm going: don't make a thing of it.' But Cécile kept her back. 'Listen to this. I'm going to sing you a song I made up this morning as I was translating.' And she began in a flat, thin voice, laughing to keep herself in countenance:

> 'We have been Kings, you and I,
> For a couple of months,
> We who were nothing much,
> Keep that in your heart, Marlene.'

And Laura bit her lip to prevent herself from giggling. She was embarrassed too; but then she said kindly, 'It's not bad, but it's a bit dated. And you'd have to change the tune, too. The best bit is the last line—*Keep that in your heart, Marlene.*'

This was life, wasn't it?

3

The family celebrated Marc's forty-ninth birthday; Marc had been made a senior principal a few months before. His promotion had come through during one of those periods when he laughed and talked too loudly, never refused any invitation as though each had a charming surprise in store for him, asserted that he would go on beating the young at tennis for a long time yet, wanted to see all the shows and be up to date in everything, put his arm round the necks of girls the age of his own daughters, and flung hundred-franc notes about in restaurants as though he had won them in the *Loterie Nationale*.

At the party Cécile gave in honour of this promotion Marc had been in splendid form. Cécile always gave one big party a year, but usually at the beginning of autumn, for theirs was more of a winter flat, and as soon as it was spring people preferred seeing one another out of doors in gardens. Marc seemed very young for the post he held and he was so much congratulated upon this point that he had put on the airs of an infant prodigy. But after so many late nights, and with the coming of the first really hot weather, Marc bogged down in depression, just as he had done for some years past. All at once, nothing could rouse him. He continued to go out, but he did not talk and he no longer enjoyed himself. He went to the country, but there he invented pains in order to remain in a deck-chair. He grew humble. His eyes, like Nathalie's, looked inwards. All he wanted was gentle kindness, affection, carefully prepared

99

dishes, his family around him, and the strange wonder of exhausted embraces.

'Christ, what an athlete's body!' he would say, looking at himself in the mirror. Cécile laughed and could not stop, laughed until the tears came. Whereupon Marc also managed to snigger a second, and said, 'How it stinks, getting old.'

Yes, it stank. For so long it had seemed to apply to other people, another race, an unfortunate caste: and then suddenly there it was—the old, that meant you.

'But Marc, you're not old. Fifty is the prime of life for a man. Besides, no one would think you were forty. What would you say if you were me? Growing old is much rougher on a woman.' That was not true, at least as far as she was concerned, not with all the hopes she pinned on age. 'Besides, I'm ageing faster than you. You haven't a single wrinkle. Look at all mine. Before long they'll be taking me for your mother.'

He scarcely protested. He found Cécile's ageing quite easy to accept. 'The reason I have no wrinkles is that I'm too fat,' was all he said.

'Well, that's how I like you best.'

Her youthful liking for well-rounded men, whom she found reassuring, was one of their established jokes. But in those days Marc had been thin. He used to groan, 'I shall never manage to get a pot belly.'

'Unfortunately I'm not the one you try to please nowadays.' Nowadays, alas, she also knew what feet of clay her stout men had.

They joked about it. 'What on earth is happening to us?'

If only they had been able to talk about it clearly once and for all, say all they had to say, and then, hand in hand and with their eyes open, go forward together towards that torment, old age, which they would certainly reach in the end if they did not die first, and towards that inescapable abyss, death. Together, eyes open and hand in hand, set free from their responsibilities, they might perhaps have behaved wildly and given away their possessions, like those under sentence of death.

But that was not the way of it.

When Cécile said, 'Not feeling ill, are you?' Marc said, 'No, it's just that there's nothing I look forward to.'

'That happens to everyone,' Cécile said.

'Maybe. But that doesn't make me feel any better.'

'When something is the common lot it seems to me it's more bearable.'

He gave her a sad, childlike look, as though it had been in her power to offer him better comfort.

He never asked if she ever felt that way too. And yet God knows she did, though admittedly less often than she used to. It was chiefly when the children were small and the family needed all her attention, above all in their early years, that it used to come over her. Sometimes she would get up in the morning with such a feeling of revulsion that it seemed to her quite impossible to bear the hour ahead. She washed and did her hair. She got the three children out of bed; they were as heavy as lead. She washed them, dressed them, fed them, answered them, coaxed them, and reflected that they would grow up and experience this very sadness. To talk to them, play with them, make them eat (they were never hungry)—it was beyond her strength. She held out the spoon and waited, her arm in the air; she became exhausted, she longed to die. Then she felt guilty: what kind of a love was this that did not give her heart and strength? She kept quiet about it, ashamed of not being able to cope as well as other women. Suffering and death seemed to her the only points of certainty.

If Marc had known about it in those days, if he had been

worried by it, perhaps she would have become intolerable. But he had such confidence in her, such a delighted appetite for life, so little idea of neuroses or weariness, and such a plentiful lack of imagination. She had had to cope all by herself. She used to bend over double, with her head on the smallest child's stomach, and wait for it to pass. It passed. It had no connection with their real troubles. On the contrary, during the months that followed Stéphane's poliomyelitis she had been energetic and stimulated, in spite of her feelings of guilt. But now it was Marc who, without warning or shame, was beginning to lose his pleasure in life and said so.

'There's nothing that worries you particularly?'

'No . . . but . . .'

'But what?'

He made a wide, vague sweep of his arm. 'All this,' he said. They remained silent for a moment, small, fragile, hemmed in by 'all this'. 'Sometimes I get up in the morning and think that I am going to start a pointless day,' Marc went on, 'and that the world would go on in exactly the same way if I weren't there. If I have to go on doing this for another sixteen years, presiding over commissions I don't believe in, trying to find answers in cases where I know perfectly well there aren't any, scribbling away, begging for special missions, all this just to be able to keep my family in something like decency . . .'

She saw him again as he had been in the years of the Occupation, with the simple, direct choice of those times: hard towards the waverers, pitiless towards those on the other side, certain of the future: 'How easy it would be to breathe if our streets were swept clean of them.' He had broken off his studies; he had no job; but he took on responsibility for her too (which after all was something Emmanuel had not wanted to do) and got her with child straight away; and then he had done so again, so that they should be a real family to celebrate the future.

With the streets at last 'swept clean of them', proud of his job, he set about rebuilding France. Who could tell what would happen if Marc had to go on doing this for another sixteen years? Most probably nothing would. He would be a thoroughly successful man. With his membership in the Resistance, his fine career and the list of his books, to say nothing of his little successes at games, it would be possible to write a very creditable biographical entry under his name.

Cécile comforted him like a big baby, waiting until his days of glory should return. But the evening of his forty-ninth birthday, getting ready to blow out the candles on the big cake, Marc still had a glum and melancholy look.

The children did not present a particularly cheerful spectacle either. Nathalie was ravaged and worn by late nights and looked dangerously thin. Stéphane, more withdrawn than ever as the examination drew near, was grey-faced and ineffectual-looking. Laura was hideous—greasy-haired, pasty. She had suddenly decided to do her utmost to be moved up into the top form, and for the last two weeks she had been working prodigiously in her own particular way.

Cécile had no patience with them. When she saw them like this round the table, all failures, doing nothing to help her, she felt like leaving them for ever. She was particularly cross with Laura—the child might at least have washed her hair for this evening. She had spent the whole year primping in front of the glass, and now she had no time even to be clean. She was a third-rate creature. And she was ratting. Weren't parties any of her business? The whole family was being third-rate for their father's birthday. A family the world could very well have done without.

The table was laid for a feast. They had eaten caviar and cold salmon and drunk vodka. But nobody really contributed anything. They had to be carried along—dead weights. Oh, that dreary voice of Marc's!

The time for the presents had come. Today's gifts were modest and conventional—a tie with a matching handkerchief; a book. It was impossible to know what to give Marc. There was nothing he needed: they had never been able to part him from his old razor or from the aged cough-lozenge box he used for his cuff-links when travelling. He did not like gadgets; he did not know how to use them and he ruined them almost at once. But he uttered an exclamation of delight on discovering the handkerchief. 'That's good,' he said. 'I could do with one of those.'

Their faces lit up. Marc had unfolded the handkerchief and was beginning to arrange it in a manner that indicated to Laura that he was under a misapprehension.

'But it's not a cravat, Papa: it's a handkerchief.'

'Are you sure?'

'Of course it's a handkerchief,' they chorused.

But Marc persisted. 'It seems too big for a handkerchief.' He managed to get the fabric with its masculine colours round his neck, where it formed a thin string with a tiny knot. He gazed at them, unsure of the effect. 'Isn't that right?'

And as they all burst out laughing, he put on his half-witted look, bit his lower lip with his two slightly protruding front teeth, and in an earnest, childish voice, imitating Maria, said, 'I thinked she was a cravat.'

They all kissed him. 'Poor Papa, is he disappointed, did he want a cravat and get only a handkerchief! Poor Papa, but what did he want a cravat for?'

'It was for the country,' he said, still with his half-wit's air. 'I should have worn it under my shirt, so that I didn't have to put on a tie and had my neck free.'

How they loved him when he was like this!

'Heavens! Papa with no tie, wearing a cravat like a dandy! If only we'd known. But you shall have your cravat. There was one that matched the tie and the handkerchief. If only we had thought. You shall have your cravat, Papa: don't be disappointed. We'll get it for you tomorrow.'

'It's not that I'm disappointed,' said Marc, removing the handkerchief. 'This handkerchief is a beauty and so is the tie. But if I have a cravat I shall be even happier.' Once more he gazed at them all, still biting his lip with his two teeth, and he repeated, 'You see, I shall be even happier.'

They coaxed him, they kissed him, they petted this father who wanted to fling his tie into the air for his forty-ninth birthday, this senior principal in the Audit Office who had a particular brand of humour and melancholy which they alone knew.

'You know,' said Marc when he was alone with Cécile again, 'I'm old enough, God knows, as it is; but there are times when I wish I were older.'

'Go on!' said Cécile.

'I'd like to be rid of the children. I want them all to have a job and be done with being brought up, so that their livelihood no longer depended on mine, if you know what I mean.'

If she knew!

'I'd like to be rid of it,' said Marc again. 'It goes on too long.'

For twenty years four times a day he had plunged, frowning, briefcase in hand, into his car or into the Métro, to force himself back into the same mould. For twenty years, ever since he left the civil service college (the whole class had consisted almost entirely of young men who had fought in the war before returning to the lecture halls to follow their courses), he had earned the right to go and sit in an office eight hours a day, six days a week, then five and a half days, and then five. For twenty years he had kept them by his own unaided work. All the clothes they had worn, everything they had eaten, all the heating of all the winters, all their holidays, all their schooling, everything had been paid for by Marc: they owed everything to Marc's servitude.

'I wish I were five years older.'

'Would you retire?'

In his eyes she saw the same little hunted gleam so often seen in Stéphane's.

'I don't know what I should do. I don't know. But at least I should do whatever I liked.'

She almost said, 'How like Stéphane you are, how like Stéphane you are at this moment, darling.' All she said was, 'Darling,' with a little smile.

He was fixed, settled, done for, the handsome young man all wild for liberty. Never again had the magnificent freedom of their first days returned.

'You don't know how I think about it sometimes; it seems to me unbelievable that you have fed us all, clothed us all and housed us day after day for so many years.'

'Fathers of families, those great adventurers,' said Marc.

Secretly, illegally, they crossed the demarcation line into unoccupied France. In the free zone they waited to get a residence certificate that would allow them to marry, for they had never even thought of living together in any other way. This was a real holiday. The open air made them hungry. They threw stones, knocking walnuts off the trees in the fields. They settled in Paris again under a false name. She was pregnant; she was ill; and Marc often left her on her own. She waited for him. She learnt to cook with nothing, on a spirit-stove. To have an alibi and to buy the baby's cradle and pay the rent, he used to work several hours a day in a friend's office, but he was away for whole evenings at a time. The unlit twilight dragged on. She dozed; she was perpetually sleepy. She queued to buy onions off the ration, and peeled them, weeping. She passed the last subject for her degree. She waited for Marc. There were more and more arrests. Marc came back. Together, at midnight, they bathed their baby. They were cold and hungry. After Nathalie's birth she began to be afraid. They made love, love, love. They themselves were their sole happiness. At least, it was her sole happiness. Marc also exulted in plots of which she knew nothing, and in hope. Stéphane was born.

Now the excitement of the party, nostalgia for the past, the sense of the vanity of life, surprise at the changes that had come over them—these, together with Marc's sadness, wrapped them both about.

'We really were adventurers to begin with,' Cécile said. 'Only we didn't fully realize it. Besides, we could hardly be anything else. Yet it seems to me that our greatest adventure has been all this time spent together, day after day. A family really is something quite out of the ordinary: a trifle excessive, perhaps.'

'The other day,' Marc said, 'when I was looking for a piece of paper, I came across the address that young priest gave on our wedding-day. I wanted to show it to you, but you were telephoning, and then I forgot it. Wait a minute and I'll find it. I put it away.'

The priest had guessed their situation and liked them, though sad that he had been unable to convert Marc. 'Nevertheless, you will be married in a chapel. Since my address is fairly long people won't even notice that there is no mass going on.'

People, indeed! There were only their witnesses and their parents.

Marc came back with a sheet of paper in his hand. 'I've given you a drab, restricted life,' he said. 'If we were to have our time over again, would you still marry me?'

'What a question,' she said. 'What a question to ask after twenty-three years!'

'Do you think you'd still marry me?' Marc insisted. 'You've never regretted it?'

You who are marrying without knowing where you will live tomorrow, without knowing what your position will be, you who are giving each other this splendid gift each of the other for yourselves alone, you show us love manifest and I salute love in your persons.

Just as before, just as twenty-three years before, she longed to cry and felt herself unworthy.

While the priest was speaking she bowed her head. She was in tears. She saw Marc's hand. She had a wild longing to clutch this hand and escape with Marc before the rings should be put on their fingers. She was not worthy of what the priest was saying.

'Of course not,' she said, pretending not to take Marc seriously. 'Of course I've never regretted it.'

It was the truth: she had never regretted anything. But if it were to do all over again? What fire had been in their blood in those days; what poverty they had all lived in, what total disorder!

It was as well to remember those days when one had children of twenty.

'You are the man I never could have left.'

That was the naked truth. Other men, yes, no doubt—so many other men. Other lives—so many other lives. But never without him.

She very nearly added, 'And what about you?' But what

was the point? When he looked at young women and girls with that expression she knew so well, when he came home late without any good excuse, did that mean he regretted their marriage? There was no relationship between all they would have liked to experience, the little they had experienced, and them as a married couple. That was how it was. That was what they had had; and, all things considered, what they had wanted. What was human love? They were far from being pure love and nothing else the one for the other; the life, the small-scale life they had led together, was far from being the only one they might have led. But they could never have left each other. A doubt came into her mind. Certainly not. She did not believe that from now on Marc could leave her either, even if he were now suffering more from the deprivation she had experienced when she was young. In fact they had probably loved each other more than they had loved themselves and more than they had loved love itself. Or at least they had behaved as though . . . Like a great many couples. Was that wrong?

'You are my life,' she said. 'And that's that.'

Indeed, it appeared to her that what they had failed to be for each other bound them as much as and more than what they had been; that their failures represented the closest, most private of their shared intimacies, their deepest alliance.

And, as she had done so often, she sat down at Marc's feet and rested her head on his thigh. 'Perhaps everything depended on our bodies,' she said, 'on our physical good fortune.'

As usual he put his hand on her hair. 'No doubt you could have done much more than you have done with me,' he said again, 'and much finer things.'

She did not like him humble. 'Everyone might have done

much more than he has done, and much finer things. You too—you most of all . . . Everyone.'

'Oh no,' he said in his dismal voice, 'I was never particularly bright.'

She drew away, shaking off her heaviness. 'But why talk about us in the past? We aren't as old as all that. Our life's not over. In one way it's only just beginning. What is over, or almost, is this great adventure of the family. But presently you and I are going to be alone, just the two of us, and freer than we have ever been in our lives. We are on the right side, Marc. Worry about earning a living is over; and the worry of being the provider and the guardian is over too. At last we're going to be able to do what we want and show what we're capable of. There'll be no one to worry about any more. No more prudence, no more of these everlasting scruples. Why don't we think about our future instead? Why shouldn't we set off on fresh adventures? You and me, all by ourselves? Free. Can you imagine how free we shall be, presently?'

He looked at her with his sad eyes, which had a hint of mockery in them. 'You are young,' he said, in his wretched voice.

'No, I am not young. On the contrary, I am fully mature. But I'm still so very much of a virgin.'

He was about to be facetious when suddenly his expression changed and he said, 'That's just it; you put it very well. From time to time I have that feeling too—the feeling that I shall die uninitiated. I see retirement looming up, and what shall I have accomplished? It's unbelievable.' He shrugged. 'Oh, damn! Maybe everyone's in the same boat. You have to make a good choice at the outset. And once you've made your choice it's all over—you've had it.'

What would he not have done, what risks would he not have taken, without her and the children? She knew him.

She knew his dash and courage. He might have written, travelled; he might have lived without working, or at least without working like a slave: he might have launched into politics. He might have aimed at making a great fortune or risked being really poor; he might have had countless women. Was it not ill-luck that he should have met her so soon? She felt the weight she had been round his neck.

'A few more years and then, when they've all got jobs, you'll be the one to decide. We'll sell the flat and buy a house in Provence. We'll live in espadrilles and jeans. Life will cost nothing. We'll read all the books. We'll go swimming. We'll listen to music. You'll write. We shall be free. We'll be lovers.' But I shall dream in your shade, she thought, like a child under age.

'In short, retirement,' said Marc.

'Yes, as you were saying just now. You'll retire and you'll do just as you like, just as you choose. When there are no more children at home, no more helpless creatures to look after, and when you don't have to worry about anybody, it's easy to plunge into adventure. Adventurers really make me laugh.'

'The trouble is that I no longer want anything, there are no more adventures which tempt me. You didn't marry a very outstanding man, my poor Pépette.' Oh, he made her feel like screaming. 'But what about you,' he added, 'don't you have the feeling of living again through your children?'

'No, not a bit,' she said. 'No more than you do. And maybe even less. Now that they're grown up, at least the two eldest, their life's their own affair—an affair that's not the same as mine, not the same as ours.' She surreptitiously touched the wood of the armchair. 'Of course,' she said, 'if something awful happened to them . . . But so long as everything goes reasonably well for them . . . I have the impression, if you understand me, that I'm only just beginning to live without a screen. All these years there was always their weakness coming between the world and me. It was as though I couldn't walk at my own speed; as though every time I moved I was afraid of breaking someone. I never benefited by the two or three journeys you made me take without them. I didn't see Rome, I didn't see the Acropolis, I didn't see anything. When they weren't with me it was even worse.' She laughed. 'And then I've got rid of men, too. In the old days I daren't do a thing. I couldn't move a step without bumping into a man. Now I can stop where I like, look at what I like, sit on a bench, put my dress on inside out or look quite mad—men don't worry me in the very least.'

That was not entirely true. She had not yet lost the gift of chance encounters. But these days men hardly bothered her at all unless she wanted them to. Then she had a sudden vision of Marc as she had sometimes seen him, hurrying about the beaches and the sports grounds with his eyes ablaze with thoughts of rape. You can never take your oath on anything, she reflected. Up to the very end, up to the last sad collapse, all marriages are threatened. Who could take his oath, even about me?

'You've infected me a little,' said Marc at last. 'Once upon a time I never used to think of the possibility of misfortune. Now I sometimes hurry to get home because I wonder what I am going to find there. By the way, what's happening to Nathalie? It seems to me that we don't see much of her these days.'

Had he needed the children to bring him back to her from wherever his silence led him? She felt like answering, 'Do you mean you've actually noticed that she's not at home very often?' But she confined herself to spreading her hands in her usual gesture and raising her eyebrows.

'Is there something up?' Marc asked.

'It's more some*one*.'

'Who? That pianist?'

'Yes.'

'Is that why we don't see Alain any more?'

'Probably.'

Then, as though he were very sorry he had ventured out on this limb, Marc asked, 'Now I come to think of it, you've seen this Jo, haven't you? You've never told me about him.' And as she did not reply, 'Why have you never told me about him?'

'You never asked,' she said.

'That's no reason. I'd forgotten. Tell me, what's he like?'

'Good-looking,' she said.

'Well, what more?' asked Marc, as she relapsed into silence.

'There's really nothing much I can tell you. He's a young Israeli who wants to go on living in France. He was wearing jeans and an open-necked shirt. It suited him.'

Marc closed his eyes and nodded. 'I see,' he said. Then a moment later, 'Is he talented?'

Talented. Talented. Nathalie too had wanted to make her say that Jo was talented. 'Judging by his appearance,' said Cécile, 'I rather imagine he is. But obviously I know nothing about it.'

'Do you think it's serious?' asked Marc.

'What do you mean by serious?'

'I mean, do you suppose they are thinking of marriage?'

'Oh, that . . .' said Cécile. Then she added, 'It wouldn't surprise me if Nathalie was. But he's not the kind of young man to think of marrying anyone. No, I don't think so.'

'Well?' said Marc.

'Well, it's obvious, as you would say.'

'What's obvious?'

'The situation.'

'You seem very fatalistic.'

'Nathalie can't be shut up,' said Cécile. 'She's twenty-two.'

'She can't be shut up, but still she can be told . . .' He fell silent.

'Told what?'

'She can be warned.'

'Against this foreigner? Against this musician? Against love?'

'Well . . . yes,' said Marc.

'For years now you've been telling me that times have changed, that girls are free and that I worry too much; and you blame me for lecturing them too often. And now you want me to warn Nathalie when I feel I have no right to do so and when I have no wish to do so either. It would be more to the point if you were to do your share and see Jo.'

'If the opportunity crops up,' said Marc. 'Yes, if the opportunity crops up I'll see this fellow. But as on the face of it I don't care for him all that much I'd rather the meeting looked as though it had come about by chance: I shouldn't like him to suppose . . .'

'It may be that you come across a young man like that only once in a lifetime.'

'What romanticism!' Marc said.

'Perhaps you could no more help going to him than you could help running through a summer storm,' Cécile murmured.

'What?'

'If only you could see how lovely they are together.'

4

Marc's pains grew worse. He spent a week at home, getting up only for meals which he ate in his dressing-gown, ill-shaved. The doctor could find nothing wrong with him. Cécile was unwell too; her symptoms were said to be of an allergic nature and she had to take drugs which had a depressant effect. Once more the dream of a place in the country was aired in the flat, while at the same time the picture of retirement lost its charms and gave way to an uneasy vision of a helpless, ill-tempered and domineering confrontation.

Marc made up his mind to go back to the office. Cécile felt better. Festivities were going full blast; parties grew more and more frequent as the holidays drew near, as though people were afraid of dying on the road or in the sea before they could see one another again. Friends from the country and strangers poured into the town. Cécile and Marc began to go out again and to entertain. They were not averse to friendship or the civilized pleasures. It was delightful, it was charming, they were very fond of everybody. But it was rarely so delightful or so charming as they said it was: it was not unforgettable. It was almost always the same—the same traffic jams, the same nervous exhaustion, the same people, the same districts, the same flats—all either traditionally middle-class or 'full of character'—the same wonderful ideas, the same 'see you soon' that meant nothing, the hostess's drawn looks, the anxiety of reciprocating, the threatening sky on the day of a garden-party—

'And what shall I wear? It's dreadful: I have ten dresses but never the right one'; the difficulty of parking—'It can't be helped: we'll leave it here. But it'll cost ten francs again—next time we'll take a cab.' No cab to be found, and Cécile spoiling her gold shoes and her hair-do waiting in the rain: 'It can't be helped: we'll take the Métro'; but they had to change twice to get to Neuilly or the fifth arrondissement, where they often went, and then walk another quarter of a mile and crowd in, absurdly dressed, among people coming back from work: 'Oh, I shan't go out any more. You go, Marc, since you enjoy it and it's more or less expected of you; but so far as I'm concerned it's a waste of time and a pointless grind.' The ageing of certain people who only a short time ago still had the look of lords of creation, first one war, then another, and the enduring threat of a general flare-up, all these threw their shadows over the knick-knacks, the party dresses, the gardens and the plans for the holidays. Sometimes there might be an epigram or a piece of inside information that would be in all the papers a few hours later: sometimes the happiness of a brief encounter. Sometimes it was so pleasant to come across people one had lost touch with that it was impossible to understand how one had managed to live so long apart. There were promises to meet again before the holidays: 'We really must, it's too silly: a quiet little dinner just the four of us: we'll telephone—it's a promise', and then the promise grew burdensome—one more social obligation—and life was running by fast and what was one doing with it?

And there were all these women, who had come into bloom during the years of peace, these young ones springing up on every side, gleaming and sparkling around Marc: these girls, these young women in crazy dresses, were nearer to the flappers of the twenties or the women of

Edwardian days than they were to Cécile. There was nothing like these women who proclaimed that life was a party for making Cécile aware of loneliness, of time's passing, and of the anguish of death. She was like those proletarians who cannot take life lightly because they are waiting for great promises to be fulfilled; she was like those refugees, from whatever side, who cannot find human friendship and solidarity outside the comradeship of fighting and of prisons; she felt herself to be an everlasting survivor from the war. Only women who had been twenty during the nineteen-forties were her sisters. The continuity of the generations had skipped hers. Cécile gazed at the be-jewelled, chattering old women with as much astonishment as at the young ones covered with costume jewellery. When she was at the age of bosom friendships and first love she had known the secret world of the Resistance, hunger, cold, and deep spiritual joy. She still hankered after that severe austerity. Yet she too dressed up and took part in the game. She discovered that in spite of everything said and written to the contrary, a woman in her forties is still attractive to men; it was pleasant, life was long, and it was always the same ones who were attractive. But the human comedy no longer interested her very much. In any case she would soon have to dispense with being a woman. Above all, she would be obliged to leave this world before she had found out what could be done, as far as it was in human power, to deal with the vast unhappiness, the huge distress that was forgotten in the Paris of the month of June. She would never have been able to come to grips with it; and Marc, who had had such a clear idea in the days of the Occupation, could not see any solution either, or none that was not very, very far away. For the twenty years to come, that is to say, the twenty years that statistics still gave them to live, he could see nothing but the approach of famine and the escalation of disorders. And that was what the top civil servants and the big businessmen were saying as they stood among the flowers and the glasses at cocktail parties.

But what of it? You liked the people you met, but not all that much: you took care never to see them again. Perhaps you might have liked them better, but there wasn't the time; there never would be time any more. The cards were dealt. From now on you could count the people who were irreplaceable. The others were only extras. Sometimes a look or a word made you think that friendship might spring up, or love burst into flame, but it was no more than the quickly silenced echo of the thunderclap of former days. For a moment the extra held the front of the stage. You were seized with a longing for another love, another life, a completely fresh start. 'Well, goodbye.' Your spouse was tugging at your sleeve; you shook hands; couples went off together—'Goodbye.' You thought of it for a little while; you even dreamed of it sometimes. Were dreams to be the innermost, most certain aspects of your private wealth from now on? Did the future hold at least these nocturnal surprises and discoveries in store? It was lovelier than reality, so much power and more full of meaning; it was as moving as first kisses, and it was bathed in a light that even memory no longer possessed. Compared with dreams, memory was mere black and white. Sometimes the wonder of dreaming lasted all day; the physical tenderness and gaiety of heart remained until evening, and you made a date with them for the following night. But nothing ever came of it and dreams left fewer memories than memory itself.

Cécile wondered whether old people dreamed, but dared not ask those she knew. Yet what was unseemly in dreaming after a certain age? She told herself that in order to retain the power of dreaming, she would certainly drug herself a little, if necessary. Death had already eroded some of those irreplaceable beings who made up her human landscape. Whose turn next? She retreated within herself. From now on the unseen seemed to her the surest.

Often, amid the din of a party, she would think: in fifty or sixty years at the outside, all these people here, so full of bounce, so full of themselves, will be under ground. All of them. There was not one face over forty that did not already acknowledge its defeat, in one way or another. Some were already the colour of the earth for which they were bound. There were some whose appearance in a drawing-room was embarrassing: a kind of holy dread emanated from them. Everyone, themselves perhaps included, knew this was the end. At next year's great reception it would be better not to think of what had happened to them. People said, 'Poor old So-and-so has come unstuck.' Or ought it to be, 'He has taken off'? Taken off for heaven? Or did they really mean unstuck, no longer holding together? After all, *décollé* could mean either.

The talk carried right on. 'We rather think of becoming your neighbours in the south. We had a notion of buying a flat at Villefranche. But the price! Three hundred and fifty thousand for three hundred square feet; though admittedly there was a terrace and a flat roof. It's out of the question. Besides, we'd rather have a house; a house has more charm than a flat. Though to be sure, a house is frightening.'

'Go inland ten or fifteen miles and the prices are much lower.'

They were told the names of villages and Marc wrote them down in his diary.

Talking to other people, Cécile said, 'We should like to find a farmhouse in the real country. No, not a weekend house but something quite far from Paris for those impossible months when you're really only happy in your own place.'

She was advised to try the Eure, Burgundy, the Sologne, even the Corrèze—yes, why not?

But when she met Edith and Julien it appeared that Neauphles was the place to settle in; there were still some houses to be found there, not in Neauphles itself but within a radius of a few miles; the district was not included in the scheme for Greater Paris—she must beware of that scheme. So it was at Neauphles that laughter and affection were to be reborn, Neauphles that would see the reconciliation of the generations every weekend.

But Marc did not like Julien, and in any case prices were rising everywhere. They really should make up their minds. On the other hand land was not selling so well. It was said that Marc's was included in a development plan, that it would be impossible to get a building permit for it and that it would be completely worthless. They ought to do something about it.

And then, like a 'what's the point?' there came back the vision of all those people buried under the ground, Cécile and Marc among them.

They went home. St John of the Cross, Teresa of Avila, Proust, Kierkegaard, Musil, Karl Marx, Günter Grass, *War and Peace*, *And Quiet Flows the Don*, Samuel Butler, Aragon, Plato, Saint-John Perse, Sade, *Le Communisme*, the Bible and all the music on earth were there waiting for you, but Marc said, 'I should like a slice of ham and some salad: I had nothing to eat,' there was a telephone call, you talked to the children for a while, glanced at the papers, listened to the news and all at once it was midnight. Proper reading and escape would be for later, and as for the time one ought to take for basic problems, Cécile would die before knowing.

'I don't really wish to travel in this world emptied of its wonders: unless you can expect everything you expect nothing . . . The young are potential adults, but I am interested in them: the future is in their hands, and in so far as I can discern my plans in theirs it seems to me that my life stretches out beyond my grave. I like being with them: yet the comfort I derive from them is ambiguous—in keeping this world alive they steal it from me. Mycenae will belong to them: so will Provence and Rembrandt; so will the fortified Roman towns. How superior the living are! All those eyes that gazed upon the Acropolis before mine seem to me out-of-date, superseded. In the eyes of a twenty-year-old, I see myself already dead and stuffed.

'I have always lived reaching out towards the future and now I am recapitulating: it is as though the present had been filched away . . . As I review my own history, I always see myself on the near or far side of something that has never been accomplished. It is only my feelings that have been wholly and perfectly experienced.'

If she had possessed the writer's talent and intelligence, reflected Cécile, she might have been able to put her name to those lines; but with this difference, that, unlike the authoress, the only feeling she had experienced in perfection, the only love she had truly known in perfection, was in the last analysis the family. The family as a whole, that is; for each separate love, her love for Marc, her love for Nathalie, for Stéphane, for Laura, remained hopelessly incomplete. But the family, yes, that was something fully experienced. Sufficiently experienced. Almost over. Another time was about to begin. Was this time, this real time of love, merely that of solitude and dreaming? Or was it that of a single question for ever unanswered?

'Mycenae will belong to them: so will Provence and

Rembrandt . . .' Love belonged to Nathalie, music belonged to Nathalie, Emmanuel in the physical aspect of Jo belonged to Nathalie; everything that Cécile had not dared to grasp, had not been able to grasp, belonged to Nathalie; but Cécile was aware of the danger that all this might not yet be enough. Mirrored in the eyes of twenty-two, she saw herself not as 'dead and stuffed' but as the genitrix, the ring of a tugged-at chain, the means of another's freedom, innocently murdered by her offspring. All that Marc and she had not dared grasp, had not been able to grasp, would belong to the children, down to the last drops of their blood. Nathalie could possess what her mother had been deprived of only with Cécile's connivance; she would never get there all by herself, for she and Jo were too poor, and Nathalie too middle-class. Either she would have to be subjected to pressure, mutilated as women and young people have always been mutilated for the sake of convention, or else Cécile would have to make her a present of what was left to her of her future. And Nathalie would not even notice it. Yet, said Cécile to herself, I shall never be sorry that I had children. Whatever happens. And the future might well be worse than what she saw coming, what she saw was only life, only happiness.

'The Peking opera, the arena of Huelva, the *candomble* o Bahia, El Oued and its dunes, Wabansia Avenue, dawn in Provence, Tiryns, Castro addressing five thousand Cubans, a sulphur-yellow sky above a sea of clouds, the copper-beech, the white nights of Leningrad, the bells of the Liberation, an orange moon above the Piraeus, a red sun rising over the desert, Torcello, Rome, all those things I have spoken about and others that I have never mentioned—nowhere will all that ever come to life again . . .'

Apart from the bells of the Liberation, dawn in Provence, five days in Rome, an afternoon at Torcello, and the

Piraeus; apart from the sky and the trees, and the sea, she had seen nothing at all. But neither had Vermeer, it seemed; for he never went out of his house.

Of all the things that she had never mentioned, and never would mention, nothing would ever come to life again, for it is not true that you live again in your children. You live for them, sometimes; that is all. You put them before yourself; it is a habit you acquire, a duty you do not shrink from; you can no longer do otherwise. But it would be untrue to claim that it is done without effort.

Now, at the end of June, insomnia was rife, and the thought of the day ahead made her almost weep for her inability to sleep. The city was hot, airless, dusty. They would still have to spend the whole of July in Paris and the first half of August, since Marc was fortunate enough not to start his holidays until the fifteenth. They would thus have three consecutive months of peace, first in Paris, which would be empty, and then on the beaches, which would be less crowded.

At last Cécile went to sleep. A new day came into being with the strength of a thrusting spear. For a moment she withstood it. Then she opened her eyes and everything became gentle: the light filtering through the yellow blinds caressed the furniture; a sunbeam pierced the shadow and struck the balcony geraniums, lighting up one secret and voluptuous bloom in the pattern of the carpet. She loved these things as she would have loved others like them, richer or humbler. She did not know why she loved them, but she gazed at them and felt a glow of affection. She loved them more than Vermeer's pictures, more than the Acropolis, more than the future, more than the prospect of adventure, more than art; they were her life, they were her own things, her inner citadel; surrounded by them, she had loved, worked, dreamed for all these years; they might have made her feel sick—they had done so before and would do so again—and maybe they would all go up in smoke one day; but so long as there was no one ill in any of the beds Cécile could not prevent happiness from springing up inside her as she gazed at them. Yes, in spite of the two-thirds of the world dying of hunger, in spite of Nathalie's scorn and Stéphane's reproaches and everything that was said all round her to make her feel disgusted with herself, even in spite of Stéphane's leg and the distress of growing old, in spite of the vision of all those people so soon to be laid beneath the ground, she and Marc among them, and the children too, a little later—but no, that particular horror at least was no concern of hers and must not be—in spite of this she found life good.

They lived on ice-cold milk, tomatoes and cocktail snacks. But they made the children eat proper meals because of the examinations and because of the love that was burning Nathalie up. What can parents do, at certain times, except feed their children and remember the heat of the examination room where the future was at stake, the torment of self-doubt and the youthful feeling of how powerless one is to make one's way in the world, and the novel strangeness of caresses?

Stéphane had made up his mind that as soon as the examinations were over he would fly to Cuba with some friends and then go on to New York, where they would buy a second-hand car and travel through the two Americas. 'It will cost nothing,' he said.

'It will cost at least two thousand five hundred francs,' said Marc.

'Two thousand five hundred francs for a three months' stay, including the airline tickets, is pretty much nothing,' Stéphane retorted.

'If only I'd been able to make trips like that at your age, and spend all that money . . .' sighed Marc.

'You'd have done it if you could.'

'You can only do it because you have a father,' Marc pointed out.

'If I hadn't been born in this set-up I've no doubt I should have done a whole lot more things.'

'Certainly, if you'd been born a Rothschild.'

'If I'd been born a working-man's son.'

'I'd very much like to know how.'

'I should have been freer, had more incentive.'

'In that case it's a great pity you weren't born a working-man's son,' said Marc, 'for as regards incentive . . .'

Cécile broke in to ask whether Marc would or would not allow Stéphane to go to America. Marc replied that things had been said which would have been better left unsaid. Stéphane turned to Cécile and explained, 'You see, Papa just can't accept the fact that my youth is different from his. But it's not my fault if there was a war on when he was my age.'

'No, it's not your fault,' said Marc. 'But you might at least say thank you when I stand you a journey I've not yet made myself' (here he swept his arm in Cécile's direction and added, 'nor your mother either, for that matter') 'instead of informing me that two thousand five hundred francs is nothing—it takes me a fortnight to earn it, I can tell you.'

'All right, I'll pay you back,' Stéphane said.

'I'd like to know what with.'

'Come off it,' Cécile said.

'Besides,' Stéphane went on quickly, 'if you and Mama were to make a similar trip you'd need more like twenty thousand than two thousand five hundred.'

'That's true enough,' said Cecile, chipping in before

Marc had time to retort. 'But I can't help thinking your plans are a bit ambitious. Cuba, North and South America in three months—isn't that rather much?'

'Perhaps,' Stéphane conceded. 'We're all going to meet to discuss the programme. But in any case we'll make up our minds on the spot. It'll all be very flexible. With a car we shall be able to do what we like.'

Car, accidents, August heat, dirt, sickness. But Stéphane, more than most, had to become a man. He was going off with three very pleasant boys. It was fine. Far away, at the end of the journey, in Chile, there was Marta—Marta, who was no longer in love with Stéphane and who would not be overjoyed to see him reappear. Marc had immersed himself in *Le Monde* again.

'At all events,' said Cécile, 'you agree he should make the trip, don't you, Marc?'

'Oh, sure,' said Marc, shrugging his shoulders. 'Splendid, splendid!'

At the journey's end there was Marta. But Stéphane must become a man, even if the metamorphosis had to take place so far from his mother.

Nathalie said she had not yet made up her mind about her holidays, but that no one need worry about her. She would not be going before mid-September. She wanted to earn a little money in July and August.

'How are you going to do that?'

'I've been to the job listing service. There's nothing much except being a temporary assistant in the big shops and the chainstores.'

'What do they pay?'

'Not bad. Eight hunndred francs a month.' Nathalie had put on her antagonistic look.

'Do you need this money?'

'Yes.'

Cécile looked at her. She opened her mouth, she spread her hands; she did not like to ask 'What for?'

'I really don't advise you to take such a tiring job,' she said. 'You don't know what it's like being on your feet all day long in an unhealthy atmosphere; and you're about as fit to be a saleswoman as—as I am. Working yourself to death for such a pittance when you're already tired from a year's study—you're likely to spend all that and more in recuperating right afterwards.'

'Pittance: you speak for yourself,' said Nathalie.

'And where will you live when we're all away in August?'

'Here, of course.'

Floods, explosions, everything topsy-turvy, and Jo spending his nights at the flat. Whose fault was it if his name was no longer mentioned and if, in spite of the freedom she was granted—indeed because of it—Nathalie was as it were in solitary confinement?

She needs a flat of her own, thought Cécile. There comes a moment when lives must separate. Presently she will have to set up on her own. Once she's earning her own living. We are all of us paralysed by age-old taboos. We accept the situation, but we do not know how to cope with it. We haven't the nerve. We are tongue-tied, and Nathalie doesn't make things any easier.

Sometimes early, sometimes late, she always came back to sleep at home. Despite her hollow eyes, her attitudinizing, her pallor and that air of snatching at life, of proclaiming that she had cut herself off from her kith and kin, that they were unworthy and that her lot did not lie with them, she still came back when it suited her and sat at the family table in front of her plate and the napkin with her initial on it. Laura stared at her. Marc did not appear to notice anything unusual. The first time Cécile would have liked to tell her daughter, as Marc had told Stéphane, that there was no point in putting on such airs and that she was free to do whatever she liked.

But she remembered the two ghosts, the two restless spirits who nevertheless owned her narrow, schoolgirl-like room. To make contact with her daughter, Cécile always came back to these two intercessors who had been wandering now for close on twenty-five years, these two poor, lost young people who had been dragging so many chains for so many centuries and who for so long had been travelling towards Jo and Nathalie, making their way towards her girl in bloom and towards Jo, her boy, and who might now, at long last, be able to love each other.

'The main thing, you know, is that you should pass your exam in October. After that you will be independent. That's much more important than spending two months earning one thousand six hundred francs that will just vanish, one way or another. Instead of working in a store it would be better to go to Spain and improve your Spanish.'

'I'm going in September, anyhow,' Nathalie said.

'Who with?'

'Friends.'

'With Jo?' I'm the one who named him, thought Cécile.

Nathalie's eyes flashed darkly. 'Yes, with Jo. And two friends of his.'

'By car?'

'Yes.'

'Does he drive well?'

'Yes.'

'What friends?'

'You don't know them.'

'Musicians?'

'Yes.'

'Married?'

'No.'

'Where will you live?'

'We'll camp.'

No address. 'We'll camp.' Two couples. We'll camp. They will drive too fast on bad roads. It will be hot. They will look for empty beaches. They will find them. They will make love under the summer sky; they will make love under the sky in the summer nights. In three months Nathalie will be twenty-three. At her age I had already had two children.

They will find empty beaches. They will make love in the summer nights. When I was her age it was six years since I had seen the sea. At her age I had only seen it twice in my life. At her age I was dragging along in queues; I was travelling in second-class carriages with babies, bags and feeding bottles.

'Why do you answer in that tone of voice, Nathalie? I'm not against your going on this holiday. What's more, I'm not against anything, as you know very well.'

Now Cécile's eyes were full of tears. Nathalie saw them and was irritated. 'I'm not answering in any tone of voice,' she said. 'But you're so tense and edgy: I can feel it. Anyone would think I was doing something extraordinary instead of trying to earn a little money during the holidays like everyone else, and then going camping in Spain with friends, like everyone else.'

'I'm afraid,' said Cécile, with her little old woman's look, 'that's all.'

'Who for?' Nathalie asked rudely.

'For you, of course: for all of you. And even for us, if you really want to know. Your brother's going off too—going to drive all over America. Here you are, children at home, and yet at the same time you want to live like adults —run all the risks, do everything, experience everything. No one's allowed to say a word to you, or protect you, or even ask your address: but we're still responsible for every-thing. It's exhausting, Nathalie. Your father and I are tired. It goes on too long, and you all of you take it too much for granted. There's something wrong nowadays: there's a lack of balance between children's freedom and their everlasting dependence. Being a parent has become too difficult. You're horrifying, all of you—there you are, like huge monsters. And never, never do you look in the least pleased. You're horrifying, I tell you, horrifying.'

'Oh!' cried Nathalie, 'don't get worked up, don't cry. We aren't monsters, honestly. Not compared with the rest.'

'No, you're not monsters. But you're hard. Young people today are hard. You think only of yourselves. You make a tremendous fuss about your own lives, but you don't give a damn, no, not a damn about what becomes of us. So long as we're there to pay and pick up the pieces.'

'All this fuss just because I want to work during the holidays,' said Nathalie.

Now Cécile really burst out. 'I won't have you working during the holidays. Not in a chainstore, at all events. I still have the right to forbid that. I want you to work for your exam: I want you to have a proper job after the holidays. It's the only way to manage your life and ours. The money that you can earn by wearing yourself to a shred for two months isn't worth wasting time on. What your father and I want is for all of you to grow up, really grow up. After all, we're beginning to want to be free too.'

'Can I still stay on in the flat during July and August, if I don't go before September?' Nathalie asked dully.

Cécile opened her mouth, but it was as though she had forgotten what she was going to say. She had a lost look; sad, sad. 'Of course you can stay on in the flat,' she said. 'I don't even mind if you find a part-time job in an office, if you want to earn a little money. But I'd much rather you

130

had a change of air—I'd much rather you went into the country. You're not looking too well, you know.'

Was it her strength or her weakness that was so frightening in Nathalie? If she were deprived of anything, she always threatened to punish you with some disaster—always had done. When she was small her blood-count went down if she was crossed too frequently. Once, after a scolding, she had stepped straight off the kerb and crossed the street without looking, like a hunted doe; on being told to come down from a roof she had jumped and broken her leg; and when her best friend did not like her overcoat she cut it to pieces with a pair of scissors. There was always an 'it's your fault', explicit, implicit, lurking in the background. It's your fault if I've gone on with studies you admit don't suit me: it would have been better if I'd written a novel or studied music or worked at a publisher's; and as you see, I *am* setting about learning music all the same; but it's too late. It's your fault if I go to bed with Jo; it's your fault if I do not go to bed with Jo; it's your fault if I'm not ready to share a musician's life and if I'm afraid of everything—you brought me up surrounded by fear. If you had been peasants, working people or gipsies I should have had to manage for myself. I loathe Paris. It's a revolting city where human relationships are impossible. Callas is singing at the Opéra. And Nureyev is dancing this winter. I'll crawl there on my knees. Catherine is expecting her second baby. Of course she'll go on working and her mother will bring up this one just as she's bringing up the first. It's natural. What else has her mother got to do?

Being twenty years older than your children is not enough: it should be a hundred. Then you would look at them from another world, and all you would see would be their wounds. Even within a family, even with all that love, there is a struggle for life. Nathalie's right: when she has her diploma and has earned the right to work eight hours a day in an office and then go back to her own place and do the housework and the cooking, where will her freedom be? Her freedom is being fed, housed, laundered, looked after by us here, and then going off to make love elsewhere. Go on, Nathalie, go on. These days will never come back again. Never again will you be a girl-woman. These days of youth and light-heartedness will never return.

All this talk is beside the real point. The one fear is the child. An anachronistic fear, an ancient ancestral fear. Who would bring the child up? Who will bring it up? Not me, not me! Is that fear over and done with? Is it really at an end?

It isn't something one dares to speak of. Yet before Jo appeared we did speak of it. I told Nathalie everything. She knows it all. Of course she knows it all. Let them go off to Spain in September if they like. Let them make love. There will never be such freedom, youth and beauty again.

Sometimes you say to yourself that money is the only thing that counts. Yes, you're reduced to that. Cécile felt herself threatened to such an extent that she thought of taking a job as a refuge. 'Let everyone lead his own life,' she said, reverting to the well-known slogan that had thrilled her adolescence. 'Let everyone lead his own life.' If only one could.

'Why don't you give me a small allowance, Papa, so that I can have a little flat on my own after the holidays?' Nathalie asked one day in the middle of dinner, coming out of a total silence to deliver an unexpected statement, as she sometimes did. 'The Giraudons do for Isabelle.'

Laura had gone pale; Stéphane was watching his sister attentively.

'I'm not Giraudon,' Marc said at last, stiffly.

132

'Isabelle is much more balanced since she's been living on her own. She used to be so tensed up. That was why she did all those silly things,' Nathalie explained weightily.

'But Isabelle is twenty-six,' Cécile said. 'And she has a job.'

'Still, it's her parents who pay for the flat. If you did the same, I'd manage for the rest, like her. Besides, I'll have a job too after the holidays, if I pass my exam.'

'Let's wait and see whether you do,' Cécile said.

'Yes,' said Marc, 'let's wait.' He gave his daughter a long look, shook his head, and added, 'You aren't treating us very well, Nathalie.' There was so much hurt affection in the way he said it that Laura hurried from the table.

'What's the matter with her?' Nathalie asked.

Marc and Cécile joined Laura in her room. They kissed her, they petted her, they took unfair advantage of her tears, her youth, her weakness.

'Darling, we've not quarrelled; no one has made a scene. Nathalie says anything that comes into her head just now— she's all on edge. But she'll soon get over it.'

They comforted her, they told her that the time for separation came in all families, but that it was still rather early, Nathalie wanted to go off too soon; she had to be restrained, protected, even if it were against her will.

'It's all over, it's all over: we aren't happy any more, not like we used to be,' Laura said.

'Yes, that's true, in a way; for you three, childhood is over. But something else is going to begin, another kind of happiness, other kinds of life. You'll see, Laura. You too, presently. For Nathalie it has already begun. But we still have to protect her a little. We can't let her go off yet.'

When the three of them came back to the dining-room Stéphane and Nathalie were still at table, and there was a silent agreement between them. Nathalie had gone a shade paler and the blue circles under her eyes were more marked. But she picked up the dish standing in the middle of the table and handed it to her mother, saying, 'It's getting cold.'

5

The plan for Laura's exchange visit to England, arranged with so much trouble back in February, fell through because of illness in the English family. After frantic activity, with telephone-calls and telegrams, they managed to get her on the waiting-list for the most expensive school in Cambridge.

Marc did sums. He said, 'It can't be done: it can't be done. I'm going to have to spend ten thousand francs these holidays. Perhaps we could postpone this visit until next year.'

'But what could we do with her during July and August?' Cécile said. 'She can't hang around in Paris for two months with nothing to do.'

'And anyhow she really must go to England before her exams,' said Marc. 'Even so, her chances aren't too good.'

'If it's too dear,' Cécile went on, 'there are those student camps, you know.'

'She's too young; and it's too late. It's the end of June—everything is sure to be booked up: besides, she'd never learn any English in those camps. She'd talk French all day long with the French students. No, we did the others proud when they were learning their languages. We must do the same for Laura.'

Marc read the prospectus again. ' "A tutor for each group of five pupils." This is obviously quite something. It must be a wonderful place. Tennis-court, swimming-pool. She's going to have the experience of a first-class English school.'

'If we'd known the exchange was going to fall through, we shouldn't have taken this house in the Camargue. A hotel wouldn't have cost any more for three. I shouldn't have minded having no housekeeping to do.'

'Yes, of course, if we'd known . . . But we didn't know.'

They telephoned the Principal again, and he said that there was a good chance that Laura would be accepted for one of the courses, but it would not be possible to accommodate her at the school. Bad news. Laura might not be hanging around in Paris during July and August, but she would be hanging around in Cambridge.

Cécile was coward enough to reflect that she would at least be out of sight.

They found a room in a boarding-house kept by a lady who seemed eminently respectable, but the house was a long way from the school and was also very expensive. Laura was cross when told that she would have to share a room, and claimed that the first time she had been in England, two years before, she had had to defend herself against the advances of the girl in the other bed.

Cécile lost her temper. 'Then you'll just have to defend yourself again, Laura. If you could manage it when you were fifteen you can certainly manage it now you're seventeen. You can't be kept in cotton-wool for ever. We're doing the best we can. These holidays are an absolute nightmare. If only one could skip them altogether.'

'All right, all right,' said Laura. 'Only I loathe sharing my room with another girl. I loathe other people's untidiness.'

'You loathe this and you loathe that. Maybe your roommate will loathe *your* untidiness. There's enough of it.'

'You can be really bitchy sometimes. And how you do go on.'

'What really worries me,' said Cécile, 'is how you'll get

136

to the school. There's a bus service, according to Mrs Brown's letter, but it doesn't seem very convenient.'

'I'd much rather hire a bicycle.'

'Oh, I'll have to go with you and see what it's like on the spot. I can't make head or tail of it from here.'

'It would be the last straw for you to go with her,' said Marc. 'I went to England for the first time when I was thirteen. I was alone, I went by boat, and I managed to catch the train for London, and then the train for the suburbs, without knowing a word of English.'

'Oh, you,' Cécile said, 'you've always been a leader.'

'Wait and see if I get a place before you start quarrelling,' said Laura.

They soon learnt that she had. So once again everyone's holidays were more or less organized.

O Lord, may no misfortune befall them in all these countries, on all these roads, beneath all these skies, in all these seas, in all these streets. May these three children return to us as surely as they are eager to go. What lies between doesn't matter. Far from here, far from our sight, it is as though they were nothing but frail, defenceless creatures. Let October soon come round again, and autumn's still splendour reign over Paris regained and the family reunited.

As expected, Stéphane failed in the preliminary examination for the *Ecole normale supérieure*. His marks were so low that there was no further question of trying again next year. This failure put an end to his ambition.

'At your age it's impossible to tell how anything will turn out in the future,' his parents told him. 'Doors which people were only too pleased to open sometimes close behind them like prison gates. The best thing to do now is to write *finis* to what couldn't be managed and look elsewhere. You can never tell where opportunity lies.'

'But you'd have hung out flags if I'd passed,' said Stéphane.

'Naturally,' said Marc.

And a shattered silence hung over the event.

During the days and nights that followed, Cécile began suffering about Stéphane's leg again. Sometimes the disaster would jerk her violently out of a deep sleep: once again she took her fine little boy from his bed; she tried to set him on his feet but he could not stand. While she was sleeping he had been changed into a broken-jointed puppet. She called out, 'Marc, quick, quick . . .'

Marc dozed in his bedroom. He was gloomy and dull. His son was a drag upon his spirits. He no longer dared be himself and he resented it. In the same way, after Stéphane's illness, he had played no games of any kind for more than a year.

He spent his weekends at home in a dressing-gown, kind to everyone, too kind. He slept prodigiously.

Eyes closed, but wakeful in the night, Cécile groaned. If Marc was lucky enough to be asleep she was not going to disturb him so that he could hold her hand. Besides, who in any of the rooms of this flat did not feel like shrieking these days, except perhaps for Laura? And what did they know about Laura? She was the most hidden and closed of them all. Which of them was not too weak to bear the marvel and misfortune of being alive?

It was over. Over so long ago. It was thirteen years now since that terrible morning. In any case, the child of those days no longer existed. What is left of the children of thirteen years ago? Everything streams away headlong into the past. Happiness and unhappiness too. Why give painful memories a front place? It was over. Stéphane was not a cripple. He could do everything, even ski. He was going to travel through the Americas. Suppose they gave him a camera?

The violence of the pain was abating. It was merging with the old suffering of the world, retreating into the dim crowd of undying sorrows that have been tamed.

One morning Cécile found her son's room strewn with papers, the overflow of his crammed waste-paper basket—history, English and philosophy lecture-notes torn up by the bundle. Notes carefully taken down and annotated in the margin. Essays, too: a pile covering the last three years. Kneeling, Cécile read 'Good. Interesting notions, but sometimes muddled'; 'You do not get to grips with the subject'; 'Woolly'; 'Construction still poor'; 'Good'; 'Don't let your political opinions intrude.' She gathered some of them together and sat on the floor to read them, remembering how they had discussed this or that subject at home and how Stéphane had arrogantly rejected his father's arguments. Here, in the tutor's hand, she found just what Marc had said. She set some of the pieces to one side, meaning to stick them together again. In his involved sentences, Stéphane had been striving towards the realm of the Good, the Just and the Beautiful; but he was the only one to whom it had made sense, and he had not gained even average marks. Cécile let the pages fall to the floor—there were too many of them. She looked at them lying on the carpet, like a flight of doves shot down. Then she lay flat on her stomach among all this paper, and with her head on her arms she wept. She wept quietly for a long while, for as long as she felt like it. Then she sat up. Her tears had dropped on some of the pages and made the ink run. Gently she stroked this mixture of ink and tears, which made long pale marks on Stéphane's work, pale and already as it were remote.

She stood up. First she emptied the waste-paper basket.

Then, picking up paper by the armful, she filled and emptied it again several times. The dustbin was overflowing. 'There's as much again in Stéphane's room,' she said to Maria, pointing to it and laughing.

'What you say?' asked the Spanish woman.

Cécile spread her arms wide. 'Lots of paper,' she said.

'Lots of paper,' said the Spanish woman, thoroughly pleased.

Laura had had unexpectedly high marks for her end-of-term exams and had been moved up into the top form: during the few days before she was due to fly to England she had been more scatterbrained than ever. Cécile took her to Le Bourget, lost her way and began to fuss. When they reached the airport they discovered that her father's authorization was necessary for the trip.

'But I'm her mother, monsieur. Surely if I am here . . . Look, here's my driving licence.'

'I'm not the one who made the regulation, madame. It's explicit enough. The head of the family's authorization is required.'

Laura was eyeing the young man.

'So she can't take this plane?' said Cécile. 'You mean I'm not the head of the family?'

'No, madame.'

'But this is terrible, monsieur. It's all arranged. The woman my daughter is staying with is coming to meet her at Cambridge at the bus station. There's only one bus a day that goes straight from the airport to Cambridge. Can't I phone my husband?'

Laura had got into conversation with an English youth. Time was slipping by. The official was busy with someone else. But he looked at Cécile again. 'Couldn't your husband come?'

'How on earth can he get here before the plane leaves, monsieur?'

'She could take the next,' said the man.

'When?'

'Nineteen hours forty.'

'But there's no bus that late. She'll have to manage all by herself, and at night. Perhaps you have children yourself, monsieur. Surely you must understand.'

Laura was zealously sounding her consonants: '*Mar-vel-lous.*'

'She's not a child any more,' the official said lightly. 'She'll manage all right, don't you worry.'

'Laura, listen a moment, *please.* Do you think you could manage to catch a train to Cambridge all by yourself, once you get to London?'

'What does your husband do?'

'He's in the Audit Office.'

'Give me his number. I'll ring him.'

From the receiver Cécile could hear Marc's authoritative, convincing tone. The passengers for the London plane were called. The English youth lingered. Laughing merrily, Laura told him that she was having difficulties.

'Can you tell me the date of her birth?' the official asked.

Cécile crossed her fingers, for Marc could never remember when his children were born.

'Just this once,' said the man, 'just this once . . .' He hung up. 'All right, madame, we'll let your daughter go.'

'*Is it OK?*' asked the English youth.

'*Yes, I think so,*' said Laura.

'*Bravo, monsieur, merci,*' said the English youth, and waving his bag by way of a salute he went through the barrier. Laura kissed her mother offhandedly.

'You've five pieces of baggage, counting your raincoat,

your tennis-racquet and your handbag,' Cécile said. 'Remember: five things. Get your boarding card ready.'

'Oh, all right,' said Laura, entangled in her possessions.

'Don't worry, I'll take care of her, ma'am,' said the English youth from the other side of the barrier. Laura caught up with him, and they went off, side by side, without turning back. At this point Cécile saw Laura's identity card fall from her pocket.

'Laura, Laura!'

Laura turned haughtily.

'Your identity card! There! On the ground!'

Laura came back, bent down, thus causing her bag to slip from her shoulder, picked it up again, picked up the card, winked at her mother, twirled about and hurried after the English youth.

'Oh!' gasped Cécile.

At the last moment, just before she vanished, Laura glanced back at her and waved.

'*Don't worry, ma'am. I'll take care of her.*' The young man, like Laura, was nothing but youthful flesh; he would be no more use in case of an accident than an ashtray in the plane. Perhaps it would be better, sometimes, to listen to the warnings of fate than to press on regardless.

Cécile went back to the car, which now seemed extraordinarily empty. There was no trace of her child left in it. Slowly she drove to the fork for the throughway. The afternoon seemed to her wide open. She had nothing to do. She looked at the road signs. The *autoroute du Nord* ran between woods towards the sea. At this very moment cars were driving along it at eighty, ninety, a hundred miles an hour. Single men, couples.

The throughway cut through the fields of sugar beet, flat beneath the sky. She would telephone from the other end: 'I don't know what came over me. I saw Rouen on a road sign. I suddenly remembered that Paris was quite close to the sea and that I had never seen Varangeville. You know that little hotel Jean is always telling us about? That's where I'm spending the night (laughter). I don't know what came over me. I turned left instead of turning right, towards the sea instead of the suburbs. I couldn't help it. Your Maminette has lost her wits. She bolted (laughter). There's some roast beef in the refrigerator, and the salad is all ready. I'll be back tomorrow afternoon. Oh, and I mixed the salad dressing too. It's in the cupboard over the sink.'

She spread her hands wide, lifting them from the wheel. Psss, psss, psss, the cars sped by. At eighty, ninety and a hundred miles an hour, the cars were running towards the sugar-beet fields, the woods and the sea. Single men, couples, scarves streaming in the wind.

The Peugeot waited at the fork until another car hooted behind it. Then it turned to the right.

Cécile came home through ugly, busy, dusty suburbs and found the flat empty. On the pad in the hall Stéphane and Nathalie had written that they would not be in for dinner, but in case anyone telephoned, they would look in during the afternoon. She reached her den, telling herself that she would have had time for a dip in a swimming-pool. She looked at the big books piled up at the bottom of the bookcase. St John of the Cross, Teresa of Avila, Proust, Kierkegaard, Musil, *War and Peace*, Karl Marx, *And Quiet Flows the Don*, Samuel Butler, Plato, Aragon, the Bible, Saint-John Perse, Céline, Sade, Mascolo's *Le Communisme*, and all Jean Genêt and Lévi-Strauss and the structuralists—people she knew nothing about though Stéphane thought the world of them; all the books of which people had said, 'You simply must read it', and all the books she had read already with the feeling of having skimmed over the surface; all the books she had put on one side and all those others she did not possess at the moment; and an edition of the *Bucolics*, edited and revised by her old Latin teacher—there they all were, waiting for her. So was music—the records and the record player were in Laura's room; and so were painting and sculpture in all the great museums of Paris.

It was half past six. Cécile told herself that by now Laura's plane had already landed at Heathrow, and it seemed that in so short a time nothing could have happened. She tore open the wrapper of *Le Monde* and read it, waiting for someone to come home.

The first key to turn in the lock was Marc's. Cécile told him about Laura's eventful departure. They laughed as they pictured the arrival of this hare-brained creature at the boarding-house. They said there was no point in telephoning since the eight o'clock news had not spoken of any plane accident; but at nine o'clock they could bear it no longer; and when, after Mrs T. H. Brown's even tones, they heard their daughter's beautiful calm voice, as though she were talking from the next room with the door open, they looked at each other like a couple of schoolchildren. Mrs Brown, who was so delighted to have this charming girl for six weeks, might perhaps have time to change her mind. Laura managed to whisper into the telephone that Mrs T. H. Brown was a joke, but rather a dear. As far as she had been able to tell, the other girls in the place were all more or less 'nanas'.

'What exactly does *nana* mean?' asked Cécile.

'Don't know, my poor Pépette,' said Marc, looking as much like an antique as he could.

'What exactly does *nana* mean?' Marc asked Nathalie a little later. She shrugged and answered, 'Nothing: it's part of Laura's vocabulary. *Nanas* are drips, rather like her.'

Stéphane managed to pass in the last two subjects for his degree—an important success because of the reform of higher education. It became possible to talk to him once more and he returned to his habitual bickering with his father. Although the *Ecole normale* was out of the question, the *agrégation** did not seem entirely beyond reach. Yet Stéphane now declared that he no longer had the slightest wish to go into teaching. But what else had he in mind? Stéphane explained that he had started off on the wrong foot with Latin and Greek and had wasted his best early years on them. 'All because I got a mention for Latin translation in the general schools exam. What balls these general exams are! I did not like to say so,' he went on, 'but I've been wanting to give it up ever since last October. The whole thing made me feel absolutely sick the entire year.'

'You ought to have said so,' Marc retorted. 'It would still have been possible to change.'

'Change to what?'

'The School of Political Science, for example, or law.'

Stéphane laughed derisively. 'I know very well you wouldn't have let me change at that stage. Not with your principle of always having to finish what you have begun.'

'At the beginning of the year you hadn't begun at all,' said Marc.

'Oh yes I had,' Stéphane said. 'I'd begun the preparatory year. In any case, political science isn't really my line.'

'Not your line—not your line! You've got to earn your living, one way or another. You can't go on saying no to everything. If you don't want to go in for teaching, what *do* you want to do? Tell me.'

'I want to study ethnology.'

'What for?'

'To be an ethnologist,' Stéphane said. 'At least that's a subject that's alive.'

*A difficult competitive post-graduate examination for lycée and university posts.

145

Marc seemed lost in thought and fell silent.

But a few days later Stéphane said that he had submitted a subject for a diploma to one of his tutors. He would do some work on it during the holidays and would be able to finish it while embarking on other studies. 'But it's only to please you, Papa,' he repeated. 'Whatever happens, I shan't go in for the *agrég*.'

'All right,' said Marc. 'We'll see.'

So the camera did not look too much like a consolation-prize and Stéphane was so astonished and so ingenuously delighted with it that it brought tears to their eyes. They drove him to the airport.

With his camera slung over his shoulder, already caught up with his two friends in the companionship of adventure, and about to take off for a night flight across the Atlantic in a four-engined plane, Stéphane for the first time really looked like a man. In her mind's eye Cécile pictured him, sunburnt, among vast landscapes, vast crowds. Marta frightened her less. And she said goodbye to her son with an ease that surprised her.

On the way home they said how sorry they were not to have had time for a serious discussion of Stéphane's future with him. But in any case he had been too much on edge these last weeks. They would see in September. He had his degree at twenty, and that was not a bad start. So let him set off on his long trip without having to worry. He could still wait some years before he had to earn his living, thank God.

'I shouldn't be altogether surprised if he were to stay out there,' Cécile said.

'What would he do over there?' asked Marc, changing from one lane to another, a manoeuvre that Cécile watched attentively before replying, 'They must need young men like him in those countries.'

'Yes. But he hasn't much in the way of qualifications as yet. It would be better for him not to break off his studies at this point.' He gave her a sideways look and added, 'It's curious in you, the mother hen—anyone would say you were glad the children were leaving us.'

She opened her mouth, hesitated, and then said, 'No, it's not that I'm glad, but . . . but I should like their lives not to be our business any more.'

'There I'm with you,' Marc said.

Without giving any explanation, Nathalie abandoned her idea of working in July and August and decided to go and stay with a girl-friend in Normandy. For a long while her world had been peopled with beings called Catherine, Bernard, Pascal and Philippe, vague characters who were scarcely ever seen in the flat. Cécile had long since given up keeping an eye on the people her daughter mixed with. Yet she still had a prejudice deriving from her disappoint-ment in the first dreary groups that Nathalie had joined at the age of thirteen and that made her think of her daughter's mysterious friends more as accomplices—as people with whom she herself was in a vague state of hostility.

This time Nathalie was going to stay with one Pauline. She stated that there was no telephone in the house. But as soon as she got there she would send the address, which she did not happen to know by heart. Or else she would telephone from a post-office.

'But since you're going there you must know the address.'

'Philippe's taking me.'

'Well then, Philippe knows the address.'

'I suppose so.'

'Ask him for it.'

'He's not on the phone.'

'Write to him.'

'There's no time.'

'Write special delivery.'

'Oh really, for such a trifle! And force him to send me one in return?'

'Ask him when he comes to fetch you.'

'We're meeting at his place.'

'So you can't be reached in case of an emergency?'

'But I told you I'd telephone when I get there.'

'Give me Philippe's address.'

Nathalie was pale. Cécile looked at her. No, no, it couldn't be *that*. At twenty-two she might already have been married and living elsewhere. One would not have known where she was or what she was doing at any hour of the day. Cécile stretched out her hands, opened her mouth and began, 'You know . . .'

But Nathalie interrupted. 'You ought to be glad I'm going to the country, since that's what you wanted.'

Yes, Cécile was glad. And yes, that was what she had wanted. But it was never just how she wanted it. 'I should have preferred you to go rather later. As it is, your grandparents won't see a single one of you while they're here.'

'Pauline's only got the house to herself until July 20th.'

But that same evening the grandparents telephoned to say that, all things considered, they would not come. It was too hot. No, they were not ill; everything was fine; no one was to worry. It was only this summer weather that was so trying. They would rather stay at home and enjoy their garden in the evenings. Besides, Cécile and Marc must be tired too. So let them make the most of the children's being away to rest. No doubt Cécile would be able to stop for a day or two on her way to the Camargue. As for Marc, they would love to see him too, of course, but he was not to cut his holidays short for them. Not at all, they were not in the least unwell: above all, no one was to worry. Otherwise they would come in spite of everything.

'No, no, I'm not worrying. I understand perfectly,' Cécile had said. 'So I'll come and spend a few days with you in August, then.'

When she had hung up she stayed sitting by the telephone for a moment. She could still hear her mother's small, hurried voice, a voice that never let her get a word in edgeways. This was the first time the grandparents had given up their annual visit to Paris before the main holidays began. In a family whose traditions were strong and where the repetition of gestures and activities had been found to be the best way of getting through life, this break with routine was a serious reverse.

Cécile at once wrote to her parents to say she thought their decision was the right one, and took the letter to the post-office so that it should get there the next day. Marc was watching TV and as she went by she said, 'My parents have decided not to come. It's the heat.'

'They are quite right,' said Marc. 'They're much better off in their garden.'

The next day a letter arrived from the grandparents. They too had written directly after the telephone call and made a special trip to the post-office. They too wanted to bridge the gap, to explain away their first sign of weakness and transform it into a rational decision.

In her unchanging hand, a delightful, free-flowing, regular hand, as modest as the fashions of her day and as neat as her own cupboards, Maman wrote that there must be no mis-understanding, and that truly there was no need to worry about them. Indeed, it was rather to allow their children to rest that they had decided not to come. With a poetic enthusiasm unusual in her, she described their evenings in the garden, where their neighbours came to sit with them. It was many years since there had been a summer like this. Poor Stéphane would be roasted alive in Cuba and America.

But still, he was young. A pity he had not had time to come over and say goodbye. But of course with all those examinations he had not had a moment to spare. Laura would certainly be better off in Cambridge. England could be relied upon to be cool. And what about Nathalie? What was she going to do for her holidays? If she would like to come to them for a rest they would be delighted. It was not the country, but still it was not Paris either. And there was the garden that Nathalie loved so. She could pick currants and raspberries, as she had done when she was little. There were masses of currants and raspberries this year.

The sentences ran on pleasantly, like a little train winding through the countryside. Indeed, it was an unusually lively letter. For after all, what did the grandparents have to write about, apart from the weather, the books they had read, the radio programmes and the flowers in their garden? Generally their letters did little more than reflect their children's: 'So you spent a pleasant day with your friends the So-and-so's'; 'And Laura went to a dance on Saturday . . .'; 'Our little Stéphane has had the last laugh, doing so well with his degree.'

Only a few years ago they were still describing social activities, luncheons and dinners; they related events in the town, and retold films and lectures they had been to. They would enclose a newspaper cutting, a menu or a group-photograph in which they could be seen, usually rather towards the back, somewhat hidden.

How everything had changed in the course of a few years. One after another almost all their friends had died, and those who were still living no longer went out. But the grandparents were still getting about, they were still together, still active. They said people envied them, and no doubt they did. Yet Cécile saw them, as it were, on a rock surrounded by a rising tide, pressed together, pressed tighter and tighter, uttering their pathetic, weak-voiced chorus to comfort and protect their ageing child: 'We are fine; don't you worry about us. Let us pray to God that everything goes on as well as this until the end.' But the brave voices could no longer drown the threat. When? How? Would she really have to see it?

When had old age seized upon them? Since when had there been arthritis, a stick, a shrunkenness, the pale uncertainty in the now bottomless eyes, transformed by operations and spectacles? Since when had there been greyness in Maman's splendid, thick, dark hair? Since when had her hands given up their perpetual mending? Maman's darning was instantly recognizable: it was as beautiful as embroidery.

Cécile looked at her own hands, which were like her mother's. They had the same prominent veins, the same swollen, rheumatic joints and the same fine oval nails, cut short. Cécile looked at her hands, and she had the feeling of being the last in the line of working women who had bequeathed them to her. Women of the lower middle-class, given to gardening and embroidery, women who could not tell at the end of the day what they had done to be so tired and whose only alibi was their hands, resting at last on their lap.

Maman's hands had taken on a bluish tinge. Cécile's were still white, but there were two or three pale marks that showed they were ageing. The ring on the fourth finger of her left hand could only just slip off and on. Maman's had sunk so deeply into her flesh that a cyst had formed, and it had had to be operated on. There are some things that you never do except in dreams: for example, kissing your mother's hands.

It was she who had changed most during this last period.

Apart from having shrunk a bit, Papa was the same as he had been for the last fifteen years or so. Still the same wrinkles and the same ivory-coloured skin. But it needed an effort to remember Maman as queen of her own household, the tall woman in a severe blouse whom one had looked up to from a lower level for so long.

One day—it was during the war—Cécile had taken her mother's head between her hands to kiss her and had found that beneath the deceptive hair it was tiny: between her hands was a little old woman's head. That only happened once. Maman regained her substance and her usual look. She continued to reign over her household, always on her feet, always carefully dressed, her head perhaps a little bowed, that was all; she was taller than Papa now, and so she went on until, suddenly again, Cécile saw that she was fragile and slow; her joints were stiff, she felt the cold, and in her face there was a kind of bewilderment.

This time her reign was really over. Was it the coming of the new liturgy, the adolescence of her grandchildren, or the first wrinkles on the faces of her own children? With a lost expression and a sigh she took to saying, 'I'm too old to understand; I can't get used to it . . .' Or else she would listen without saying anything, shaking her head from time to time, puzzled, childish, or mysteriously radiating a youth no one had seen.

But in spite of her seventy-six years she was always on the go; moving from cellar to attic of the house which was too big for them; the first in the street to get up, quietly opening the shutters so as not to wake the neighbours (for she had always been most considerate of others), and so accustomed to being on her feet that she could not sit down without dropping off. She slept even when she was listening to music, though she said she did not—she had only closed her eyes; and perhaps she was right, for the

152

music that reaches us as we doze is indeed the music of the spheres.

She had been busy so long that she could not be still. If anyone called she would break off the conversation to offer a drink, a cup of tea, some flowers or fruit, anything—she had to give something. She never believed that people could come merely for the pleasure of her company.

Cécile's father had made better use of his retirement. He was a great reader and a great sleeper, and during the bad weather he hibernated. In summer the garden was his kingdom. He worked there, he rested there, he ate, read and dreamed there. His eyes would run lovingly over his little patch of ground, the last remaining open space among the tall buildings. This was summer, he reflected: he preferred not to look beyond. The last winter had frightened him.

'You have to die some day,' he said, 'and that's not what I'm afraid of. But your mother—oh, she's not ill, or at least not seriously, or at least I don't think so—your mother can't cope any longer. And you know how she is . . .'

Yes, Cécile knew how she was. She could not bring herself to accept help from anyone, apart from her husband.

Winter was frightening. Two old people struggling against the cold, sweeping the snow from their steps and their piece of sidewalk, opening a path as far as the letter box, the source of their manna, the stir of life, their children's letters. Papa saw to the shopping: he walked very carefully, afraid of slipping, anxious for his leg, which a war wound had broken in his youth and which had not improved with age. He took great care of his body, which had never stood him in such good stead; he wanted to keep it going to the end. What would happen to him and Maman if either were left without the other?

Once Cécile had heard someone say, 'Presently everyone

will live to be old, barring accidents.' And she had replied, 'So there will be no hope left, then?' 'On the contrary,' said the speaker with a smile, and she had felt foolish. It was only later that she understood what she had really meant: there comes a stage, a moment in one's life, when one has nothing to look forward to other than decline and death. There is no possibility of anything pleasant happening or of any further adventure whatsoever. It is said that God does what men dare not do: He condemns the old to death.

But now it was summer and Papa said that Maman was very well—indeed, she stood the heat better than he did. He had wondered what his new rose would look like. And behold! one morning it was in bloom. He called his wife, but she was busy. She put her head out of the window and asked, 'What do you want now? Can't I have a moment's peace?' And Papa said, 'Come and see the rose: it's out.'

She appeared. She came down the five stone steps. Flowers were the only luxury she allowed herself without a feeling of guilt. She bent down over the rose, found it beautiful and smiled with that smile reserved for flowers or small children alone. 'It ought to be photographed,' she said. But she had found some chore that needed doing in the garden too. Putting her duster down on the iron table, she went off to get her clippers from the tool shed. She clipped and tidied, and he, the begetter of the rose, was rather disappointed. 'Madame Blain is ill,' said Maman. 'Who is ill?' asked Papa, for he was a little deaf and it always took him some time to leave any train of thought. 'Madame Blain,' she said again, cross already. 'I'm going to pick a bunch of flowers for her, and you can take it round.'

I make the children too much of an excuse, thought Cécile. I ought to go and see my parents more often.

Yet she could not repress a feeling of cowardly relief at the thought of this whole week—no, more than a week: these ten days—that still lay before her, ten days in which she would not have to look after anyone except Marc, and in which they would be just a couple, just the two of them, something that had never really happened to them in their life. In families there is always someone, either old or young, who is not up to scratch or who needs care, and it is the mother who stays with him. At the idea of spending ten days alone with her husband, Cécile felt as if she were about to take off.

'Well, here we are like a pair of lovers,' she said to Marc.

The words were part of their private language. They dated from one of the first big parties they had been invited to after the war: they knew no one in the crowd, and when their host found them, sitting side by side in the background, young and left to themselves, he had said, 'Ah, there you are, all by yourselves like a pair of lovers.'

'Yes,' said Marc, 'a pair of lovers.'

They had seen all the shows they could bear: the parties were over. They no longer felt like seeing anyone. Cécile went to the museums and the galleries; she strolled along the banks of the Seine, through the old streets on the Left Bank, the Palais Royal, the Marais. But the city which had seemed so attractive when she had been obliged to stay at home in her own district no longer appealed to her. It was full of dust, it was in labour, with its streets dug up and great heaps of rubble lying about—one huge building site; it could not manage to get rid of its cars and the heat smelt of petrol. She gazed at the reflections in the water, the great buildings and the pale narrow houses, pink, yellow and blue, along the river. She lingered in front of the antique shops, in front of all those fancy shops that were gradually ousting the bakeries and the bars, and rigidifying certain districts in a state of preservation. Decoration, preservation, she thought, with an odd feeling of powerlessness and disgust.

Sometimes she went to meet Marc at the office. They would cross the Cour carrée, and then the Pont des Arts, and go and drink white burgundy in pretty glasses in the café on the Ile de la Cité, or go and sit under the arbours of the Closerie des Lilas. They had nothing to say to each other; they grew bored; they were tired; they went home. Sitting opposite each other, they drank orangeade, listening to a record, with a feeling of emptiness. There was something missing: they could not tell what. They told each other it would not be long now before they heard from the children. There were books, and there was the great tidying up before the summer holidays. Cécile moved from the one to the other without much conviction.

On the evening of July 14th they wandered among the tourists and the crowds were just about to go off on their holidays with pay. They sat at an outside table in a secularized monastery that had been turned into a firemen's barracks. A dance was being held there, a real village feast with children asleep in their mother's arms, and bucolic jollity. They danced under the twelfth-century arches. 'Laura and Nathalie would have loved this place,' they said. They could see them, with their long legs and their shining eyes, and eager young men all around them. Cécile had a vision of Nathalie with Jo, the handsomest couple in the dance, and the most abandoned. 'But Nathalie would never have spent the evening with us,' she said to herself. 'And she has never wanted me to see her dancing.' *She's pretty, isn't she, madame?* Perhaps Jo would have induced her to go with them. Jo would certainly love festivities. Jo would bring the generations together. Marc said he would gladly ask a girl to dance, if only he knew these modern steps.

'Oh, go on,' Cécile said. 'It's July 14th—you can dance how you like.'

And while she was surreptitiously watching Marc as he revolved with a pretty, rather common dark girl in his arms, she herself was asked to dance by a thirty-year-old fireman, who made her feel as stiff and awkward as a poker. She did not know whether she ought to assume the look of a middle-aged woman having her fling or pretend to be young. Over his partner's head, over her partner's shoulder, they exchanged winks. Then they were swept away by the dance. They had great fun.

But after an hour everything went flat. They remembered that someone had told them of another 'very amusing' place to dance near the flea-market. They went there and found everything shut up, though the front of the house was still lit, festooned with four dreary garlands. The quarter was completely empty; apart from this one façade, it was as dark as though the police had raided it. They drove home through the traffic jams and blaring horns. They really ought to have got in touch with some friends, they told each other. You can't celebrate July 14th in a party of two.

'But she wasn't bad, that girl I danced with, was she?'

'No,' said Cécile. 'A nice girl. Not at all bad.'

During the days that followed cars drove at top speed through the empty streets, Cécile's car among them. It was possible to lunch near the Louvre, walk at Bagatelle and go to the cinema on the Left Bank, all in the same day. The restaurants overflowed on to the sidewalks. The narrow streets of Saint-Germain-des-Prés made you think of Venice. Bare legs, bare shoulders, the town rippled with youth and beauty. Sunburnt men walked past, a wolf-like gleam in their eyes. It was said that respectable heads of families were picked up, dead drunk, in the gutters. Is there any place on earth where the holidays are more felt than in Paris?

Cécile frequented the streets, the gardens, the parks, the swimming-pools. She walked through the lovely summer among groups lying on the grass and heard the penetrating, caressing music of transistors. She saw the couples fondling one another. She went as far as the Muette. She took the little chair-lined walk between the fine trees. There nurses, young mothers and grandmothers were watching over pretty children who had not yet left Paris and who were busy squabbling and digging with their little spades. She smiled at them, but she walked on with the fine swing of a free woman. She remembered the days when she had walked here with children who cried to be carried, clung to the railings, fell down, stuffed earth into their mouths, and were always wanting something. She reflected that if her parents had come to Paris they would all have tottered along this path together. Phrases came into her mind, words, jets of pleasure, because she had seen a spaniel running, the upward soaring of a tree, the gleam of water. She remembered the rasping happiness of love's beginning. She spent a whole afternoon at Bagatelle, which was curiously untouched by the weariness of summer; once more the middle years and old age seemed to her life's great holiday. The landscape entered into her, filling her, a world as happy as the Impressionists' paintings. Bagatelle is a happy place for the old.

Sitting behind a hedge of rhododendrons, she saw women walking alone, their gentle faces lit up. She saw couples, holding hands, slow, decent couples, who seemed to have been together for years and years. Some had white hair. Watching their faces, their joined hands, their way of looking very much alike, their limbs, features and clothes all matching, their habit of bending over the roses with the same movement, she wondered whether a long-lasting love were not the most desirable of all endings.

She could not say that she and Marc made up one of these couples, but it did not worry her. These couples seemed to have in common their love of beauty. Their eyes lifted from the flowers to meet and find their confirmation each in the other. They could not lie. Their lives had been neither base nor empty. These flower-loving, hand-holding couples signified much more than the painted characters of Watteau or the Impressionists. A long-lived love never just happens; a long-lived love is a work of art. Might not these old lovers have said, like Joan of Arc before her judges, 'We had the strength to believe'? By strength of will, faith becomes truth. Yet she did not envy them. There was something quite different, a greater love, coming to life again for her, here in this garden; something wonderfully strange that called out to the sky, a nostalgia, a gaiety, a loneliness, an unquenchable pain, a greatness: and success of that kind would have deprived her of it.

She reflected that to live together and remain faithful to each other, young people as good-looking as Jo and Nathalie would have to disfigure themselves; 'It's being young that is so hard,' she said to herself, 'and being young goes on and on. And every person born must start all over again from the beginning.' Cécile cried out against the idea that she might be robbed of her old age as though she were threatened with having the best part of her life cut off.

A man of about thirty-five, a thin, pallid, dusty moth of a creature with the hollow, lightless eyes of those who pore over books, came and sat down on her bench. She was angry with him for having chosen to come and settle next to her when there were so many empty places elsewhere. But she waited a moment so that her getting up should not seem insulting.

In an educated, smug voice—which seemed to her

pathetic—the man asked her about the château and the garden, and 'that little belvedere over there'. She told him what she knew and pretended to immerse herself in her book again. But a peacock came towards them, spread its tail and then flew high up into a tree. She was obliged to exchange expressions of surprise with this dismal chance companion. Cécile got up and walked away, leaving the man alone on the bench, with his striped trousers, his black jacket and his useless umbrella.

Along the lawns, amid the brilliant flower-beds and the trees, she reached the far end of the garden. Her inner light had been darkened.

It was here, at a bend in one of the most secluded walks, that she came upon Françoise and Yves. She knew Françoise had left the nursing home. She had been to see her there a few days before she came out and Françoise had shown her the hole near her shoulder. Françoise was wearing a long-sleeved flimsy dress with a green scarf tied round her lovely hair; she was leaning on Yves's arm and they were walking very slowly. Cécile saw them and hid.

She went back to the roses. Going from one to the next, red, pink, orange, mauve, faded, dried up, aged beauty, open, over-blown, almost dead, in bud, proffering themselves, swollen, male, female, treacherous, she looked at them one by one with extreme, almost obsessive attention, until she could bear no more.

Then she walked all the way home. She could feel the organs in her body: her ovaries, of course; her liver; her stomach; her joints. She was no longer a happy co-ordinated machine, capable of running on and on until the end of time. Somewhere, in one of these organs, perhaps the factory of death had already set to work. Every living being, every plant already possessed this cancer, hidden or clearly visible, even the freshest rose, even the flesh of pretty children, even the muscular flesh running along the avenues over there towards the Athletic Club. Along the edges of the footpaths stood grave, motionless, commanding figures with the massive heads of donors. There were others, furtive among the trees, and they drew nearer at the sight of Cécile, whispering as she went by and sometimes going so far as to call out, 'Hey, hey! Look here, you fool!'

She was afraid. Panic. Holding herself straight, she walked on. But she was tempted to stop and look gravely, understandingly, once and for all, at where abandonment and desire could lead a man. The taste of the roses clung to her lips like a sugared funeral. Cars with questing men in them swished by her, too. They called to her, psst, psst, as though to a dog. It was crazy of her to walk home along these paths. Lunatics who see women going along like this, alone, on foot, through the woods and public gardens, recognize their kindred. She would never do it again. The town emptied its refuse into the Bois: summer was rotting in the city. A woman of forty-four has nothing ahead of her but decay and death.

She walked on. This anguish would pass. So often, over so many years, it had come and had gone away. But what if, as she grew older, it did not go away? What if the freedom of her later days opened only on to horror? Suppose old age were nothing but a torment? She was weak, flimsy, worn out by motherhood and by chores, and there was no guard-rail at the edge of this abyss. She ought to have begun much earlier, have found out what her potentialities were at the outset, and disciplined herself; she ought to have taken part in history, politics, business, like a man; she ought to have sunk her identity in that of a team, to have specialized, found a hobby, an engrossing interest, to have furnished her mind, and then one day to have died without a moment's warning, like a man. It was unbelievable how things ran round and round in the head of a woman who did not work outside her own home, a woman like her, middle-class, her hands always busy but her mind too free. The great problems confront a woman directly. She has no way of outflanking them, of nibbling away at them, of playing with them. Her thoughts are directly and solely concerned with life, death, love and fate. And if she is given back her freedom, if she is no longer tied by housework to her home, if no one really needs her any more, then life, death, love and the absence of love can drive a woman mad: she comes to be like those sex-ridden men among the trees or those fathers of families who are found drunk in the gutter in summer dawns.

Cécile walked on. She was back in the broad civilized walks, advancing towards the tragedy of lives which have not ended. She saw the vanity of all created things. 'A hobby,' she said to herself, 'I ought to find a hobby, or else go in for charity, or else quickly get back to the bringing up of my children's children. That's the best thing to do. People are quite right, you can't look death in the face.' But everything seemed to her so petty, so limiting—a form of suicide. This bitter distress was hers by right. It was the price she paid for her freedom, her personality, and even her honour.

She came back through the peaceful alley where the children were playing. Once again she looked at the grand-mothers on duty. Some of them had pleasant round faces and in their eyes shone love for the youngsters in their charge and a trust in life not unaccompanied by a certain disillusionment—gifts of grace. These were women who must be loved in their families, and who were certainly not useless. Yet Cécile had no wish to be like them.

These walks were part of her very private life. Not that from time to time she did not say to Marc, 'I went as far as Bagatelle today: the roses are still lovely.' Or, 'I was in the park at Saint-Cloud during the storm. You'd never believe how green everything was. I took shelter in the speed-cops' hut. They aren't at all the same once they're off their motor-cycles and shut up in a little house. They are awkward little men. The place fairly reeked of leather and old goat. After the storm I finished my walk. There were a few broken branches, but heavens, what a scent! And the funny thing is, the roses had not suffered.'

Marc said, 'It's a pity there's no one left to play tennis with you at Margency. It would be more fun than walking by yourself.'

'I'm very fond of walking,' she said.

But she also concealed from Marc the fact that once a week she stood in for a friend and helped transport children who had had polio. She and another woman filled a coach with the cripples and sometimes their little wheelchairs too, and drove them out into the open air. The hobbling and hopping, the pitiful band that they unloaded on to the dusty grass, the innocence of these unfortunate children who did not even have any family to sustain them, and—for her at least—the falsehood of laughing with them, was almost more than she could bear. She tried in vain to hearten herself by thinking of the part compensation certainly played; or telling herself that perhaps these children would derive extra vitality from the very fact of their disease; or that in comparison with them her Stéphane had got off very lightly. For all that she could say, these little bodies that dragged themselves about on the ground were her own flesh; they pursued her into her dreams and continually asked her the same question. Marc would have said, 'Why inflict this upon yourself?' Yet she had made up her mind to go on with it after the holidays.

She made the most of the quietness in the flat to tidy the

cupboards and sort papers. Sometimes she re-read letters. As soon as their immediacy was past, even the most commonplace aroused sorrow for days that had not been fully lived. They expressed an absurd desire for communication, for reconciliation, for order. They made it clear that everyone lived upon two planes, yearning for 'another life'. But the mere sight of the handwriting was enough to show that some long-preserved letters had, by heaven knows what kind of wear and tear, lost their emotive power. Cécile tore them up unread.

She came upon the notes that, from her earliest childhood, Laura had been in the habit of leaving in the hall or by her bed. 'I've borrowed your grey jacket. I hope you won't need it. I'll take great care of it.' 'I've gone to the cinema with Hubert.' 'Laura got home at one o'clock on the dot.' That one had been written when she had been given leave to stay at a party until one in the morning. Cécile kept all these notes. She could see a whole crowd of grandchildren just like Laura.

In the mornings, Cécile and Marc read their daughter's letters together. She had been to spend a weekend with friends of friends. 'It is a low house, ivy-covered, with french windows opening on to the garden. As soon as you go in you catch the lovely smell of old wooden floors and lavender. The walls are distempered or done with striped white wallpaper and hung with old humorous prints, all crooked. The furniture is lovely. My hosts are fabulous, and the most terrific snobs. I love that. Sir Andrew is a big man with a moustache; he has thick lips and teeth like a horse; his eyes are bright blue and his hair is thick and short and curly and he plasters it down. Since I got here I haven't met a single man I didn't think it would be fun to live with. Of course the setting helps. A man would have to be hopelessly devoid of charm to miss being attractive when he's sunk deep in an armchair, with a pipe peering out from under his moustache and his feet on a flowered pouffe. We had dinner in a freezing dining-room . . .' 'Yesterday evening I went to a dance with two of the other girls at the school in a sort of smoke-filled jazz club, a Cambridge *cave*. You should have seen me! The English boys have hair to their shoulders and high-heeled shoes. They dance all by themselves, writhing, opposite you. They ask you to dance, but it's as though you weren't there at all. Everyone says they take drugs.' 'I have been lent a bicycle. Mama's not to worry. There are masses of bicycles in Cambridge and the cars and buses are very careful of them.' Cécile immediately began to worry. There was no longer anything she could do for anyone: she could not prevent them from setting to sea in a howling storm, nor from driving too fast, nor from climbing things; she could do nothing about contacts, smoking, drugs, illness, abortions or indeed anything. It really was a great mistake to have sent Laura to Cambridge, living out. She was too young.

Cécile only worried vaguely. That was life. They had done everything they could. Now whatever was to happen would happen. There was a sort of great cotton-wool screen between her and the children. But behind the curtain where he was having his shower, Marc said something.

'What?' The water was coming down in torrents. 'What did you say?'

'Nothing, I was groaning because soon there won't be any children left in this house.'

Over. Yes, almost over. Thirty years, if they were to live to be old, maybe thirty years of life alone together; that was the best they could hope for. That had been their own parents' lot. It never occurred to you that the last part of your life might very well be the longest.

Sometimes they looked out at the night and at their

t: angely empty avenue. At one of the few lighted windows in the building opposite a woman was ironing, anxiously preparing up to midnight, no doubt for a forthcoming holiday departure. A couple came out of a door, arm in arm. On these stormy evenings when the town smelt of earth and leaves there was something touching about all the couples. These two walked to the corner of the street and then stopped. The woman was wearing a short summer dress which left her arms and knees bare. They kissed. The woman's thighs showed as she strained up to reach the man. They unclasped. The man kept on kissing her hand interminably. The woman turned back into her house with an indifferent air. A man on a motor-cycle came down the empty avenue, waving his legs in the air for fun.

They lay down. They slept together more often in the empty flat. They were naked, with the doors and windows open, astonished at not having to hide, finding in their unwonted freedom both the physical emotion of fresh beginnings and the sensual grief of that which is going to end: they swam in the warm darkness and the silence, soothed by the moving air, castaways on a loving shore.

Sometimes, towards three or four in the morning, they would hear Nathalie's furtive key in the lock. 'There she is,' they said. And at that hour of the night their own pleasure and sensuality and a certain shame prevented them from saying any more.

Yet on one occasion they did discuss it. 'She mustn't let herself get pregnant,' Marc said.

'No,' said Cécile. 'She mustn't. But these days it shouldn't happen.' She stopped and then went on, 'Unless, on the other hand . . .'

'Are you certain that . . . ?' Marc asked.

'Oh no,' said Cécile. 'I'm not certain of anything. Yet she comes home so late that it seems to me they must be . . .'

'I should have thought a mother would have sensed these things,' Marc said.

'I should have thought so too,' said Cécile. 'But the young are more surprising than you think. Anything's possible. Even chastity. Anyhow, I don't want to think about it. I don't consider it my business any longer.'

'She's never talked to you again?'

'No.' They were silent for a moment; then Cécile went on: 'She's right. From now on she ought to live on her own. But if we consent to give her this little flat she's asking for, it seems to me that wouldn't be right either. Don't you agree?'

'Yes, I do,' said Marc. 'We've had that out already. She doesn't leave until she's married or got a job. We're not going to discuss it again.'

'If we were to let her go now, it would be as though we were abandoning her for the sake of peace and quiet, don't you think? We must be firm, at least until after the holidays.'

'But what about this Jo?' said Marc. 'What does he want?'

'The lot, I expect.'

'Perhaps I ought to see him.'

'You've been saying that for ages.'

'She would fall for a fellow like that.'

'A fellow like that is what she's been looking for from the start. It's quite understandable.'

'You understand her,' said Marc, after a pause. 'But you leave her too much to herself.'

'And what about you?' said Cécile.

'Tell her to see a gynæcologist.'

'Oh, Marc!'

'You're still full of archaic taboos. You know perfectly well that's what really matters. And it's up to you to tell your daughter.'

167

'But I *have* told her: I've told her a thousand times already in one way or another. And the details are in all the papers and magazines, all over the place. Dear God, if you really want to know about these things . . . So far as I'm concerned, the taboo is quite the other way round. What I recognize in Nathalie is my own idea of love itself, a romantic idea of love that I can't and won't give up. It's not that I'm afraid of talking about these things; it's just that I have a great respect for love. Even if I'm wrong and if Nathalie has to suffer for it—and we too, into the bargain—I don't feel I can talk to her along sensible, prudent lines.'

'Well . . .' said Marc. 'Ten years ago, no one would have dreamt of such a conversation in a family like ours.'

'Yet this situation isn't exactly new, thank God,' Cécile said. 'It's very ancient—eternal, everlasting.' She stopped again and added, 'It's not the young who have changed: we have. We're not prepared to mutilate them any more, that's what it is. We're the real revolutionaries!'

'The dreadful thing is this everlasting responsibility for the children, this never-ending friction.'

'Still,' said Cécile, 'if we were dead, they'd just have to . . .'

'Yes, but so long as we're not . . .'

Tidying a drawer, Cécile found letters and photographs. 'If I could come and see you in France, we'd go and wander about Versailles at the weekend and eat oranges . . . Don't forget, Cécile, after the war you're coming to England, and you'll stay with my people . . . The war is something that I just cannot understand. I'm on an anti-aircraft gun—do you understand what I mean?—my French is rotten—and we wait and wait and it's ghastly; and when you wrote me that letter I was so happy, Cécile. I know you don't like writing. But do write, Cécile, because I wait for your letters as though I were off my head. It's funny, but I'm always, always thinking of you, always, do you understand? I'm not joking now: it's true. But you are too far away from me. I can't see you or speak to you and it hurts. I pray for peace all the time. But if the war goes on long enough I may be sent to France and then I may see you, Cécile.'

She had loved them all, Marc, Jimmy and the others whose letters and photographs were there in her drawer, as well as those whose letters and photographs were still at her parents' house, in the room she had had as a girl—Yiyo, the Chinese; and Arthur, the Californian—she had a lock of his yellow hair somewhere; and Jean, the sculptor; and Hubert, who had died in his blazing tank; and Bernard, whose dawn-clear eyes had closed in a concentration camp. And Emmanuel, who was love itself. She still loved them all; she would love them until the end of time; it was enough for her to chance upon a letter or a photograph of one of them and he was the one she wanted. To each she could have said, 'How lovely you are. You are the only one. There is no one but you.' And then, 'That was my last word as a woman: my heart will never leave you. God bless you for ever, my dear.'

She hung the photograph of Jimmy in uniform in her den. Only his face and the top half of his chest could be seen, so that the picture was not old-fashioned. Jimmy might have been one of Stéphane's friends. She saw that he was handsome: she had not remembered it and she said to herself that now perhaps he was hideous or even dead. But what did it matter? Now at last this young man found her love, this young man for ever imprisoned in his battledress, with his look of expecting to be taken dead or alive, more likely dead, dead like a hero, falling from his plane, falling from his gun, dead in an open field, his eyes wide for the last time, full of ardour and disappointment and everlasting promise, this soldier who seemed to be saying, '*It might have been.*'

'Who's this?' asked Marc.

'An Englishman, a childhood friend almost. I wonder what's happened to him? I found his photo when I was tidying a drawer. Don't you think he's handsome?'

'Magnificent,' said Marc. 'Was there anything between you?'

'No, nothing.' She added, 'I can scarcely remember him. We didn't know each other for long. It was just before the war. It's as though the things and people of those days were part of a dream. Yet I'm dreadfully sorry to have lost them. Don't you feel that way?'

'It was our youth,' said Marc.

Games of ping-pong, walks in the park and through the streets of a provincial town; whatever had happened before the war belonged to a kind of vague prehistory. In fact she had been a silly little goose in those days, and Jimmy had probably been much the same. Memories generate their own poetry: a fraud. It was only now that Jimmy so moved her that she felt like writing to his old address, like getting a detective to seek him out, like sending him a lock of her hair. It was only now that she heard the lament of dead, ill-used youth, the unavailing lament to which one can only reply with a little shrug, saying, 'Bah . . .'

Marc looked at her with a wry expression, half making fun and half shame-faced, and said, 'It seems to me you've got it bad, Pépette.'

'Yes,' she said. 'I'm going through my second adolescence.'

'Good for you,' said Marc.

They played the fool; they horsed around. She felt the nakedness of her face and hid herself in him, laughing.

'Don't you get it bad too, when you look at girls, Marc? At least I only go all mushy over photographs.'

'Oh no,' said Marc. 'I don't get it bad any more.' And he added foolishly, 'I make the best of going gently, gently down the slope.'

They were alone in the flat. There was no one to see them. Empty space and silence lay all around them. They rocked each other, like poor old babies. They went on for a while, quietly, not laughing any more, and then sat down.

'Do you know what Nathalie really means to do over the holidays?' Marc asked.

'I think she's still going off to Spain in September. But she no longer talks about anything.'

'Still, you ought to try to find out.'

'Why don't *you* ask her what she's going to do? And when are you going to have this talk with her that we hear so much about?'

'How edgy you are,' Marc said.

She turned round on the couch to look straight at him and he noticed that her face was suddenly drawn. 'It was lovely a moment ago, just the two of us,' she said. 'Why go on about Nathalie? Why always hark back to the children? Nathalie's grown up and I'm nearly an old woman. It was lovely, a moment ago, just you and me.'

'Do you think they would marry, if we had money?'

'How can I tell? Certainly, if we had money Nathalie would be less frightened.'

'Is she frightened?'

'Of course,' said Cécile. 'Aren't we all?'

His eyes far away, his mouth pursed, Marc remained silent for a long while before he went on, 'Still, we ought to find out what this musician amounts to.'

'What he amounts to?'

'As a pianist.'

171

'And if you feel he doesn't amount to much, you'll put Nathalie off him?'

'Well, maybe.'

'Nice work.'

'But if it's for her own good? We can't let her marry just anyone.'

'Who's talking about marriage? And this young man isn't just anyone.'

'How do you know?'

'*I* took the trouble to see him.'

A memory came back to her, a memory of Emmanuel's time, of wartime. One Christmas Day she had lunched with Emmanuel in a restaurant in Montmartre. Not far from them, all through the meal, a man old enough to be their father had been watching them. When they got up to go he had smiled at them and given a little wave that was both of friendship and farewell.

'Did you know him?' Emmanuel had asked.

'No. Did you?'

'No.'

'But you felt you had known him for ever, didn't you?'

Because of that look, that little wave, they had felt heartened all the afternoon.

'Your attitude towards Nathalie is ambivalent,' said Marc.

'Do you think so?'

'Don't you notice it?'

'Yes,' she said, 'though perhaps it's only because you can't have two women in the house at the same time. In spite of myself I hamper her freedom and she restricts mine.'

'What would you like to do with your freedom, my poor Pépette?'

'Oh,' she said, 'if only you would take me seriously just for once. I don't know what I want to do with my freedom. But it seems to me that what with always putting the children between the world and ourselves and of minimizing what happens to us personally, we've ended by doing ourselves real damage . . . We can't take each other seriously any more. We are ashamed of our own tragedy in front of each other. To be together, we've always got to go by way of the children, and that's bad. Very bad. I don't know what I want to do with my freedom. But I do want to get away from the children's problems and from this perpetual screen between the world and us. The children's problems are beginning to bore me. Nathalie's love-affairs, Stéphane's difficulties, Laura's follies—sometimes I really wonder whether we're not using them as an alibi, something to keep us from danger. Suppose Nathalie has a baby, married or not—and she'd already be older than I was when she was born—does that mean that now she would no longer have the right to do anything but look after it? Would her life already be over? What is there that we can do from now on about Stéphane's difficulties or Nathalie's affairs? In a very little while there'll be nothing more we can do for Laura, either. We're not going to go on perpetually feeding on our children's youth, like a couple of vampires. Sooner or later you and I will have to come to terms with each other, and come to terms with the outside world, just the two of us alone.'

'A little while ago you seemed to think it was the children who were the vampires.'

'It's all the same,' she said. 'It's the family that is the vampire.' She looked at Marc and went on: 'What are children? Will-o'-the-wisps, and we fly round and round them, fascinated, as though they promised us a world unlike our own. But in a few years they belong in the grown-up world, they have children, and a job, and everything begins all over again. Who *does* live, in fact? Who *does* rise up to the heights? It's all a great fraud. Why shouldn't the years

173

we have before us—thirty, more or less—why shouldn't they be as good as those that are behind us? Why shouldn't they be even better, with no anxiety about money and no chores? Why shouldn't they be the years of our real adventure? It's not possible that there should be such waste in human existence. Oh, of course I'm speaking as a woman, and as a woman who's never been anything but a woman.'

And as Marc looked as though he were going to argue this point she hurried on: 'It's not that I regret it. But now I should like to bring about a great change, so that life isn't merely waiting and then the memories of that waiting. Look at writers: they've nothing else to tell us about but waiting and the memories of having waited. Something ought to be done—change ethics, change society, change family relationships, I don't know what: but life oughtn't to be like a tadpole, all head and a tiny body—life ought to be life right up to the last day of it. And perhaps that's the best thing we could do for our children. They'd be less afraid of their own future if they saw us still alive.' She fell silent, then added shyly, 'Don't you think so?'

'I'm not really sure what you mean,' replied Marc. 'The children, me, this home—isn't that the essence of your life? Motherhood is your life. Would you rather have worked in an office? Just you ask women who have not had children whether they feel they have lived fully.'

Now she looked at Marc, somewhat bewildered. 'I don't really know what I want,' she said. 'I don't want to be parted from my children: but still, to be a little farther off— a little more responsibility on their side . . . You know . . . I'd like . . .'

'What would you like?'

'When you go off on another long trip, I'd like you to take me for once.'

Now that it was the beginning of August life was easy-going in the extreme. It was not only Laura and Stéphane's being away that made it so much lighter, but the rhythm all around them had changed. They got in touch with friends who had stayed in Paris; they had fun; they wondered why they did not live like this all the year round. It might be that ease and rhythm depended merely on the season, the summer dresses, the fact of not being hungry, of drinking a lot, on the ease of movement in the streets, and on other people's being on holiday. Yet there was a simplicity and a friendliness in human relations that might have been preserved, that they longed to preserve: this simplicity and friendliness would still be pulsing with life in the fine October days when sunburnt women went about without stockings, only to grow stiff with the first frosts, muffle themselves in furs, cars, winter drawing-rooms, and then vanish among the chores and the nagging cares of winter.

Cécile brought out plates, cups and glasses that they did not generally use. Living as a pair became an aesthetic experience. She made bright, colourful dishes for Marc's return. This pleasure in material things, this taste for objects, was certainly one of the delights of middle age. Cécile had been astonished at its early appearance in the young: having breakfast on fine china, drinking out of the best glass and using embroidered linen was one of the minor pleasures, to be sure; but she observed with regret that the children already put such a value on the future setting of their lives—the material setting—that in their dreams of what was to come objects often had more importance than people or ideas—indeed, they even made a virtue of good taste. Yet certainly it was a joy for the middle-aged.

For too long they had drunk out of glasses the mustard had come in because there was too much washing-up and because they could not replace the easily-broken best glasses: for too long they had had meals off plastic tablecloths because of all the glasses that were spilled and the stains they made: now at last it was delightful to be able to use the charming, unmatching things that dozed in the cupboards, sometimes engrained with the immovable dust of succeeding generations who had let them doze likewise, because these objects had always been too beautiful for use and then, quite simply, had been forgotten.

Cécile laid the table for two. Opposite each other she set the flowered plates and the old goblets with their engraved bunches of grapes. The pale yellow tablecloth matched the curtains and the flowers. She looked at her little table, and the sight filled her with restful happiness and a sensual pleasure.

Yves and Françoise came to dinner. Françoise was wearing an enchanting dress with long sleeves, like the one Cécile had seen her in at Bagatelle. Her flesh had changed: it was a little puffy. When she smiled you could see that she had lost two teeth. She had taken on a gentle look of awareness, of disillusionment and a strange acquiescence. The talk was utterly commonplace, but they did not allow it to flag. The evening's main features were a lack of ease and a continued striking of the wrong note: Françoise was the only one who escaped from this, as though the others had been obscurely hag-ridden adolescents and she the only one with experience—but an experience that could not be conveyed, privileged and at the same time accursed. She even seemed to feel a certain compassion for their youthful blundering. Sometimes the two women's eyes met and Cécile knew that the truth of what she was thinking was perfectly obvious in spite of all she could do. It also seemed to her that in a certain way Françoise was lovelier than ever.

On the landing, during the rather early farewells, they at last congratulated her on having come out of it all so well.

'Oh, I'm not out of it yet,' she said. 'They're still doing all sorts of revolting things to me. But at least they've stopped the hormone treatment. That's quite something. I was beginning to grow a beard.'

Yves laughed. 'Can you imagine Françoise with a beard?'

And they shook their heads, smiling sadly at the absurdity. 'How ghastly,' they said. 'What a good thing they've nipped it in the bud.'

'Well, goodbye,' said Françoise.

They shook hands. Again they assured Françoise that any-one could see she was on the up-and-up. They watched her affectionately until the moment she vanished, still smiling and regal in her pink muslin, leaning on Yves's arm. Then they were ashamed of themselves and of the game they had played, yet unable to say what else they could have done. Perhaps there was nothing, they told each other. They and Françoise and Yves were not such very close friends, after all.

Nathalie had come home in an excellent mood. Laura's letters made her laugh heartily. It was obvious she was delighted that her sister too had gone over to the side of independence.

'When I was her age,' she said, 'you would never have sent me to Cambridge living out like that. I always went to boring families.'

'Boring? We sent you to delightful families. And it wasn't our fault that the exchange we arranged for Laura fell through at the last moment.'

'Still, you parents have come on since the time I was seventeen. It's extraordinary how lucky the young are now.'

They smiled. 'Your youth is in the distant past, of course.'

'It's all very well for you to laugh, but things have changed in the five years between me and Laura. When I was her age I was held in like a little girl and dressed like an old woman.'

'But you wore the clothes you wanted to wear,' said Cécile. 'You were mad on stiletto-heels and you wanted to dress like a widow. Personally, I'd much rather have dressed you like a seventeen-year-old today.'

'Nonsense. You'd have liked me to wear socks and white collars—to dress me up as a little girl.'

'It's what they do now,' said Cécile.

'Not at all,' said Nathalie.

And what about me, thought Cécile, with my provincial hats, my beige cotton stockings and my little puffed sleeves. I was a fine sight at seventeen. But there was no point in shedding tears over that: it was really too far away. Nobody cared.

'When I was seventeen,' went on Nathalie, 'I was never allowed out after midnight. You used to come and fetch me when I went to friends. Oh, you don't realize it, but you two have certainly come on these last few years.'

They admitted it. 'Well, what do you expect? The older children pave the way for the young ones. You're tired of fighting by the time the third comes along.' But they added, 'We've come along as regards you, too. Everyone's evolved during these last five years. Indeed, when you come to think of it, it's extraordinary. Tell me, do you think drug-taking is very widespread among the young?'

'It certainly is in England,' Nathalie said.

They looked at each other. Perhaps at this very moment their little girl was in some foul den, running even greater risks than Nathalie whom they worried about so much. What was she hiding behind her sweetness and her kisses? What was happening at this very moment to Laura, who answered reproof with 'How do you expect me to have the strength of mind to have strength of mind when I haven't got any strength of mind?' They remembered all the weaknesses she had displayed at the time of puberty—her run-

178

ning away, her lies, her cheating, even the mysterious emptying of the bottles of liqueurs. They were seized with panic. They longed for her to be there, at once, between them: they longed for their little girl, with childhood still in her face and eyes, that heavenly gift, that charm which would never return and which they had sent away to be spoilt in England.

'Oh, don't look so dismal!' Nathalie said. 'Laura's not as mad as all that. Besides, if she meant to play the fool, she'd never tell you so much.'

'Listen,' said Marc, 'you write to her. Warn her. She'll pay more attention to you than she would to us.'

'If you want me to,' Nathalie said.

And now, seeing that he was under way, Marc went on, 'And what about your own plans? Are you still going to Spain?'

'Yes. At the beginning of September.'

So all you had to do was to hit the right note and ask her, thought Cécile.

'You mean to stay in the flat alone for a fortnight, then?'

'Why, yes,' said Nathalie.

Gas, water, leaks, explosions, the meters, screw the bar across the front door, leave by the back stairs, not even the daily woman, shut all the cupboards, the wardrobes, spray against the moth, and Jo, Jo, who would be living here . . .

'I must have a talk with you.' This time Marc had put on too solemn a voice and Nathalie froze.

'All right,' she said.

Cécile could hear her heart beating. 'Am I in the way?' she asked, laughing.

'I'd rather speak to her alone,' said Marc.

'Fine.'

Cécile went to her den, and as she sat there on her couch,

her hands pressed together, something very like a prayer rose within her.

When she saw Marc again, an hour later, in the bathroom, she asked, 'Was it all right?'

And Marc said, 'Of course it was all right.'

That evening they said goodnight to each other rather ostentatiously, so that Nathalie should see that they were not going off together to gossip over her love.

6

Cécile left Paris on August 14th, but without Marc. He had to finish what he called 'a little homework'—a report on a special mission. He said he would rather get it out of the way before the holidays, and also he did not want to miss an American friend who was passing through Paris; she was the first woman he had ever felt drawn to and he was curious to see what she was like now. Cécile suspected that the second reason weighed heavier than the first. She also suspected Marc of wanting to dodge the little family reunion at her parents' home. But she had no wish to make him come. Maman would put herself out less if Marc were not there. In any case, Cécile was very fond of being alone with her parents and of taking up the old family life once again.

They teased one another as usual. 'If I were you, I shouldn't take the risk of seeing this old flame again: I'd stick with my memories.'

'She was very lovely, you know, at twenty-five.'

'That's just it.'

'She wasn't stupid, either. And so charming . . . But for the war . . .'

When Joyce had shown signs of life again in the fifties, Marc had been openly delighted.

'You're not cross because I shan't be here to welcome her too, are you?'

'I should certainly have liked her to meet you,' said Marc.

'Come on, she'll be much happier with you alone. By the way, how old is she now?' Cécile knew very well how old she was: four years older than Marc, nine years older than herself—fifty-three.

Marc pretended to work it out. 'She must be round about fifty.'

'At least,' said Cécile. She nearly said something catty, but refrained. She could see her big baby of a husband, her nearly-fifty-year-old who, speaking of women, said, 'I always go for the same age, about twenty-five . . .' Might he not have said to her, 'What about taking *me* seriously too, now and then?' He was waiting for his wife's little jab; he was ready to engage in the game and had a swift counterstroke on the tip of his tongue; but the far-off light of boyish love was trembling in his blue eyes. Joyce could appear with her thirty extra years or so, and he would forgive her for having aged: he would take her to one of the best restaurants in Paris, he would treat her like a girl, and he would gaze at her with the expression that he had in his eyes at this moment.

'Yes,' she said, 'I should very much have liked to meet her too. But still it's better that you should see her alone.'

Driving down to her parents' home, Cécile made a détour to see an old friend of the family whose wife had died and who was therefore ending his days in an unfamiliar house. This took her through several villages that were celebrating the day, and she arrived later than she had said.

Her parents were both in the garden waiting for her, and she had scarcely drawn up at the kerb before her mother, the quicker of the two, had opened the garden door, kissed her, and was reaching out to help with her luggage.

But into these outstretched hands Cécile put a great pot of delicately coloured primulas with a ribbon round it. 'Happy birthday, Maman, happy birthday!'

Maman laughed with pleasure, clasping the flowers. They

kissed again on the sidewalk, and then Cécile held her off, inspected her and said, 'But you look splendid!'

'Of course I do,' said Maman. 'Everything's fine. You *have* been extravagant! How lovely! I'm so pleased. I was just wanting something to fill my jardinière.'

Papa had limped out to wait his turn, and he laughed to see their meeting.

'Yes, it's the right side,' said Maman. 'The second fortnight in the month. You can leave your car right here.'

'I'm not too near the corner?'

'No,' said Maman, who had never driven in her life. 'It's perfectly all right for a little while. We'll unload and then you can park in Monsieur Riou's yard.'

The greenery was bursting through the railings. The dahlias and the roses were an explosion of colour.

'How lovely the garden is, Papa.'

Papa beamed. 'Yes, isn't it? People stop to look.'

Maman gave him the flowers to look after. 'I'm going to help Cécile.' Because of his bad back Papa was not allowed to carry anything heavy. Once more Maman stretched out her pretty, knotted hands with their network of blue veins. She wanted to take the heaviest bag; Cécile protested; Maman insisted. Finally they carried it between them and Cécile felt her mother's tense fingers against hers. Each thought the other had all the weight, so they both crooked their arms to lighten the other's burden.

The big table in the dining-room was laid. They had waited tea for Cécile. Ever since her children left home, Maman had treated them as guests—white tablecloth, best china, silver: everything gleaming. But they sat down as though this welcome was quite usual. They talked of other things. 'Another cup of tea, Cécile? Some ham?'

'No, thank you, Maman, no ham. I wouldn't be able to eat any dinner if I ate ham. It's six o'clock already.'

'But you must be hungry. I'm sure you had no lunch. Come, just a thin slice . . .' She was on her feet, hurrying about.

'If you really want me to,' said Cécile. 'But in that case we won't have dinner.'

'Oh yes we shall,' said Maman. She smiled. 'There's a chicken.' Maman's chickens were better than anyone else's. She said she had no secret, she just roasted them: that was all.

'We'll have your chicken tomorrow.'

Maman hesitated, glancing at Papa. 'We had rather thought . . . When are you leaving?'

'The day after tomorrow.' Cécile had prepared her little lie to excuse Marc's absence. 'I have to meet Marc at Lyons. His parents wanted to see him too, of course. He went by train yesterday.'

'That's very short,' said Maman. 'So we shan't be seeing Marc? Well, it's perfectly natural that he should go to see his people. You could both have come here and then stayed a couple of days in Lyons together. But of course if you tried to see everybody you would have no holidays left. And since you've taken the house from the fifteenth . . .' She hesitated and then went on: 'We had rather thought you might be able to take us to Vrigny tomorrow.' As usual, Maman explained that with these new timetables it was impossible to go to Vrigny by train without staying the night. And where could one spend the night? She went on: 'I have to go to the cemetery and see the curé and the tenants. You've no other plans?'

Behind the soft voice Cécile could hear the ceaseless, touching supplication: 'Lord, don't let anything happen, don't let me be responsible for an accident because I have asked Cécile to drive me to Vrigny. Now that she has arrived safely, and since she has to leave the day after, is it not tempting fate to drive again tomorrow?'

'But I had counted on taking you to Vrigny,' said Cécile. 'I should like to go there too.' Not so very long ago she had thought these visits to the graves and the curé ridiculous.

'And then,' said Maman, 'I'd very much like to call in and see my cousin. She's all the family I have left on my side.'

'What about us?' said Cécile.

'Of course,' said Maman, and she went on, 'Do have a little ham. It won't interfere with your dinner. It's very lean.'

'Don't force her,' said Papa.

But Cécile had foreseen this overeating and had taken some pills on the way. She ate the ham.

'There you are, she was hungry all the time,' Maman said.

The dining-room, with its windows open behind the half-closed blinds, was full of yellow light—the familiar, gentle light of summers at home. The garden could be sensed the other side of the blinds; it could be heard, with its murmur of bees, its birdsong and the rustling of leaves. Motor-cycles roared and sputtered outside the windows, it was peace they ripped apart, the peace of the old street, of the old house.

Next morning Cécile deliberately stayed in bed for the pleasure of hearing her mother creep up the stairs, tap at the door, carefully open it, come into the dimness and whisper, 'My poor child, I'm waking you up. Did you sleep well? Not too hot? I'm sure you would have liked to stay in bed a bit longer, but your father's always in a hurry and he wants us to leave in half an hour. He's outside now, all ready and waiting.'

Papa was indeed in the garden, leaning on his stick.

Neither age, infirmities, nor more than fifty years of living with his wife had taught him to wait in any other manner than on his feet.

Cécile had not yet grown used to having to bend to kiss him. He laughed, 'You sleep soundly in the old house, don't you, child?'

He felt responsible for the smooth running of the day, which was to be divided in two by a good luncheon. He pulled his watch from his waistcoat pocket and looked at it.

'I can see you,' said Maman. 'I can see you looking at your watch. I'm hurrying all right, don't worry. Of course there's no danger of your being late. You've only got to put your hat on and there you are.'

She had picked flowers for the graves and packed sweets for her cousin and clothes for the tenants; she had shut all the shutters and filled all the bowls scattered about the garden for the birds, who were dying of thirst. She put on her little black hat with the mauve ribbon. She locked the front door, the cellar door and the garden door. She got in the front of the car because she was always afraid of being unwell during the drive and this queasiness spoilt her outings. In spite of his stiff leg, Papa settled into the back as best he could. Maman put away her keys in her big black handbag—it still looked new for all its years of service, she never dirtied or spoilt or tore anything she wore. She looked back. The house, with all its shutters and doors closed, was like a box. 'I don't think I've forgotten anything,' she said.

The car moved off.

Maman turned round. 'We're not late, you see. It wasn't worth fussing . . .'

He looked at his watch again. 'I said that to do it properly we should leave by half past nine. It's ten o'clock.'

Cécile and Maman laughed. 'We'll not change him now, my poor child,' Maman said. 'Always in a hurry. Do you

remember going on holiday, when you were little . . . ?'
She was glad to have an ally. And Papa was glad to see his
wife and daughter getting on so well together.

'Women have no notion of time,' he said. 'They never
stop deceiving themselves. They don't believe a minute
here, a quarter of an hour there, really matter.' Everyone
knew Papa's views on the equality of the sexes.

'So nothing has been forgotten, then?' Cécile asked.

Presently they were on the familiar road that ran through
the vineyards and the villages of yellow stone, perched on
the hillsides.

'Good grapes again this year,' Papa said. 'That makes ten
good wine years in succession. The growers are doing well,
they are indeed.'

They looked at their Burgundy. It filled their gaze in
every direction. 'You'll have to turn right soon, you know,'
Maman said.

Vrigny sprawled over a plain closed in by distant woods.
Papa was dreadfully stiff. They had to help him pull out his
rigid leg, which had got wedged under the front seat. He
had almost to lie down in the back. 'What acrobatics,' he
said. He put his stiff leg out first. As soon as it touched the
ground he grasped his stick to get ready for the next movement, and there he was on his feet, waiting for the blood
to flow in his veins. To make them laugh he sang the old
song of the light infantrymen, *When your sure-footed rapid
pace* . . .

And Cécile remembered how fast he used to walk in
former times, in spite of his lameness, with the whole
family trailing along behind him.

They went into the church to say a prayer. They called
on the curé, who lived alone amid piles of dusty papers.
'Impossible to get any help,' he said. From time to time his
blue eyes flashed with merriment, shining through a cloud

of mild disappointment in claims, demands, collections. Maman sympathized with him. Papa urged her to hurry. 'You know we've still got to go to the cemetery and to see the tenants.'

'And my cousin,' said Maman.

The first house to be seen from the entrance to the grave-yard was the grandparents', the house where they used to spend the holidays. Maman looked at it without speaking, and Cécile looked at Maman, whose expression was that of an aged child. They opened the boot; they took out the flowers, which had lost a few petals; they stood in silent reverence at the family tomb. What did that mean—to stand in silent reverence? You stood there, and you went on standing there. Maman's countless little wrinkles quivered, and she still had that lost, orphaned look on her face. She lingered by the tomb. 'That's where I want to be buried,' she said. She smiled and added, 'François promised me.' She always had more confidence in her son than in anyone else.

Did she ever speak more fully on the subject of death? It was a topic upon which Papa was very happy to philosophize. But no one knew what Maman thought about death: perhaps she did not think about it: perhaps she was afraid: perhaps she did not understand, and that was all there was to it.

They fetched water, they arranged the flowers, they threw away the old pots and set up the new ones. They stood in silent reverence once more.

'Well, we must be getting along now,' said Maman.

Papa climbed into the back of the car. 'I'm not getting out again,' he said. 'You can go and see the tenants without me.'

They drove back to the church down the beautiful avenue lined with chestnut trees. At the end of the holidays in the old days, chestnuts used to lie there shining, uncountable treasure that sprang from white-lined green cases, the object of an enormous greed in which there was more sorrow for what could not be carried away than pleasure in the booty gathered.

'Poor curé,' said Maman again, as they went by the presbytery. Now they were at the cousin's house. They stopped in the front courtyard.

'I'm not getting out,' Papa said again. Once more he looked at his watch. 'Ten minutes,' he said. 'You mustn't stay more than ten minutes. Otherwise we'll be late for lunch.'

'We know all about that,' Maman said.

The cousin hurried out and said, 'I'll persuade him to come in.'

'Good morning, cousin,' said Papa from the depths of the car, all the more friendly since he was determined not to be persuaded. 'No, no, I'm not getting out. With my leg it's too much of a business.'

So the conversation took place out of doors, everybody standing beside the car. Maman asked eagerly after everyone she knew, mentioning unknown names. Cécile longed to calm her down. 'Take your time, Maman; gossip in peace with your cousin, the only witness of your past; take no notice of Papa. Don't you know him yet? He'll wait quite happily.' Maman had assumed her own highly personal look of compassion, with her eyebrows raised, her forehead creased, and she still seemed to be saying: Why suffering? Why death? Why does nothing ever stay the same?

'Come on, we must be going,' Papa said.

They kissed; they held one another's hands. Cécile said, 'Yes, yes, Papa; we're coming. Just let us alone for one more minute.' And she deliberately restarted the conversation. After all, it was she who was driving.

Maman got in next to Cécile again. She was grateful to

her for her co-operation and they talked with unusual freedom.

'You're happy to have a good gossip with your daughter, aren't you?' said Papa.

Yes, they were happy, all three of them. The weather was fine. They had had an excellent lunch. The road among the vineyards was splendid. Keenness of vision diminishes with age, but the gaze is more sensitive. They drove through woods. Now they were on their way to see Papa's family.

'I remember walking through this wood after a party,' he said. 'I can't have been twenty at the time. I'd been seeing a girl home . . . D'you know, I can't even remember who it was . . .'

'Not Laurentine, by any chance?' asked Maman slyly.

'I can't remember, I can't remember at all. But what I do remember as clearly as though it were yesterday is coming back alone and hearing the nightingales. Such singing! The night was filled with it. Never had I heard them sing like that.'

He fell silent as they drove slowly through the wood. The nightingales of his youth were singing louder for Papa than the memories of his earliest loves.

Suddenly, on the way home, Maman, with an embarrassed gesture, said very quietly, 'Cécile, I think you'll have to stop. I don't feel very well.' But almost at once she said it was over and insisted on getting dinner ready that evening.

The next day she urged Cécile to be on her way, anxious as usual lest her daughter should be late and therefore drive too fast. She had picked flowers, prepared sweets and a picnic lunch. Each little parcel was pretty, carefully wrapped and tied in her own inimitable manner with the same long discreet loops that decorated her handwriting.

Once the car was loaded and the farewells said, they

stood on the sidewalk as always, waiting for their daughter to settle behind the wheel and drive off. At this moment Maman—it was surprising in her and illogical, since she had just been speeding Cécile's departure—said, 'Wouldn't you like to come back into the house and sit down for a while?'

And Cécile longed to do just that. But the goodbyes had been said. A kind of shame held her back. The two women exchanged a gentle, puzzled, nostalgic look. 'I must be off, you know,' Cécile said.

Sitting in the car, hoping, as always, to throw out a bridge towards their next meeting, she said, 'I'll stop again on the way back. And I'll drive you up to Paris. The weather will be better in September.'

'Yes, yes,' said Maman, not listening, 'don't worry.'

Now Cécile spoke directly to her father—words meant more to him. 'You will come, won't you, Papa?'

'Perhaps we will. Yes, perhaps we'll come in September.'

Maman shut the door and said, 'Don't look back: we're going to watch you go.'

For years now, every time she left them, side by side on the sidewalk, Cécile had felt that the car was drawing out a thread to breaking-point between them, and breaking it with an awareness of that last farewell which must come and which in turn filled her with a wild desire to turn back, to put into words this love, so battered by life, which yet spread and grew in separation.

'Don't look back: we're going to watch you go.'

She was leaving the town by a road she did not usually take, a street with others crossing it at right-angles; she obeyed, and did not look back at the two old people who she knew were still standing there, side by side on the sidewalk.

7

She was sitting on a stone bridge, with her legs dangling over the parapet. Down below was a crowded mass of plants and insects, with creeping things moving among them and unseen running water that set some leaves trembling so that they fluttered wildly above heaven knows what mystery lurking beneath countless others, motionless, fascinated. The hot breeze caressed her neck, her arms, her fingers. She looked at her knees as though they did not belong to her, yet as though the whole of her being dwelt there, in that sunburnt body that was so pleasant to look at; yes, and still pleasant to own, this year, this summer, in spite of a few marks that she was almost alone in knowing, whose advance she watched over and which already condemned this happy flesh in contact with the warm roughness of the stone. She had picked blackberries in the hedges, devouring them by the handful, staining her face, and she had washed in spring water. An arid country with water murmuring everywhere astonished her. She was forty-four: what of it? Forty-four was not old: vital statistics were a mere invention. Youth lasts long—that was not sufficiently known. It lasts all your life, or very nearly.

It's not that you forget it; it's not that you can possibly forget it; but the delight always springs up anew. You can never have enough of it.

She had walked among the murmurings of water and leaves, down sunken lanes that opened on to a vast landscape rimmed by the white wall of the Alpilles, a landscape with its own sense of order, a paradise in which the cypresses and olive trees showed black in the sunlight.

And now she was sitting on this bridge, not far from the partner of her life, who was having fun at a club and did not much care for walks, but a great way from her children, who had gone, or were about to go, each in his or her own direction with unknown friends to three different countries, and who, so far as she knew, were perfectly well even though hundreds of miles away from her carefully kept flat, so full of cherished pieces of furniture and irreplaceable carpets: it could catch fire for all she cared—she was ready to take in whole towns, to bake in the sun, to skip among the reeds, she was a thousand times a virgin and a thousand times a lover, she worshipped life and she despised death; she was alone, no one could see her, and she began to feel a little frightened and furtive like those men who roamed among the trees. She looked sharply at the road and the hedges, thinking she felt eyes upon her: she was a wanderer who might get herself murdered.

From the moment they arrived they had loathed the village of Les Saintes-Maries-de-la-Mer, where they had taken a little house. So they made the most of their last days of being alone to go up into Haute Provence, for they were sure of having their fill of the Camargue during the three weeks they were still to spend there with Laura after her return from England. Moreover, Laura had asked whether she might bring a friend from Cambridge, saying that his parents were delightful people—teachers—and that perhaps another year they might be very glad of having been kind to him. Only too pleased that she should have made such suitable contacts, they had replied, 'Bring your English friend by all means; you'll be less on your own with him here, and since we have taken this house we might as well do someone a good turn.'

So almost every day they drove up from Les Saintes-Maries-de-la-Mer to Saint-Rémy-de-Provence, where they had found tennis-courts and pleasant walks. Cécile had taken up playing again. Marc encouraged her affectionately, saying, 'It's coming back, you see.' And she ran about the court, astonished that not so long ago she had quite given up this pleasure and thinking Marc remarkably seductive with his little linen hat on his head and his long sunburnt legs. So long as they kept their health, they still had many good years ahead of them.

They looked at houses and chose those they liked. It seemed to them that if they were to settle in this part of the world neither age nor illness would have any hold on them. The city and its rat-race seemed to them ridiculous; the human comedy was no more than a childish game, from which they would gladly opt out. They were enough for each other: they were old friends, enchanted by the same landscapes and the same pleasures, accepting the difference between them, moving apart, coming together again, one flesh, a double outlook, forgetting even their children, eyes open once more, as they had been in adolescence, to the longing for the absolute, yet knowing that nothing and nobody could ever satisfy this longing, which was rather the absolute of longing and which had the very savour of life.

At night, in the little house, they grilled fish with the herbs that scented the whole countryside, they drank vin rosé, they read aloud passages from their books, they listened to records, and music threw its limitless promise over their future. In the morning they went to bathe far from the village, on the long beaches where sheets of salt and egret-haunted lagoons shone among the sands. They ate a second breakfast on the terrace of a café by the sea. They drove up into Haute Provence, returning at sunset, driving slowly across the marsh, sorry not to be able to walk along the canals because of the mosquitoes, and stopping the car until the very last ray disappeared, the last tinge of colour from the water.

But then it began to rain and blow and they stayed at home, sleeping, reading, getting a little bored, watching the mud-covered hordes of young gallop by, streaming with sweat and rain; and regretting they were no longer twenty nor enormously energetic, for they saw that this country did not lightly give up its secrets and that it could quickly turn against mankind. Hemmed in by the marshes, tired of the wind that penetrated every crack of the little house and flaked the whitewash from the walls, they grew anxious and began to count the days until Laura should appear, and to live for the post.

Nathalie wrote to say that her holiday plans had been changed because Jo had been asked to take part in musical festivals in various Italian towns. They hardly minded at all. Seen from the Camargue, Nathalie's examination no longer looked so important. She would go to Spain later, and this year she would improve her Italian, which would also be useful to her.

They were afraid they might not have left her enough money and they sent her five hundred francs. 'After this,' said Marc, 'I've only got a hundred francs in my account.'

'Now I come to think of it,' said Cécile, 'you never told me the details of your conversation with Nathalie before we left Paris.'

Marc hesitated a moment and replied, 'She told me nothing that you didn't already know.'

'But how did it go?' asked Cécile.

'Well, Nathalie seemed to me very sensible. She told me that the reason she no longer brought this young fellow to the house was not to hide him from us nor us from him, but that she did not want their relationship to seem on an official footing; she said she was very fond of him and admired him, but as for marriage, that was something else again; it was a question of knowing whether they could live together, and they would probably know more about that by the end of the holidays because they were going to try it.' Marc reddened slightly.

'What did you say to her on the subject?' Cécile asked.

'Which?'

'Did you tell her to see a gynæcologist?'

Marc's colour deepened. 'No. It was not for me to say it. Our conversation was on quite another plane. Anyhow, Nathalie seems to me so grown up now, so reasonable.'

'Oh, reasonable,' said Cécile. She knew Nathalie's deliberately vague way of defending moods and situations when protective grown-ups interfered with her private life. She kept her harsh rejection and her air of superiority for her mother. With everybody else, including Marc, she played the part they expected her to play. With an open, serious look, as pleasant and reasonable as could be, she would answer everything in soft, padded words, a thousand miles from the person who was talking to her. People would say to Cécile, 'You're quite mistaken to worry about your daughter: I've had a chat with her, and I am truly surprised to find how mature she is.' And God knows plenty of people had 'chatted' with Nathalie. Cécile nodded and said nothing. 'Oh, but in any case, Papa . . . If a boy doesn't wear a tie . . .' She wondered whether Nathalie had really been open with her father. But she reflected that their daughter might be quite as sincere in deliberately casual conversation as she was when trying out her claims and formulas on her mother.

'We talked about Jo's career,' said Marc. 'I think he will be a great pianist.'

What on earth did Marc know about pianists' careers? She felt like kissing him. 'So you think he will be a great pianist, do you?'

'I'm not the one who thinks it,' said Marc, hurt, for he had not yet recognized the tenderness of the teasing. 'It's people who know more about these things than I do. The Israeli government has given him a grant. He's won an international prize, and one that counts for a great deal.' Even without a tie, Jo, wrapped in official approval and encouragement, became a most acceptable match. 'If they love one another, I don't see why they shouldn't marry.'

Marc loathed extravagant attitudes and wild outbursts, but as soon as anything was put to him in quiet, reasonable terms he became the most romantic of romantics. From now on he would have a blind and total faith in this adventure dressed up as an intelligent, reasonable engagement. He's the adventurer, thought Cécile; he's the really adventurous member of the family—the maddest creature I've ever come across. That was what attracted me so much in the first place.

'Our little Nathalie is quite attractive,' added Marc. 'This young fellow would be a fool not to want to marry her.'

'That is, if he wants to get married,' said Cécile. 'And in any case . . .'

'And in any case what?'

'He might look for a girl who knew more about music, or who was more fit to share a pianist's life, or was a better cook, or richer . . .'

'He might well look for a richer one,' Marc agreed. 'Still, we'll try to help them if they do marry. To be launched, Nathalie says he would have to be able to give a concert. I asked her what that would cost and she said approximately ten thousand . . . Well, if they marry we won't give a wedding reception, and he shall have his concert.'

Sitting side by side in the little wicker chairs belonging to this holiday house with peeling walls, they looked at each other. Outside the rain was coming down in torrents. They were not sure how the butane fire worked and they had not dared light it. They felt cold in spite of their flannel slacks and a smell of damp drifted about the room. This house had been taken for an Englishwoman who was not going to come after all: they were not having much fun in it . . . They would have been just as well off in a hotel, or even if they had stayed at home in Paris: they might have travelled, they might have gone to Greece, Tunisia, Scandinavia: they had never done anything really out of the ordinary together. Instead, they looked at each other, saying nothing; they could hear applause. Jo bowed, elegant, handsome—oh, how handsome!—triumphant: his genius burst forth, it was a revelation. Nathalie was pink, wild with happiness, wild with love. Searching through the crowd, Jo found Nathalie's eyes as she sat there almost invisible in her box; it was a triumph, and they, the parents, saw this look passing between their children, and they too had some part in it.

'You told her we could help them a little?'

'Yes,' said Marc. 'It was better she should know.'

'I'm glad you did,' said Cécile.

The day before Laura was due they found that Air France was on strike. They wired to Cambridge to tell their daughter she would have to come by another airline and asked her to let them know when she would arrive. There was no reply. 'Of course,' they said, 'she has no money left. We ought to have sent it reply-paid.' But it was too late to send another. Fortunately she was bringing this boy with her: he would help her to cope.

They telephoned, but the information they were given

was muddled and uncertain, and they decided to drive to Marignane in the morning, to be there to meet all the planes that flew in from London that day.

The mistral had swept away the clouds and was still blowing furiously. Marc looked at Cécile out of the corner of his eye, and teasingly assured her that aircraft did not crash as easily as all that. Cécile knew that Laura did not like her in trousers, so she was wearing a light frock, and in spite of the sweater she had put on over it she was shivering. As each plane from London or Paris (Laura might have had to change) was announced, she tidied her hair and her scarf. Marc, sunburnt, wearing a pink shirt and a reddish-brown pullover, was a father it would be a pleasure to produce. When the passengers came out they looked at them intently, already smiling, keyed-up, disappointed.

There was only one more plane due in from London before nightfall. They had little hope that Laura would be aboard. They were tired and cold. Where was Laura? Where were they themselves going to sleep? The next plane after this arrived at five in the morning. The idea of going back to Les Saintes and getting up again at three did not appeal to them.

When Laura appeared they did not immediately recognize her. She had a Beatle hairstyle, she had put on weight, and as to eye make-up, she had lost all sense of proportion. She was less pretty and less of a child than they remembered, and she said hallo in an offhand way. Cécile noticed that she smelt of tobacco. With a critical look at her mother and a pleasant one at her father, she introduced a red-headed youth who at once began stammering in English; then, with a movement which seemed instinctive, she led them all towards the bar. Her teeth chattered as she said, 'Brr, and I thought we were going to be warm at last. You'll stand us a drink, won't you?' After this she said that she was dying of starvation—she had been hungry for so long in England—and wanted to have dinner right away in the restaurant. 'What on earth is that sweater you've got on over your dress?' she asked Cécile as soon as they were settled.

'Well,' said Cécile, 'I didn't bring many clothes, and as you don't like me in trousers . . .'

Michael ate bouillabaisse for the first time, and did not like it. Laura smoked before the meal was over.

'*Sorry, the place is middle-class,*' she said to the English youth in an affectedly careless tone, and 'This is an awful shack,' when Marc and Cécile showed them the house.

'An old house furnished by people with taste,' said Marc.

'Oh, do you think so?' said Laura.

The children unpacked their bags and there was a pleasant moment when Laura seemed something like her old self as she gave them their presents. They did not like to prevent her from straight away putting the English records she had brought back on the record player; they seemed to recall particularly cherished memories—rather disturbing ones, to judge from her expression. Each took a turn in the bathroom and then the parents went up to their room. For a long while they heard the children chattering below.

During the night it began to rain again and Cécile wondered what they were going to do with this Michael if the bad weather went on. She was low-spirited. All this wind, all this rain pouring on to the terrace frightened her. She would have liked to be back in Paris. It seemed to her that she no longer loved her Laura as much as she had done; and even that she had been delightfully at peace before the child came back.

Although Michael did not care for bouillabaisse, he was mad on red mullet grilled with Provençal herbs, on Camargue rice and paella; in this he was backed up by

Laura, who furthermore wanted English tea and breakfast, with toast, bacon and boiled eggs. As Marc had no objection to this pattern of eating, the shopping, cooking and washing-up assumed heart-breaking proportions. But during the bad weather there were not many pleasures other than those of the table. The Camargue was horrible to look at. They bought rubber boots. The races were cancelled. The sea was dangerous. There was nothing more dreary than those great invisible shores swept by grey waves. The record player blared ceaselessly. The children spent their time playing cards or lying gloomily on their beds with their boots on, leafing through magazines. Meals were rendered horrible by Michael's stammering, his fierce determination to express himself in no language but his own, and his un-expected longing to be acquainted with the smallest details of the French civil service; this pleased Marc but chilled Cécile, for she was obliged either to be mute or to squeak out some observation in English—her attempts were usually greeted with laughter, for her accent was disastrous. But as she told them, *she* had not had the good luck to be sent to England when she was seventeen. And after the war there had no longer been any question of travelling.

On the ground floor there was a big farmhouse table that was used for everything. Every time it had to be laid for a meal it had first to be cleared of letters, books, flat-irons, cards, photographs, water-melon skins, magazines. Every-thing was piled on the chest-of-drawers and one hour later it was all back on the table again. The children had a knack of vanishing at times when they might have been useful.

Cécile—and let him who has never read a letter left lying about throw the first stone—noticed that one letter written by Laura kept stubbornly reappearing on the table, and in the end she read it. It was addressed to an Italian, alluded vaguely to 'orgies', to a quarrel at a fair, and in the last unfinished sentence said: 'The worst of it is that I've not dared tell my parents that after all the dough I've squeezed out of them I've still left a good many debts at Cambridge. I owe Peter fifteen pounds and Johnny seven. I wonder how on earth I'm ever going to get out of this hole.'

Had Laura left the letter about on purpose? Was this her shabby little way of getting out of this hole? Respect for private letters was one of the bases of the family's ethics. What if Laura had merely left it on the table out of carelessness? It was just like her to let her secrets lie about all over the place and neither to finish nor to send off her letters. For several days Cécile held herself in. She did not like to worry Marc; nor did she like to confess that she had read one of Laura's letters. She was haunted by a memory—that of her little thirteen-year-old girl who had run away from home telephoning to ask whether they would still like to have her back, begging them to come and fetch her. 'I'm coming right away, Laura, right away: stay where you are, wait for me on the Métro platform, don't stir.' The station was a long way off: endless. Laura was there on the platform, her back turned, her school bag on her shoulder, right on the edge. She was watching a train coming in. Cécile's hands were already out to grasp her, but there were still thirty yards to go. 'I'm here, Laura, I'm here, I'm here.' She dared not call her. She ran towards her, her arms out. The train came in. She clasped her.

She made oblique references. 'I suppose you hadn't any money left by the end of your stay. Was that why you didn't answer our wire?' 'No,' said Laura, 'I certainly hadn't any money left: I'd just bought your presents.' 'You got through a great deal of money over there. I see you've developed a taste for poker. You can easily lose your shirt at that sort of game.' 'Oh,' said Laura, 'if you're going to go on blaming me for the money I've spent, I shall be sorry I bought you any presents. I brought presents for Stéphane and Nathalie too, if you want to know.'

Michael never left her for a moment; they had made friends with some local people, and they spent a lot of their time at the café. The letter vanished. Cécile, no longer equipped with demonstrative affection, did not know how to tackle Laura. By contrast, Stéphane and Nathalie seemed quite comforting: children like them kicked, but they never kicked over the traces; their course could be foretold; they only ran the not so dangerous risks. With Laura there was dissembling, strange inclinations, amorality, the unpredictable. Her conversations with Michael made it clear that she had seen a remarkable number of films and that where they were concerned she really did possess a certain sophistication. From her Michael also learnt that in Paris sweaters were bought at Renomma's, shoes at Carville's—'they aren't bad at Carel's either'—that 'the Renault pub wasn't up to the Winston Churchill', that the records were good at the King Club but Castel's line was still the best, and that after a dance the really with-it thing was to go and have breakfast at Orly. Laura said she would need a long dress after the holidays, and a warm topcoat, and a short formal dress, and a three-quarter suede coat lined with fur. This fashion for short skirts was terrific, so were the tunics that were going to be worn this autumn, the gold and silver boots, the gold and silver dresses. It made you feel like going straight back to Paris. What were they doing in this awful dump? 'But for a start,' she said, 'the minute I get to Paris I'm going to buy a matching skirt and pullover. I adore them.' But where was she going to get the money from, for heaven's sake?

Cécile was shrinking to the size of a little old woman.

The fat that Laura had put on in England seemed to her un-healthy. Everything was possible; anything might happen; it was reasonable to fear the worst. Her arms were empty and powerless.

She brought herself to tell Marc about the letter. To her astonishment he did not blame her for having read it. All he said was, 'Oh Lord, these children . . .' and so much weakness, innocence and weariness showed in his eyes that their colour seemed quite washed out.

'We must have a talk with her,' they said. 'We can't leave her to bear this anxiety all by herself.'

'But I'll have to tell her I read this letter.'

'I'll tell her, if you'd rather; but with you there.'

Yes, she would rather. She was cowardly to the point of total surrender. They summoned Laura to their room.

'Sit down,' said Marc.

They were already in their places, stiff and pale as judges. But pale with fear. Laura looked at them: suddenly she became a child again and an expression of extreme alarm appeared upon her face.

'What's happened?'

They comforted her at once. 'Nothing, nothing. There's no bad news. It's you—it's about you. Papa will tell you.'

Marc told her, slowly and with exact particulars. Cécile said, 'I read that letter because I thought you wanted me to, you see. You left it lying about so long.'

Laura was very pale: she cast about. 'What letter do you mean?'

'The one you wrote to that Italian, Umberto.'

Laura wrinkled her forehead. Then suddenly she burst out laughing. 'Oh, is that all?'

'All! Debts of more than twenty pounds, at your age, even supposing there are no others. How did you expect to get out of it without telling us? And do you think that's the right way to behave, running up debts?'

'But I haven't run up any debts,' said Laura.

'What do you mean, you haven't run up any debts? What have you just been saying to that boy?'

Laura said nothing for an instant. Then she shrugged. 'It was only a joke,' she said at last. 'For fun. To look big.'

'To look big?'

'Oh, my poor dear parents, you just don't understand the young,' Laura said sadly.

And Marc replied with the same sadness, 'No, I don't understand the young. I just don't understand them.'

She kissed them, she made much of them. But she was not entirely back with them. At what point had she lied? They were very happy to believe in this joke, but it was an odd sort of a joke and they did not care for it.

'How do you expect us to protect you, Laura, if you tell lies? We can't do anything for you unless we know who you really are and what you do and what you're capable of, at least in a general way. People who live together and feel affection for one another must know what they're dealing with. At least so far as essentials are concerned. With you, we don't know any longer.'

'But I don't lie to *you*,' said Laura. 'I swear I don't lie to you. And anyhow, lying's not so dreadful as you think. I could feel that Mama didn't love me any more these last few days, and I kept wondering why. It was awful. And even if I did lie, it wouldn't be any reason for loving me less. It has nothing to do with it. If I were to lie to you, I shouldn't love you any the less. My lies aren't against *you*. Oh, why did you read that letter, Mama?'

'Why,' said Cécile, spreading her hands, 'because I kept seeing it on the table all the time.'

Now Laura was crying. And Cécile felt herself in the

wrong and was upset. They kissed Laura. 'Go back to Michael: we believe you—it's all over—our minds are quite easy.'

Their minds were easy, but they were still sad. Perhaps Laura was right, and lying was not so serious after all, nor even gambling, debts and drinking. Young people were like that today. A certain amount of lying, a certain amount of gambling, a certain amount of debt, a certain amount of drinking: perhaps it was not all that serious. But they were afraid. They did not want anything bad to happen to Laura. Nor did they want her to grow morally soft, to become ugly. They knew very well that neither purity nor childhood could be preserved in a glass case for ever. They knew that nothing ever retained its first freshness. But they did want to keep Laura.

'Would you have played a joke like that?' Cécile asked.

'No,' said Marc hesitantly, 'no . . .'

They no longer had faith in themselves. Perhaps it was better not to try too hard to know things. Perhaps behaving like an ostrich was a sound educational principle.

'My poor dear parents, you just don't understand the young.' Cécile in her time had also made up plenty of things —deaths in the family, misfortunes, dramas, legacies. But she would rather have played the part of little angel, above all at seventeen. Seventeen: the year of the war, the first and last holiday as a young person, crowds of other young on the beach in the evening, and in the grotto café; the first night-clubs; roulette at the little casino where they were not too particular about your age; tangos. But seventeen was a long way off; as far off as the days when everything was possible, when everything was confused, fierce, simple-minded, depraved and disapproved of.

The sun came out again. The children sunbathed, swam, ran around, forgot about their English teas and breakfasts.

The redhead lost his interest in the French civil service and stopped stammering. Laura became pretty again, abandoned her haughty airs and once more kissed everybody all round. There was an alternation of being together and being apart. The house looked its best. Cécile enjoyed the rhythm of doing housework with the age-old instruments of broom and duster. All that was needed to dry the pretty tiles on the floor was sun and the draught created by opening the doors that gave on to two streets. The children were out of doors, Marc read on the terrace, Cécile was an unchanging, basic woman in a linen dress who looked after her house and gossiped with the neighbours on her doorstep, broom in hand.

They came to love the immense pale seashore and they drove on and on along it, going past the camping sites, past the last huts and red-roofed modern buildings, sometimes startling flocks of birds upon the sandy marshes, driving the car evenly and fast enough to prevent being bogged down in the sparsely covered dunes and then stopping at last, hundreds of yards from the nearest human being, in a vast desert-like expanse where they stayed for hours and hours, swimming, reading, sleeping, walking among the dreamlike objects thrown up by the sea. Unfettered by time or obligation, they were all spirit, all flesh; they gathered shapes and shells; they were enchanted when an enormous, unbelievably pink flight of flamingoes appeared and, as one bird, changed direction in a dazzle of colour when they cupped their hands and shouted, 'Hoo, hoo!'

Michael began talking French to his horse, and extended this favour to his hosts. It was he who persuaded Marc and Cécile to venture on horseback. Frightened and delighted, they rode their little white mounts over the marshes, over the tufts of glasswort and behen, through the thickets of tamarisk, across the lunar stretches of hardened mud cracked into great saucers; sometimes they even rode their mounts into the sea. Now, thanks to the children, they belonged to those splendid mounted bands that they had regarded as being part of another world. They were beginners on horseback and they made discoveries. They saw tortoises; they saw toads clinging to the reeds with their little hands and watching them go by with protruding eyes. They saw reptiles. They saw a tall flamingo dead, its neck already eaten away, but its beak and feathers splendid.

They found farmhouses hidden behind clumps of trees and they began to long to settle there for ever. Black bulls raised their heads above the reeds. They were hieratic and magnificent, worthy of being worshipped. Once they saw two mares, the one bay-brown and the other grey: their foals lay at their feet in the grass, a chestnut and a grey. They were all frozen in the same attitude, the mothers with their off hind-leg slightly bent and their heads turned towards the same point of the compass. They watched them for a long while, but neither mares nor foals made the slightest movement. The attitude, the proud head turned towards the remote distance, the immobility, were spellbinding.

Michael was a very good horseman; Laura managed reasonably well. Cécile and Marc slowed down the rides and were a general nuisance. In particular, they could not get the knack of rising to the trot. But their incompetence created a childish camaraderie between them, as though they were at school. They were the last in the troop and proud of it; perched on their twenty-year-old nags, they made game of each other and laughed so immoderately that they were in danger of falling off.

Laura came back to hurry them on a little. 'But it's not difficult,' she said. 'I'll count one—two, one—two, one—two. Rise when I say one and sit when I say two.'

Michael explained it all. Fine. They trotted. At this point Laura clicked her tongue and thump, thump, thump, there was Cécile's old nag suddenly charging off in an access of youth, with Cécile lurching about on his back. Cécile was laughing and angry at once. 'Laura, you fool! Why don't you mind your own business? You needn't be so pleased with yourself—you're not so hot.' She could hear Laura laughing.

But Lucifer went faster and faster and Cécile had to be quiet. She needed all her strength of mind and all her concentration. She was dripping with sweat. No, she would *not* fall.

'Urge him on to a gallop,' cried Laura. 'It'll be easier.'

A gallop? Wasn't he galloping already? Galloping madly. The countryside raced by. The creature must have scented his stable. He would not stop until he got there. But the farm was not yet in sight. Which way had Laura and Michael gone? Where was Marc?

Quite alone, Cécile rode at full speed across the landscape, trembling in every limb, her eyes fixed on the farm which had just come into view, a great way off. The stirrups were hammering her bare ankles: it was torture. The animal was going wherever he chose, carrying her heavy woman's body like a sack of potatoes: her heavy, heavy, heavy body—she had never suspected that it was so heavy: no, she would *not* fall. She clung to the saddle.

But Michael caught up with her and stopped her horse without more ado. As though it were nothing, he brought the frenzied animal under control. Michael smiled. Michael was strong. Michael was good. Michael was a cowboy.

'Thank you, Michael: you've saved my life.'

The others came up at full speed and rode on, Laura among them, and she was laughing. But still it had been tremendous, this ride. Intoxicating. 'It's all right now,

Michael. Don't bother about me any more. Catch up with the others. I'm going to wait for Marc.'

Far away Marc was approaching, step by step, very small in the distance. Cécile was still trembling. The sweat poured down her face. How long was it since she had had such an adventure? On what remote ski-run, during what last gruelling game of tennis? Her cheeks were hard and stretched tight, and waiting there in the sunset that lit the marsh with a drunken glow, she could hear her heart thumping in her chest.

Now Marc was within hailing distance. She laughed at him as he stroked his horse with a privet switch. 'There's nothing to be done with this old brute,' he said. 'It will not trot.'

'I'll let you have Lucifer tomorrow. He's the one for trotting. Did you see me?'

'Yes,' said Marc.

'Weren't you frightened?'

'Oh, you weren't going as fast as all that.'

'Well, I wish you'd been in my place,' Cécile said. She did not mind his meanness. Now she really understood the feelings of the great horsemen as they rode across the pampas.

Quietly, side by side, they rode back. Yes, speed was wonderful. But you had to go at a walk to get the full savour of this landscape. You really needed time to stop altogether and spy out the terrain, as hunters do. You needed to observe for hours on end, for whole days and whole nights: that way you would come to know the vegetation and the wildlife—you would really see the colours at last.

But everything was glimpsed only, never grasped in its entirety. You were there, but never wholly there, not there quite enough: you already knew that you ought to come back. Life was a succession of postponed appoint-

ments. Adoration was always for tomorrow. Oh, the intoxi-
cation of slow-moving time, the depths of perpetual returns.
The sun had set over the marshes. In a few minutes the
splendour would be quite gone.

'Marc, wouldn't you like to come back here next year?'

Marc was slapping his face violently. 'There are too many
mosquitoes,' he said. 'At this time of day it's perfectly
hellish. We ought to go back to riding in the morning.'

They dismounted, utterly finished. 'Brr . . .' they said,
looking at each other. With legs bowed out as far as they
would go, they led their horses to the drinking-trough—
the others were already there. Michael and Laura laughed
wildly at the sight of their jockey's walk: Laura was
delighted to show Michael just how funny her parents could
be.

Cécile offhandedly patted Lucifer's withers. 'I shook you,
didn't I, Laura?' And she went on, 'When I found myself
going flat out . . .'

But Laura laughed so much that her mother could not
finish. 'It wasn't for your horse that I clicked, you know,'
she said. 'It was to make mine get a move on. When I saw
you turn round in a rage and you said, "You fool, why don't
you mind your own business . . ." ' And for the benefit of
the gallery she added, 'Old Pampelune here won't go any
more. I'll take another horse tomorrow.'

'Marc, what do you say to a grilled mullet?'

'Oh yes! Papa, do let's have a grilled mullet.'

The mullet blazed on the table under the arbour of the
little restaurant. The wine was good. They were thirsty.
Their heads swam. The children went off to go and dance
with their friends. 'This is the life,' said Marc.

People were pouring into Paris. According to the papers,
six hundred thousand had returned by train the day before.
But Cécile and Marc would never go back. They were

happy here, in their little house. A tiled floor, a farmhouse table, cells for bedrooms, a balcony, the sea, the sun, scents, colours, one meal a day, linen clothes and freedom—that was all they asked. If Nathalie married and if Stéphane stayed in America, why, then Marc would retire. Here they could live quietly on next to nothing. They would buy Laura a horse—she did not really care for study. Laura would be beautiful. They would also buy a boat. They would melt into the landscape: they would no longer grow old.

8

Coming back from a ride they saw the words 'urgent message' on the letter box. Although Cécile had read the telegram *Mother seriously ill* and the signature, her mind still did not take it in: so sure had she been that the message concerned Nathalie or Stéphane, her far-away children, that she was still persuaded it came from them: but no, the name at the end was her father's or her brother's. Who was this mother who was seriously ill? Her sister-in-law's? The telegram came from her own home. She was shaken by a sob and it astonished her: the signature was her father's: the mother was her own. The holidays were being upset. Maman was going to die.

Marc and Laura comforted Cécile and kissed her. But she felt nothing. She was already packing her bag.

'There's a train from Arles in two hours,' Marc was saying. 'Do you think you can be ready in time?'

They drove slowly across the marsh. They were early. Less than an hour before, free of ties and oblivious of the past, they had been riding over this same landscape. When Marc took Cécile's hand a sob shook her afresh, but she still felt nothing.

'You'll let me know at once how things are?' said Marc.

'Yes.'

'If necessary, you can phone me at the grocer's. You're sure you've got the number?'

'Yes.'

'Shall I let Stéphane and Nathalie know?'

'How can you? We don't even know where they are: nor what's happened either. Let's wait.'

'Don't hesitate to send for me if I can do anything.'

'Make the most of what holiday you have left. Rest. Keep an eye on the children.'

The town and its heat: crowded streets, trams. The station. And milling crowds.

'Are there couchettes on this train?'

'No, only sleepers.'

'A sleeper, then.'

'No sleepers left.'

'Never mind, never mind, don't worry. I'll manage. Don't worry.'

Marc parleyed with the guard. The guard looked at Cécile. 'Perhaps,' he said. 'When the train has pulled out.'

'When the train has pulled out,' Marc repeated, 'he'll find you a place somewhere.'

'Don't worry, don't worry.'

Marc clasped her hand hard: once he stroked her cheek. Pressed against the window, the bag at their feet, they gazed at each other. They were in the way of people passing down the corridor, so they got down on to the platform again. But Cécile was worried about her bag and about dinner for Marc and the children. 'Go now,' she said. 'Go back to the children.'

But he would not leave her until the last moment. 'Goodbye, darling. I'm with you.'

'Goodbye, my love.'

The train pulled out. Through the window, she from the corridor, he on the platform, they raised their hands in a calm, discreet little gesture: 'Don't take it too hard'; 'Don't worry, I'm tough'; 'Take care of the children'; 'Drive slowly'; 'Rely on me'. They looked at each other, hands lifted as though taking an oath, and at the last moment as they were about to lose sight of each other, they each made a strange little bow of the head and closed their eyes.

The train gathered speed. Cécile was pressed tight against the window to let people pass behind her. They found their places. There were only a few left in the corridor.

'Follow me,' said the guard in her ear. He took her case and led her to a compartment with labels stuck on its windows. 'You'll be all right in here. You can lie down in peace. No one will bother you.'

She lay down. Now she saw that she was deeply tanned in her holiday dress. It came to her that this was how she was travelling towards her mother's death. At all events towards the death of what had lasted so long, towards the end of what had always been the same. For nothing less would the parents have disturbed their holidays. The train was travelling at full speed. Towards what horror?

A stroke? A heart attack? People sometimes recovered completely.

Cécile took her mother's last letter out of her bag. The handwriting was not in the least shaky. It was like all the other letters she had received every week for the last twenty-five years. Maman's last letter: would this last letter be the last of them all?

'I don't know whether François is taking his holidays soon. So I'm still going to write to him at Bordeaux. They met the Balcroix at a picnic in the Dordogne . . .' People do not die after sentences of that kind. There was nothing ominous about that sort of sentence. Had François been told too? 'Yes, Cécile dear, your last stay with us was very short, but we made the most of it.'

Not two days: she had not even stayed two full days. Maman had not looked unwell. But can you ever tell how old people look? Sometimes the young are said to have death in their faces. With men you say, 'He is failing.' To be sure, Maman had failed a little these last years, but her movements, with their slightly timid grace, were still youthful. Maman was elegant and straightbacked. There was nothing of the worn-out old woman about Maman.

She held out her pretty, knotted hands, where the veins made a blue network. She accepted her birthday flowers. She smiled.

The train was racing at full speed, with an occasional metallic clang. Maman was ill. She was very ill. Cécile had taken the first possible train. In a few hours she would know what had happened. The train ran on through the night. At the end of the journey Maman would perhaps no longer be alive. The train was doing its work. For a few hours longer let Maman still be standing there, straight, with her birdlike movements.

There she was ready to leave for Vrigny, with her little black, ribboned hat on her head, wearing a tailored suit and a mauve blouse that made her complexion look milky. They stood in silent reverence by the grave. Her face had taken on its lost, orphaned look.

'That's where I want to be buried. François promised me.'

It was already known. She had said it before. But had she said it there, in front of that stone, just like that, only eighteen days ago today?

She made haste to talk a little longer with her cousin, 'Come on, we must be going,' said Papa.

If she lived they would take her to her cousin's and to the places she had known as a child. They would persuade her to talk about her young days. What did they know of her past? If from now on she had to lead a very quiet life they would say to her, 'Write your memories down, just as they come, never mind about the style.' But what if Maman had already lost her memories?

'Cécile, I think you'll have to stop. I don't feel very well.'

Was that a sign?

'Wouldn't you like to come back into the house and sit down for a while?'

'I must be off, you know.'

'Don't look back; we're going to watch you go.'

Dawn, coming through the blue curtains, had filled the compartment. They say you never spend a really sleepless night and that you drop off without knowing it. Cécile did not think she had done so. Yet she did not feel at all tired.

'Don't look back; we're going to watch you go.' Was that goodbye from a mother to her daughter to be their last, perfect farewell?

The train was still travelling fast, bearing its load of silent travellers. In spite of the curtains it was quite light now. Cécile was seized with a sudden dread of what she was going to find at her parents' home. She got up. She saw Burgundy, yellow and massive under the morning sun; and all at once the Tour de Saint-Hilaire appeared, perched on its hill, the goal of their childhood walks, the banner of Maman's own country; then the church and the grandparents' house. But the train tore the landscape apart. It was racing towards the rising day.

Cécile tidied herself a little. She put away her travelling-bag, laid her suitcase on the seat; and sat and waited between her two pieces of luggage, with that enormous hollow dread in her heart and the thunder of the train in her ears.

Now she was looking at a deeply familiar countryside— the one through which she had driven on that last little trip with her parents. The scenery passed, and shrank between memory and pain towards that wholly familiar point, now heavy with menace and the unknown.

This was the first time there had been no one to meet her at the station. She took a taxi. It was obvious to the driver that she had come back from her holidays and he talked about the fine weather they had had that summer. The car was already in the avenue, at whose far end the trees of the garden could be seen, thrusting out over the walls.

'Have a pleasant day, madame,' said the driver, as Cécile got out.

The garden gate was open, and so was the front door at the top of the steps. There was no sound. In this still-sleeping street the open door and gate, giving on to garden and street respectively, looked strange. It was almost as though the people who lived in the house had hurriedly abandoned it at dawn, leaving it as it stood with shutters closed; as though nature were already beginning to take possession again.

In the hall, Cécile saw her father. He was wearing nothing but his trousers and a shirt without a collar. His cheeks were covered with white stubble. She heard herself call to him as she had done when she was a very little girl: 'Papa, dear, whatever has happened?'

He made a pathetic gesture, spreading his arms wide, and began to sob tearlessly.

Inside the house too all the doors were open: the dining-room door, the kitchen and drawing-room doors, the doors of the rooms at the back.

It was a heart-attack. The family doctor was on holiday and Maman had been seen by his substitute, a young man who had perhaps not immediately grasped the seriousness of the case. He had asked Maman whether she wanted to go to hospital and she had said no. But the treatment had brought on a haemorrhage and it had been impossible to prevent Maman from getting up. 'You know how she is.'

Once he had got there only just in time to catch her as she fell. And now she lost consciousness all the time. The specialist who had been called in had ordered her to be taken to the local hospital, for there was no room at his private clinic. The ambulance would be here any moment now.

It was then that Cécile heard her mother moaning down the corridor. 'I was going to take her something to drink. Here, you take her this cup of tisane. Don't say I wired you.'

The bedroom was dark behind its closed shutters. Far from the bed a nightlight gave a little glow. 'Maman, it's me,' said Cécile very softly; and at the same moment she thought, It's mad, bursting into her room like this.

Maman stopped moaning, and without opening her eyes or moving her head she listened. Her forehead was cold beneath Cécile's lips. 'It's me, Maman. I've come to look after you.'

Now she began to move her head from side to side on the pillow and, though she was as difficult to understand as if her mouth had been paralysed, Cécile heard her say, 'Oh why? Why spoil the holidays? It's nothing, nothing serious —why upset things?'

Papa explained. 'I just had to. I couldn't carry on alone.'

But Maman was vexed, and went on moving her head to and fro on the pillow. The word *holidays* could still be heard. At the same time she pushed back the sheet.

'Don't fret, Maman. Come, drink some of this.'

Her mouth made no movement on contact with the spoon. She had lost consciousness.

'It's not the first time,' Papa said.

There was a commotion in the hall. A man came to tell them that both sides of the double door would have to be opened and they could not manage it. At this point Maman regained consciousness and said, 'You have to hit it at the bottom with a hammer.' Then she said to Cécile, 'I'm going to Dr Lamy's private clinic.' And although she spoke with such difficulty they could feel the satisfaction—indeed, almost the pride—in her voice. Dr Lamy was a well-known cardiologist, and Maman liked those nursing homes where, two or three times in her life, she had had the only complete rest she had ever experienced. Had they concealed the fact that they were taking her to the public hospital, or had she not heard? She had her generation's prejudice against hospitals and it was cruel that she should be deceived at this moment.

They slid her on to the stretcher, just as she was. She gestured helplessly towards her hair.

'Don't worry,' said Papa. 'I've packed your bag with your toilet things and dressing-gown—everything you'll need.' But he took nothing with him, and he too went exactly as he was.

Maman still had the strength to point at the primulas Cécile had given her for her birthday as she was carried past them, and they understood that she wanted them looked after. Then she was outside in the sunlight, immeasurably frail.

Through the window of the ambulance she managed another little gesture and an almost imperceptible goodbye smile to the kind neighbour who had helped carry her out. Then, having very politely taken leave of her home and her street, she closed her eyes and remained in a coma until she reached the hospital, so that no doubt she did not know where she had been taken.

When the formalities were over, Cécile found her in a ward with four beds in it, one empty and two occupied by convalescent patients. Her hair had already been arranged in two short grey plaits. Was that really all that was left of the splendid mass of black curls that used to brush the ground behind her chair when Maman sat down to put it up, with Cécile passing her the pins, one by one?

The doctor came in, surrounded by his escort of senior students and nurses. With a little motion of his hand he sent Cécile and her father out into the corridor. Later he told them that there was scarcely any hope. But still, she had survived the journey—she was there. A pity she had not been brought in earlier, however. Papa tried to explain that he had wanted to, but the doctor was already on his way to the next ward.

Maman's strength had come back. It was pleasant to see her, clean and tidy in this trim bed, in the company of two women who sat up knitting and quietly asking questions. Her right arm was fixed to the rail of the bed for the transfusion.

'This doctor is wonderful,' she said, with the same difficulty in her speech. And beneath the expression she believed she was wearing but which her stiffened features did no more than hint at, they could see her trust and her wish to comfort them. Now it was Papa who seemed the more wretched of the two, with his crumpled clothes and that white stubble all over his face.

'We are going to leave you, Maman. We are going to have lunch, and then we will come back.'

Maman had already closed her eyes. Papa added that François was going to come too, for it so happened that he was in the neighbourhood. Maman seemed not to believe it; she seemed to wish to protest against this second disturbance, because she tried to make a gesture with her right arm. But she found that it was held and no doubt she was too tired to say anything more, for she merely let her other arm drop at the side of the bed.

The refrigerator held little in the way of provisions; a

bottle of Evian water, a few eggs, two small chops, some remains of veal cooked with carrots, the carrots cut very small in Maman's usual way.

Every one of Cécile's actions—picking up a saucepan, lighting the gas, spreading the tablecloth, laying the table—tore permanence apart; every one of the objects cried out that it was all over, that Maman would never again take her officiating priestess's place, would never again stand there in this kitchen where Cécile, covering her dress with the same apron, was now performing the rites, pale beneath her tan: she prepared the meal, and every movement shattered her, as though each helped to bring about some dreadful metamorphosis; as though she were obliged at every moment to take upon herself both her mother's life and her death.

It was shocking to eat what Maman had cooked, yet they did so, for nothing that had been her work must be lost. In the same way, though neither Cécile nor her brother had ever been present at the death of a near relation, or indeed at any death, they acted in an instinctive rapport during the days and nights that followed, as though they were obeying obvious instructions, known to all.

At every moment, whether they were asked to wait in the hospital corridor, or whether they were watching through the window for those minutes when life returned to her, when they came to her bedside to exchange still another word or another look, they shared Maman's last agony. Now she was almost crucified, for in addition to her arm her two feet were also bound and pierced with needles. It was the first time Cécile had ever seen her mother's feet bare. They were untouched by age and as beautiful as those of a Greek statue.

Only her left arm remained free, perhaps because it was too near her shattered heart; and when consciousness or need for her own people came back to her (yet could one really tell when consciousness left her, or what was going on in her clouded mind, or what she was asking for?) or when she was in pain or in need of something Maman raised this poor arm, lying limply beside her in the bed. Then they would come, and say, 'We are here, Maman, we are here.' Perhaps it gave her some comfort. But perhaps presence or absence no longer mattered to her? Perhaps her dry lips were merely asking for a little water? They did not know what death meant, but for all that they were dying with her.

She could no longer speak to anyone, except to moan 'I can't'. But in her wandering she still uttered words that betrayed the lasting anxieties of her life, such as this sentence that brought tears to their eyes: 'It's that cupboard that needs turning out that worries me.' Then her rough, impeded, human utterance fell silent for ever. She took on another, smooth voice, and from her paralysed mouth there issued a stream of thanksgiving. She repeated 'Oh, this lady is giving me everything I need! She is giving me everything!' Then, as though speaking under a spell: 'But where is she, where is she, where is she?' And, enchanted: 'They are all here, they are all here, they are all here.' And indeed they were all there, the family as it had been was brought together again round the bed in which Maman was dying, and they too were filled with exaltation. But perhaps those she was greeting were her own dead, or some band of saints: who could tell? Perhaps she was at that frontier where everything grows clear, both on this side and on that which lies beyond. Perhaps she was only speaking to the flickering shadows of the darkness. They wondered without seeking for a reply, for they were wholly absorbed in their love.

The next day she grew colder and colder, more and more

withered, and she spoke no more. At about eight in the evening she surprised them by taking a spoonful of water. 'You would think she was better,' they said. 'Yes, you would think so,' said the nurse, and disappeared swiftly. François and Papa were thirsty and took this opportunity to go and get something to drink. The nurse came back with a doctor and some other people. They sent Cécile out into the corridor.

It was from there that she heard once more Maman's voice uplifted—which she had thought was no longer possible. Motionless, clasping her hands, she saw twenty-year-old nurses emerge from the room, run as fast as they could along the corridor, come back.

The moaning stopped.

The doctor and some others came out. The nurse came over to Cécile and urged her to be brave. At Maman's bedside there was no one but a house physician and another nurse who was putting instruments away. The house physician listened to her heart. 'A few more beats,' he said.

Did Maman know that her daughter was kissing her forehead? Goodbye, beloved. They told Cécile that her father and brother were coming back. She went to meet them and said, 'It's the end. This is it.'

Side by side they looked at Maman's now tranquil face: all her wrinkles had disappeared. Behind the screen they could hear the breathing of the two other women, who were sleeping. They looked at Maman without knowing whether her heart were still beating and they saw that a proud rigidity was already settling upon her features. Then, without a word, they left her.

All through the following night some creature gasped and panted in a tree in the garden.

Maman's illness, death and burial had lasted exactly a week, from one Monday to the next. Three weeks from the day she had stood between her husband and daughter in front of the tomb where she said she wanted to lie, she had been buried there according to her wish.

The same high-wheeled little hearse that had borne Cécile's great-grandparents and grandparents carried Maman to the cemetery. The weather was fine, as it had been almost every day of that magnificent summer. Apart from the voice of the priest and the reedy harmonium, nothing was to be heard during the mass except the crowing of a cock, which seemed to rise up from an everlasting dawn. At the moment of communion Cécile came and knelt beside her father and brother. The action was not directed towards the God of her childhood nor intended to give her mother a post-humous pleasure. Indeed, seeing that she had not prepared herself, it may have been sacrilegious. Cécile went up to the sacrament with the rest of her family as to the symbol of the love and pain she shared with them.

Perhaps it had all been fortunate, really. So often death was unmixed horror. Horror had not been absent from this one. Indeed, it would have been possible to see the horror and nothing else. Yet it had been indissolubly linked to a strange beauty also—and by no means an imagined beauty. The modest qualities that Maman had possessed—her civility, her love of cleanliness, her very great wish not to be conspicuous, not to be a nuisance to anyone, her abnegation (which, though she did not know it, had risen to the point of sublimity in her last hours), and that quiet discretion which she had retained even on her deathbed—became more and more evident and threw a glow over the whole of her life.

Yes, it had undoubtedly been fortunate. The survivors felt they must fall in with this good fortune and rather look on the beauty that sprang from this long life than dwell on the horror of the fact of death—death, whose grin could quickly turn cynical and make nonsense of what had been enabled to appear as the liberation of a soul.

At the entrance to the graveyard Cécile in her turn looked at her grandparents' house and was filled with astonishment. In thirty years she had buried the three generations of women who had gone before her. From now on she was the last woman in the family to whom that house was a reminder of the past.

The day after the funeral François and his family left for the country, taking Papa with them for a month. He was to spend another month in Paris when Cécile was home, before provisionally settling in an old people's home which happened—another stroke of luck—to have a room free from November 1st.

'I'd rather not live in our house with your mother no longer there,' Papa had said. With the same modest quietness that Maman had shown in her dying he left a home he loved, a garden that had been his delight, and everything that had furnished his existence for the last fifty years, thus silently proving the extent of his courage and of his grief.

Cécile stood on the sidewalk until the car had disappeared, on the spot where her parents had stood when she left them.

Then she set the house in order. She shook dusters and blankets out of the windows, she dusted, polished and swept just as her mother had done, and for the first time she truly became a part of the house and loved it, happy for the sake of her mother who had kept the house so long. As she went to and fro with the windows open, she might almost have been out of doors, among the flowers. There were so many of them and the succession of bloom was such that it had been impossible to cut them all for Maman's funeral, and the garden did not look ravaged.

Indoors everything returned to normal. Once more everything shone. As soon as she had finished a room Cécile closed the shutters as Maman used to do, to protect the curtains and the wallpaper. Marc was busy with various formalities. The girls had gone to look at the museum. Stéphane had been told of what had happened by cable and had been advised not to break off his holidays. He had not yet replied.

Cécile preferred working in the house on her own. The day before, when she was getting her father's suitcase ready, she had opened cupboards and wardrobes and seen the hanging clothes and the piles of boxes labelled in Maman's hand with a list of what was in each. Later she would have to go through everything. But today it was enough to re-arrange the things that had been disordered by the sudden arrival of the entire family.

She was glad that she no longer had the feeding of them all. She had been cruelly tried these last few days by the necessity of preparing the right number of meals for the right number of people, by the overflowing life of the young who, in spite of the circumstances, were pleased at being with their cousins, by the continual coming and going, and the noise.

The day before, after coming back from the funeral, the children had rifled some trunks they had found in the room that had been opened for them; they had taken out old uniforms, swords and decorations, carrying some off 'for their museum' and leaving the rest lying about on the chairs. Cécile had felt this first hint of the stripping of the house as if it had been a wound.

On the other hand, putting things away, carrying out the actions that her mother had performed every day and would never perform again, immersed Cécile in her mother's life for the last time, and more deeply than ever.

'But what's the point in tidying?' said Marc. 'After all, we shall only come back here for the removal.'

'I don't want to leave the house in this state,' she answered.

He looked at her, puzzled: then, without pressing the point, he said, 'Would you like me to stay and help you?'

'No, don't bother. I'd rather do it alone.'

'Don't you think it would be better for you to get out of here?'

'No, I don't think so.' And so that he should not worry about her and should know that there was nothing morbid nor excessive in what she was feeling, she said gently, 'These are the great sorrows in one's life. One has to experience them to the full.'

She was grateful to him for letting her stay one day longer with a past from which he was shut out. But was it the past? It was rather the timeless reign of love and sorrow. It was the mysterious, heartbreaking participation in a shared life which had now moved on and which had never been so deeply felt as at the moment of its shattering.

Every single object cried out. But it cried without words or voice. To have wandered along the paths of recollection and lingered over memories would have been an offence against the immense, the all-embracing message of these things, above all the most humble among them.

The whole of her mother had passed into these things. With tears running down her face, she swept, dusted, put away. There had been no more happiness in this house than in the next; nor more unhappiness either. It had known the outcry of bitter grief, and also laughter, love, the sound of parties. It was an ordinary house, a house like any other, which secretly possessed its private sorrows and its ineffable happiness and through which fifty years of married life were now running headlong. Fifty years of care, of striving upwards, of striving towards happiness, towards balance and health, fifty years that were only leading—had always been leading—towards this break-up, this total defeat, against which Cécile was making a stand today, for the very last time. The furniture was in place, the little ornaments were properly arranged, summer light and shade played in the old rooms, Maman's gloves were still on the little table in her room, her spectacles lay on the sideboard and her bag hung from a coat peg; the photographs of vanished children and dead relations were neatly arranged—everything was in order, everything was the same, everything was just so; and it had all been waiting for ever for that morning when Maman was carried dying from the house; from the very beginning everything had been moving towards this emptiness in which Cécile came and went, her head held high, her eyes open, weeping as she stood before a cupboard, weeping over a mattress as she turned it, entrusted with some hopeless mission whose nature she did not understand.

Her grief because she would never see her mother again, the thought that the family would never again assemble in this house, her dread of her father's loneliness—all these united in an all-embracing compassion for Maman, who had worn out her life here, day after day; for Maman, who had not been a slave but who had not been really free either; for Maman, who had been beautiful and who had grown old; for Maman, who had never been wild or foolish; for Maman, who had believed in the moral code of her times and who had always of her own volition kept within it; for Maman, whose pen was lying there in a brass bowl among envelopes and paper and resting upon a newspaper cutting that showed the dates of the school holidays; for Maman, whose life, broadly speaking, had been commonplace; for Maman, who had exorcized dread and anxiety by going through set motions and whose ways and enthusiasms, now frozen in these objects, had all stood for a continual progress towards immobility, final accomplishment and a certain magnificence; for Maman, who so far as final accomplishment was concerned had found only death: and beyond Maman this compassion reached out to all mankind.

When Marc came back Cécile's eyes were dry and the task to which he had left her was almost done.

Together they took leave of the neighbours, for their father had left too suddenly to be able to do so himself. They walked up flights and flights of stairs. They saw the little dining-rooms and kitchens in which Maman had listened to the confidences of people of her own age. They discovered her charities. They were shown the place where she used to sit; they heard about the long summer evenings in the garden; and now old women wondered who would write their official letters for them. They found that their parents had played a hitherto unsuspected role in the district and that their lives had been useful and busy to the very end. They told each other that people were wrong to live in set layers according to age and class and that they had been at fault in knowing so little of their parents' life.

'When you're face to face with death,' said Marc, 'it's extraordinary how little difference there is between people. I was struck by that during the war. What a pity we couldn't have recorded what that old lady on the fourth floor told us: it was really a poem.'

But there was no one, least of all the old lady, who could repeat that poem of love and loss which had flowered in the first shock of grief.

Their bags were ready. They loaded the car. They dealt with the meters and locked the doors. For the last time Cécile filled Maman's bird bowls at the pool and crumbled the last remnants of the bread. So for a few days longer the birds would find no change in the house, nor would Maman, had she been able to come back to it.

They spent that night in a hotel and left the town early

next morning. Their route took them past the hospital. They saw the mortuary, the place where they had parked the car, and the place where they had stood two days ago to receive their friends' words of sympathy. Marc was driving. Their daughters, in the back of the car, were silent. It was the same old road, the road of childhood holidays, of returns to the land from which they came, the road that the hearse had taken. But this time they did not turn off to the village. They left the church, the graveyard, the grandparents' house to one side and drove fast along the main road. For a moment the Tour de Saint-Hilaire was visible. Beyond it stretched the wood in which Papa had heard the nightingales.

The children began talking quietly in the back. Presently the first round-tiled roofs appeared, the heralds of the south. It was still summer. The magnificent landscapes and sky of the Midi hurt their tear-scalded eyes.

'I wonder what Michael's been up to,' said Cécile. But in fact she did not wonder at all. She asked the question only out of politeness, to show her family that she was with them again.

At Arles they dropped Nathalie, who had decided to go back to Italy. But they did not stay to see her off. It was already dark and they were in a hurry to reach the house.

'You don't mind that I'm not coming back with you?' asked Nathalie.

'Of course not,' Cécile said. 'You go on with your holiday. But do try to get to Spain a little later. Don't forget your exam.'

'Oh, why spoil the holidays?' Maman had said.

Very sweetly Nathalie added, 'In any case I'll come and spend the last week with you in the Camargue, if I may.'

She was pale, and once again Cécile wondered why: was it only sorrow at this bereavement? But she wondered from a great way off. Perhaps this question and the weary detachment that accompanied it were visible in her eyes, for in their farewell embrace there were things unsaid, unsayable, refused, accepted: a complicity, a distance—go, child, do what you like, do what you can; come to us, don't come to us; make the most of your happiness, you only live once, have your fling, don't get ill, be yourself, see how helpless I am; goodbye, Mama, ageing Mama, face to face with death, an orphan; goodbye Mama, I'm going, I can't help it, you only live once, it's my life, my life, my life that's at stake.

Go, my life.

'Yes,' said Marc, 'come and spend the last week with us in the Camargue, Nathalie darling. It's a wonderful country, you'll see.' He looked at Cécile and added, 'She could even bring a friend or two, if she liked. The house is big enough, heaven knows.'

'Of course,' said Cécile. 'Why not?'

Presently they were driving along the narrow black lanes between the tall reeds, as they did when they came back by night from their expeditions to the Alpilles.

The house was lit up. Michael must be waiting for them. So I'll have to look after him, thought Cécile. But he had laid the table and cooked a simple dinner. When he welcomed them he was overtaken by his stammer once again. Laura wanted to know everything that had happened in their absence, and while the children were gossiping on the couch, Marc and Cécile opened Stéphane's first letter— a stream of happiness, dotted with sententious pronouncements. 'It is an error to suppose that there can be any middle ground between capitalism and socialism.' 'Cuba's case is that of all the underdeveloped countries. Famine isn't due to local shortages: it's due to a country's political regime. There is famine at this moment in India: there is no famine in China.' 'The insufficiently developed countries have only to imitate Cuba and nationalize their natural resources, without any indemnity to the monopolists who have invested in them. For a country to attain freedom on the political plane it must first be truly free economically.'

But Stéphane also wrote that he had danced all night; that Cuba was the hope of the Americas; that it would liberate even the people of the United States, that nation of lynched Negroes, persecuted intellectuals and workers oppressed by gangsters; that Cuba would waken the apathetic masses, who would put up with anything, even the dropping of atomic bombs; and that at last great mass movements of protest would come into being.

'Is it true, what he says?' Cécile asked.

But Marc only replied with a weary little gesture of his right hand.

'At all events he has danced all night.'

'Yes,' said Marc. 'That's something.'

They found that they were hungry, and there was a kind of gaiety around the table that evening, and a new friendliness towards Michael, who had cooked this meal for them.

Before she went to bed Cécile read Stéphane's letter again. She reflected that Maman's death was nothing but a minute event, which had occurred when she was really quite old, with the least possible amount of suffering and the greatest possible amount of love and attention. Compared with the immense suffering of the world and the hope that could make Stéphane dance, Maman's death was nothing, any more than Cécile's own life.

Yet it was at Maman's side that she lay down that night, as she had done every evening this last week. It seemed to her that her mother had not yet ceased dying. But already a strange, a gentler change was coming over her. Her mother was recovering the rounded face of a woman of fifty. Cécile

233

could evoke her whenever she chose, with the forgotten features of her middle years; and she did so again and again, surprised and happy at this return. At the same time Maman also became a very young ghost, an artless sister who gazed about at her particular corner of the world, embroidering, daydreaming, giving her young husband for one war and receiving him back disabled, giving her son for another, astonished, poised between the graveyard and the family home, puzzled and mute. Cécile lay down on her mother's deathbed and shared in her dying; and her mother also turned into a child whom she could comfort against her heart.

The great beach grew emptier every day, and lying there or walking side by side along the desolate shore, beyond the cars and the people, among the jetsam, the sea-washed tree-trunks, the bones, the strange shapes, Cécile and Marc led a spare, lean existence. They scarcely spoke of Maman, or of death. They talked more often about Papa, whose letters were short and beautiful. François had written to say that he was beginning to look better and that he spent hours on the terrace overlooking the lake, neither reading nor moving, so that he seemed quite overwhelmed by grief until you spoke to him, when he would raise his head and say, 'This is the loveliest view on earth.'

They agreed that if he could not bear the solitude in store for him, nor the atmosphere of an old people's home, the best thing would be to have him with them; but for the moment there was no bedroom in the flat to offer him. It would become possible if Nathalie were to leave home, but Cécile was perfectly aware that Marc only proposed this solution to please her. Living together in this way would call for a great effort on his part; it would not seem particularly attractive to her father either; and it would certainly give rise to many difficulties. Perhaps it would be better to persuade Papa to go back to his own place with a housekeeper, if he did not care for the home: they would have to see. But Cécile felt that the right solution was to have her father with them; it was the only natural thing and there was something deeply unsound in separating the generations; in modern society the old were not well treated.

They had taken to eating a pizza at noon, out of doors, and drinking coffee from a Thermos flask while the children looked after themselves. Then they rested in the shade of the car. Sometimes they saw bands of riders go by, and sometimes Michael and Laura would come to look for them.

'You ought to start riding again,' Cécile said to Marc, for it was obvious to her that he envied the young.

'If you'll come with me,' he said.

'Perhaps. But you're wrong in thinking I can't be by myself. On the contrary, I like being alone very much—it's soothing.'

'I don't want you to be perpetually brooding over the same memories,' Marc said.

'I'm not brooding over memories; it's still in the present.' And as Marc looked at her anxiously she said, 'Don't worry. It would be harder for me to be suddenly cut off from it all. It seems to me that I must go on to the very end. It's not only suffering. It's also . . .' she hesitated and said gently, 'it's also a treasure.'

'How do you expect to go to the very end of death?'

She did not really think that she would discover anything. Only it seemed to her that this mystery called for time and that, like childbirth, it could be faced only in solitude. Closer than the pain and beyond it, closer than the disappearance and beyond, something was happening between her mother and her, a transfusion of life or of death—she did not know—a kind of parturition. Perhaps it was a daughter's responsibility to bury her mother. But this was more than a burial: it was an interchange between her mother and her, an exchange through which she felt that she too was about to be born into another life.

It was infinitely cruel and necessary: infinitely gentle, too. Like childbirth, it was a woman's lot, handed down from one to another—sorrow, love.

Cécile went back and forth in her summer dresses. She talked, she laughed, she kept busy with simple tasks, she bathed, she made love with Marc: her mother lived in her.

The wave of grief broke over her. Never again would she see her; never again would another letter come from her; it was over, this long interchange between the generations, this transfusion of life, this never-ending watch over you; those watching eyes that your own met when they first opened and that never lost sight of you were closed. An essential strength had seeped out of the world, and also a fragility so frail that it was up to you to protect it. You had been balanced between the generations for so long— you looked to the right, to the left, and on either side there was life. Now behind you all that was left was one lost old man, and it was a torment to imagine his uprooting. The nurturer of life, she who understood how it was done, who protected and preserved—who was protected and preserved —had been swept away as if she did not signify at all— swept away, with her feeble movements of a drowning person. There was no mother any more. She had become nothing. Nothing. It is a mistake to love. Families are only there to make you suffer. Even priests no longer promise you heaven or hell, or even a life beyond death. You dismiss their eternal light and their spiritual comfort, their essence of the human being; what you want is your mother, just as she was, with her aged hands and her wrinkles; what you want is the happiness and the sorrow of this world without so much suffering, without death. But the dead are not yet in their graves before they are totally unlike themselves. Maman, so fragile in her lifetime, had changed in less than an hour into a mocking victory of stone.

Before this victory Cécile fled. She was not big enough, not strong enough, to stand up to her mother's sudden desertion of them—her desertion of herself—nor this triumph of the material world. She went back to love, and to the last moments of life. She lay down beside her mother, who in her last hours had been more like herself than at any other time. It was like a caress.

Luckily the suffering on that deathbed had not been long, and now it died away in the distance. Cécile let it go, let it mingle with Maman's confinements, her few illnesses, and the great sorrows of her life. All suffering was over. In the silence love poured forth like the song of the nightingale in the darkness.

'A few more heartbeats,' said the house physician.

Cécile kissed her mother's forehead.

'A few more beats.'

It is said that hearing is the last of the senses to go. Had her mother heard those words? If so, it might well be that she heard them with indifference, in an ineluctable plunge into the darkness. Darkness, or peace; the murmuring of water; happiness, rest, where perhaps her daughter's kiss had gone with her, like a caress given when one is going to sleep. Like an inner happiness, perhaps? Might it not be that eternity too is given us only upon this earth, in that final moment, upon that shifting frontier?

'I wish they would loosen them a little . . . oh, not altogether, of course,' said Maman, pulling at her bound arm and legs and in her last hour breathing forth her life's one timid, rational, overwhelming claim. The bonds were

237

not to be taken off altogether, of course; not all at once: but let them be slackened just a little.

Maman's pierced feet protruded from the bedclothes, and Cécile saw her mother's bare feet. Age had left them untouched, as lovely as those of a Greek statue. They bore witness to that fabled beauty witnessed by photographs, but which her children had never known and which had been worn out in the service of the family. Cécile thought her grief might have been less if those feet had run more often towards pleasure; unless indeed it was all one. In any case, all that a life could hope to encompass was trifling enough, no doubt, in comparison with the expectation that could be seen in the eyes of girls—in Nathalie's eyes and Laura's, and in her mother's eyes when she was a child, but restrained in her case: that repressed expectation, now breaking out in spite of her.

They had always known her timid, afraid of risks, afraid of the sea, of speed, of mountaintops, of streets—of everything that her granddaughters had already mastered: yet she listened to their tales with so youthful an expression that once Nathalie asked her, 'Wouldn't you like to go in a boat too?' She drew back at once, saying apologetically, 'Oh no, child. I think I should be too frightened.'

But it was not so much the untasted glories of this world that Cécile regretted for Maman (although she could certainly have done with a few more of them), nor was it so much all that she had been deprived of that made Cécile weep for her: it was for an altogether different kind of splendour, one of which her mother certainly had no notion; yet her being deprived of it ranked her among the oppressed. When her mother dies at seventy-six a woman of forty-four understands what a child only just set free from slavery may feel for its relatives in bondage—a helpless compassion.

It was through her children that Maman had felt even the sufferings of her last moments. Many times, lying there bound and distressed, she had said, 'How I should like to get out of this straitjacket,' borrowing the very words François had used twenty-five years before, when he lay with his whole chest in plaster after an accident and she was nursing him. So, by repeating her son's cry on her deathbed, she once more took his pain upon herself.

Cécile did not glorify her relationship with her mother. She neither raised a statue to her nor embarked on creating a myth. But she knew what motherhood had cost her. To relieve her mother's last hours, that indeed was a tender gesture which all her life she had been unable to make, a gesture that was even now unfinished, a love that had longed to give itself and had been unable to do so except in the ultimate moment when everything fled in the very instant when everything was also attained—a moment that was to be relived over and over again.

'Have you been for a walk?' Maman had asked on that first day when Cécile had come back after lunch. And having asked this question, in spite of the effort it had cost her, she had tried to smile, happy that her family should have been for a walk in this fine weather, while she lay dying.

Those last words demanded to be heard again; the last hours had to be relived in this mysteriously prolonged present which, even while grief burst over her, was in the nature of a transfiguration, for what had been veiled, imperfect, intimated during life had been apprehended in the very moment of death; and now, unceasingly, it repeated the cycle of manifesting itself and then vanishing into memory.

Although it obliged her to look death in the face and to confront the *nothingness* that her mother had become, and although every time it ended in a bewildered collapse, Cécile still returned perpetually to the same loving quest; and it carried on into her dreams.

Her mother appeared, pale, sick to death, dead already, in a wretched house, their home—a kind of cellar with cobwebs hanging down. But she did not know she was dead and she busily went up and down stairs, shaking out sheets and blankets. And they, her family, did not like to say that death was consuming her and that her labour was in vain because not one of them would live there any more, and neither would she. They were torn by compassion, by sadness, seized with dread. How could they stop this activity? How could they break in upon this sovereign independence? The house was shut up, let, sold; Papa had taken a room elsewhere. Where were they to put Maman in this new order of things? How were they to persuade her, how were they to confess to her that there was no house any more? But Papa said kindly, 'She won't come. But if she does, why then, I'll make a little room for her.' But suddenly illness struck once again; she stopped, amazed, understanding nothing, and started dying again.

Another time she appeared in a black dress, so tight round the waist and so old-fashioned that they had never seen her dressed like that except in photographs. Cécile, her daughter, embraced her, and to please her she said, 'You still have the waist you had when you were a girl,' and Maman smiled—she was happy, radiantly happy, happier than they had ever known her, happier than they had ever been able to make her.

These dreams were not nightmares; on the contrary, they formed a bridge between life and death. Cécile considered them as part of a widely-experienced phenomenon, which explained the belief that the dead did not die immediately but went on hovering about the living for a while. These dreams were very soothing to her, for they left her with the feeling that there had been a meeting and an enlightenment. She could perfectly well see that people might try to cultivate them. Perhaps she would have done so herself if she had been alone in the world and free to take the risk of exploring avenues that might end in madness. Instead, she took these dreams merely as a natural softening of grief and also as a gift, for they gave her back her suffering and her love in a degree of purity that in life was inevitably sullied, even in a life as simplified as hers was at that time.

Maman often appeared like this, dead or living, dead and living, or else in an existence shut in by strictly guarded frontiers that she would cross only to go back again, cut off from her family, a stubborn, newly initiated being, enigmatic and even somewhat cruel. Once she appeared, slim, pretty, younger than her daughter ever remembered her, and Cécile said in an imploring voice, 'Oh why did you give me nothing to remember you by, Maman?'—a prayer that she did not answer, obliging Cécile to go on, 'You have left me nothing: my sisters-in-law have more—you have left me nothing, Maman, not even a pin from your hair.' And then, still unmoved, but looking at her at last and speaking, Maman said, 'Would you like one of these pins, Cécile?' And Cécile sobbed with love and gratitude; at last she could throw herself into her mother's arms.

Nathalie came back. She was gentle, asking after everyone, enquiring about the Camargue and Cuba, with a kind of childish, straightforward politeness that discouraged reply and checked in advance the questions they would have liked to ask about her own holidays. It was impossible to tell where she had spent them, or with whom. She let on that she had seen various cities, famous buildings and resorts, but she spoke about them as if she were reading from a book. Clearly happiness had left her. Perhaps Jo had not even been with her all the time. They did not like to ask.

However, as she no longer mentioned going to Spain, they did come back to that subject. 'It fell through,' Nathalie said. And for the first time she mentioned Jo's name, saying, 'Jo couldn't make it: he had an engagement in Holland.'

'But couldn't you still go with the other friends who were going with you?'

'No,' said Nathalie.

Two young couples, roads, beaches, nights out of doors, of course not—Nathalie certainly could not go to Spain without Jo and be the odd man out. Poor Nathalie: still, it was a relief. No more dangerous roads, no more making love in the open; Nathalie had come back, she was there, among them: she looked subdued. Perhaps Jo was lost for ever, and her holidays were over.

'So what are you going to do for the rest of the holidays?'

'I'm going to stay here with you.'

They stared at their too grown-up daughter. Illnesses or disasters apart, for a long time now they had supposed themselves capable of dealing with their children's problems; they had known in just what direction they should guide them, and how. It was not true and it never had been; they had over-simplified and their moral ideas were narrow and limited; they had pretended to know and in fact they had merely been seeking their own convenience. They knew nothing, except that they were tired. All at once, confronted with their three grown-up children, they resigned— gave up.

Poor Nathalie. Poor Nathalie, whom they had brought up as well as they knew how, paying attention to dreary pedants, doing their best according to their outlook and their circumstances: poor Nathalie, whom by virtue of their habits, their ethics, their comfort, their penury, they had rendered unfit to make an attempt at living with Jo.

Nevertheless, it was all very well to know your own limits and to weep over them: you still had to see things through. If Nathalie did not prepare for this exam she would do nothing for the whole year; she would sit at home, wretched and cross, drifting from one affair to the next, making a mess of her life.

'Don't you think you ought to find some other way of going to Spain if you're giving up this plan with your friends—which is perfectly understandable, of course. You could stay here a week or two with us and then go a little later.'

Nathalie's face clouded. 'The one time I want to stay with the family, you don't want me to: it's always the same.' Then, suddenly bursting into tears, she rushed from the room.

'Perhaps it wasn't the moment to say that,' observed Marc.

Cécile would have liked to leave the room and go and cry somewhere else too; but that was not the way she had been brought up. 'From now on you look after her,' she said gently. 'Say whatever you like to her. As for me, I just don't know: I can't do anything any more. She destroys me.'

'Go after her,' Marc said. 'She needs you. You ought not to give her the impression that you wanted to send her away just at this point.'

'But of course I don't want to send her away. It's only that I think she still ought to go to Spain. If she doesn't pass her exam this year, you know very well, Marc, that now she's started having affairs she'll never pass it.'

'And what about Stéphane?' said Marc. 'Is dancing in

243

Cuba any way to prepare for an exam? Yet you think that's fine. Go and find Nathalie. And don't talk to her about Spain any more.'

She went.

Nathalie raised a tear-stained face, dry now however, and on the defensive. Cécile dropped into a chair. 'Why didn't you bring any friends?' she asked eventually.

'It didn't work out,' Nathalie said.

'Perhaps there's still time, if you've made up your mind to stay with us until the end of the month.'

'Time for what?'

'For asking friends.'

'I don't want any. And then perhaps you're not so very keen either on having masses of people all around you.'

'Oh,' said Cécile, 'it's not whether I'm keen but whether it would make you happy.' She could see the long beaches, the scoured bones, the dunes, where she could always go and stretch out in peace and be with her mother, even if the house was full. 'If you'd like to invite friends, it's really very easy. Make the most of having this place.'

'No,' said Nathalie. 'I'm fine as I am. And I'll go to Spain, if you really want me to.'

To Spain, with that little pale, tear-stained face. 'Oh, no,' said Cécile, 'I don't really want you to at all. Stay with us. We're all very happy to have you here. I only said that because of your exam.' And very gently she asked: 'Have things gone wrong between you and Jo?'

'It's not that things have gone wrong,' said Nathalie, 'it's . . . it's . . . it's too difficult to explain. Let's say things didn't work out.'

'Is there anything we can do?'

'No,' said Nathalie. She looked straight at her mother, and sadly, without bitterness, she went on, 'You're not rich enough.'

So this was what their firm ideas had led to; they were not rich enough to buy their daughter a gift of love. And Cécile knew that it was true. With money Emmanuel and she might have managed, perhaps. Youth today was no longer satisfied with mere words.

Cécile spread her hands, a very little to show that there was nothing they could do about it. But she went on, 'If it's just a question of helping Jo to give a concert, maybe we could do it. I thought your father had told you.'

'It isn't just a question of a concert.'

'What is it, then?'

'Of living decently.' And as Cécile said nothing, Nathalie continued, 'Since you hadn't got any money you should have brought me up differently.'

'In a less bourgeois manner?'

'Yes.'

Yes. If she too had been left more to herself, less protected, less loved by her people, she would have raped Emmanuel, she would have plunged into adventure with no fear of hurting others or herself; she would have been at her ease in an irregular, hand-to-mouth kind of existence.

But all at once Cécile raised her head: she could feel that old revolutionary spirit rising in her—a spirit that she had kept in abeyance up to now but that still shook her from time to time. 'If you and your Jo had any guts,' she said, 'you wouldn't let yourselves be stopped by a trifle like that. If you loved one another, why, you'd behave like Stéphane— you'd go off without looking to the right or the left. He's dancing—Stéphane is dancing in Cuba.' Then she went, but not so quickly that she did not hear Nathalie's answer: 'It's not just me.'

'How did it go?' asked Marc.

'I told her plainly that she could do whatever she liked. And love whoever she liked. However she liked.'

'Hm,' said Marc, not looking exactly cheerful.

But this time she was certain she had gone as far as her courage would take her. 'It's the best I could do,' she said.

That was probably Nathalie's feeling too, for during the days that followed she was the kindest of companions to her mother. Letters came from Paris, and telegrams: Nathalie spent hours in the post-office. Something was brewing between her and Jo, perhaps they were planning their future. Like Cécile, Nathalie came and went, ate, talked and laughed. But like Cécile too she was possessed—haunted. Cécile thought that her daughter was achieving her conversion to life as she herself was to death. It seemed to her that perhaps for the first time in a great while their relationship rang true, and that in the fresh light that her mother's death threw upon her own existence and upon all womanly life, all human life, in this pity, love, rebellion, acceptance, rejection, a distance had arisen between her daughter and herself, a distance across which they could at last come together.

But Nathalie's agitation died down and she assumed an aggressive cheerfulness that made her parents uneasy. Once, when they were lying in the shade of their car on the beach Cécile and Marc heard hoofbeats that stopped just by them. Looking up, they saw their three young people, booted, mud spattered, wearing their broad-brimmed black felt hats: their faces were scarlet, and upon Michael's and Nathalie's there was an expression of joyful avidity. Laura was laughing too, but it was obvious that her heart was not in it. The children said that they had not lunched yet, and did not dismount. Presently they rode back to their band at full speed, but Cécile and Marc had noticed that Nathalie and Michael went on galloping by themselves out in front, while Laura merged with the rest of the band.

'She's looking better again,' Cécile said. But in the very moment of saying it she was surprised to feel, like a return to the realities of life, the first pain she had experienced since Maman's death: for she saw clearly that Nathalie was taking Laura's place with Michael.

'I wonder whether she's carrying on with Michael,' said Marc.

'Very likely.'

'Has she broken with Jo, then?'

'How can I tell?'

'I'm disappointed in her,' Marc said.

'Why?' Cécile asked.

'All this drama with this Israeli, this great love, these scenes, and a fortnight later she's flirting with a boy younger than herself . . .'

'Oh well, there you are,' said Cécile. 'Youth is awful.'

But Marc screwed up his face, like a man deceived. 'So she didn't love him after all?'

Did she love him? Or he her? Whom do you love? The man with whom you can live or the one who turns you inside out. 'We don't love each other, Emmanuel; you know very well we don't love each other.' He had stopped to look at her, making her stop also in the Avenue de l'Opéra, in the heart of their city, their prison; then, dropping his arms, he said, 'What courage to say some of the things you do.' Afterwards, when they started walking again, they felt as if they had been drained of their blood.

Choice, the act of making a life for oneself, just one life, no more—is appalling. Love deprives you of love. Nothing stays pure. But Cécile thought about these things from a distance: it was a matter for the young and one could not do much about it; some had to go through it, but not all, not young men like Marc, for instance—there was no difficulty for them: live with the woman you love and that's all there is to it. But what about young men like Emmanuel and Jo; and young women like Nathalie and herself? And in any case didn't Marc have problems too at present? One single life, one single person, was simply not enough; but it was too late now, the amalgam had hardened, life together had mingled them even if Marc did dream of others, even if he did sometimes make love elsewhere. Cécile no longer found this time of life very interesting; it was a matter for the young, an everyday affair, a harmony to establish, years to be got through, turmoil, stupidities, theories, demands, anxiety over money, helplessness, beauty wasted, a working of inner essences, the surging tide of the sap. Yet she still felt sad for Laura, who had been queen of the Camargue before Nathalie came and who had been deposed; for Laura, who had seemed the stronger of the two and was in fact the more vulnerable; for Laura, who did not yet have to worry about what to make of her life and was therefore still possessed of childhood's total capacity for tragedy; for Laura, who would still allow herself to be taken in her mother's arms. But Laura was already far away on the horizon with the group of riders of her own age. She was galloping among the other children, even though she had been deeply hurt. She would come back only furtively and fling herself into her mother's arms, more from charity than from any other motive. Laura was already aware that her mother's arms no longer had the power to comfort anyone: she would return to comfort her mother rather than to take refuge there.

Someone else was now present in Cécile. Someone in whom modesty had inhibited the outward expression of feeling while she was alive but whom life no longer pulled in every direction, with whom love was whole, entire and mysterious, a love both dead and risen from the dead—an old woman from whom she had not expected to learn anything new and who had nevertheless, in her last hour, become an innocent but imperious initiator, requiring her daughter to eschew contingencies, alibis, unreal worries, unreal duties or unreal appearances, and to keep a certain distance if she did not wish to die before having really been in the world and if she really wished to be reunited with love itself.

'If Nathalie's had a disappointment, I hope she is not going to fling herself into the arms of the firstcomer,' Marc was saying.

'So do I,' Cécile said.

'That Michael doesn't amount to a row of beans.'

Cécile smiled. 'That's the point.'

'How do you mean?'

'Nathalie may not be throwing herself into his arms so much as into childhood, security and ultimate futility—into the Camargue, into the holiday. She's taking a rest from this great affair of hers.'

'She has a very domineering and possessive way of resting.'

'She's anxious. She needs to prove her own power.'

'Still, it's hard on Laura.'

'Yes, it's hard on Laura. But it's not all that serious.'

Cécile gazed at Marc with a warm, disillusioned affection that made him say, 'You're beginning to look better too. All this time you've been looking twenty years older.' He added, 'Now I know what you'll be like when you are old.' She put one hand on her husband's shoulder and the other, spread wide, on the burning sand. 'Beautiful too,' said Marc, kindly.

'You really must take up riding again,' she said.

'If you'll come too,' he said obstinately.

But Marc's shoulder, the sand, the family were no longer warm enough. It was not merely twenty years that had made their appearance in Cécile's face and then withdrawn for the moment. What took place in her was the irremediable awareness of finitude; she felt it in the marrow of her bones and in her innermost heart, and nothing came harder to her than the activity demanded of her: she had not yet fully experienced her mother's death. It was not, as the others supposed, a trial that had to be overcome but a one-way path to be travelled, a definitive change in her life whose outcome was by no means clear to her as yet. Why would they not leave her in peace on this smooth shore among the broken seashells, the feathers and the white driftwood? It was the children's turn to fling themselves heart and soul into the beauty and the filth of life. And let Marc go with them, since he found it so amusing. As for her, everything that she did not know to be everlasting was already so much dust; everything was undermined by its own mortality. She was happy there, lying flat on this seashore, and she was not happy anywhere else. She called to mind the one time in her life when she had fainted, and when her mother's voice had brought her back. Even as she heard her name, she was still aware of the alluring quality of the deathlike state from which she was being called back. Now once again she recognized that feeling of being jolted out of a blessed *tranquillity*. Now it was Marc and the children who were harassing her. The living do not allow the living to linger with death, not even for a fortnight. They grow frightened: they think you are in danger. And for themselves they feel a mysterious dread when they see the efforts of a soul struggling to rejoin the secret wellspring. So she would have to pretend that the worst was over, as Marc supposed. Out of love for them she would be obliged to force this body of hers into activity—a body that was now no more than a cradle in which her mother lay, sometimes sleeping, sometimes waking.

Another letter came from Stéphane in Cuba. Speaking of the death of his grandmother—he had been her favourite grandson—Stéphane said what the young always say of the death of the old, even the most beloved. How sad that he would never see Mamie again, to have been so far away when she died, not to have been able to give her one last kiss; fortunately she had not suffered too much and she had not known the worst effects of old age; she would leave a beautiful memory behind. He was very near to them in thought. Could they send him a photograph of Mamie? He wanted it because, though he hated to say it right now, when the family was in mourning . . . 'I should like to ask your advice about an offer that has been made to me here. Personally, I think it's a marvellous opportunity and I'm very much tempted to take it, but I don't want to decide without your consent, especially just now. I went to see the cultural attaché (that Monsieur Ehrman Papa gave me a letter of introduction to) and at his house I met a Cuban professor who teaches in the French department of the national university. For next term they need an assistant instructor, and he must be French. The professor asked me whether I'd be interested in the post. I answered that I hadn't yet got my full degree in literature. He said it didn't matter. I think we took an immediate liking to each other. Anyway he asked Monsieur Ehrman straightaway whether the technical mission could finance the post under the heading of French bilateral aid and put me forward for it. Monsieur Ehrman said it couldn't be done, at least not in time for the next university term, since this subject was not covered by the budget and there was a complicated procedure to be gone through; furthermore, my qualifications did not amount to very much, etc. The professor left it at that; but to my surprise he sent word for me to come and see him next day: his department is prepared to take me for a year out of its own funds, at the local rate of pay, of course, that is to say, my salary will be very low. But I don't care about that. I can clearly see that I can be useful here, which is something I have never seen anywhere else. I love the beauty of this country; I love its happiness—a happiness you can have no idea of; and I love it for what is left of its poverty. For the first time I am faced with a simple, direct question: do I want the world to go on as it is at present and to help in keeping it that way—for acquiescence is helping; do I want the division between the extreme poverty of two-thirds of mankind and the wealth of the remaining third to go on continually increasing like a tumour that will end up, to their amazement, by destroying the rich: or do I want, with what strength I have and backed by all the revolutionary forces in the world, to help try and change this state of affairs? So far as I'm concerned the choice is made. Do you approve? I need to know quickly because I must reply in a fortnight from now at the latest. Please can you cable your consent?

'I should add that the university is splendid—it is making giant strides. Do you remember that time when you told me I knew enough already to teach illiterate children to read, Mama? Well, I'm going to do something even more useful. I shall help shape the élite of this country, and now I am convinced that that is the first thing to be done.

'Don't worry about my future. For the moment the idea of working for another exam and of being back in our fat bourgeois quarter makes me feel sick. Please understand, dear parents, and give your consent, because even if you don't I've still made up my mind. Besides, if I have to come back in a year, I don't think my time here will have been wasted. It will even be in my own interest. I might specialize in Cuban literature and go in for the modern literature *agrégation*; I could start working for it now by taking courses in comparative literature . . .'

Stéphane bogged down among the various self-centred possibilities that, as he saw it, ought to bring his parents round. He also bogged down among expressions of affection and regret. The picture of his parents that he unknowingly reflected was far from flattering. But they did not hesitate for a moment.

They cabled that afternoon: 'Fullest agreement. Delighted for you.'

'He's right, isn't he?' asked Cécile.

'Of course,' said Marc. 'Let him take this job. It's a good opportunity for him.' He spoke in a withdrawn voice, as though he had quite given up expecting anything from anybody.

'But it's not only for himself, is it? He's going to do useful work. What he's going to do is a good thing, isn't it?'

'Yes,' said Marc. 'It's a good thing. He's quite right to take this job.'

'But it sounds as if you see it only in terms of finishing his own education. It's objectively useful too, isn't it? You do think it's better to begin by training the élite, don't you?'

'Oh, of course,' said Marc. 'But generally speaking, the first thing the élite do is to leave the country. It's all very complex.'

Cécile re-read Stéphane's letter. From now on, she reflected, her son was going to live in a world of which she knew nothing, not even whether it was brand-new or already out of date. She knew nothing; nothing at all. On one side or the other of that Christian love and charity which Stéphane blamed her for, she was continually coming up against violence, injustice and crime, and she could not bring herself to accept them. Yet, she said to herself, there are rightful revolutions, and it is one of these that the Cubans have achieved.

Why had Marc been silent for so many years now? For years he had preferred playing tennis and having fun with girls. There had been a time when he had wasted no time; during the Occupation, he had heartily approved of Germans being knocked on the head; he had been a wildly impatient man of action who did not weigh and balance overmuch. Since when had he turned into a looker-on? They had evolved in opposite directions, he and she. Nowadays you could not wring anything from Marc but weary agreement. Yet he still read, and travelled, and he was rarely mistaken in his judgments. As a rule, events bore him out. But he no longer wanted to explain his views. All he uttered now were static opinions. He would say, 'No, it won't be war this time,' or 'Fidel has made mistakes,' or 'There's nothing more disappointing than the South American nations,' or 'Of course Russia is growing bourgeois. Mao is the one who's faithful to the spirit of Marxism,' or 'Marxism certainly doesn't seem to manage to provide the same standard of living as capitalism.' 'War isn't something predestined,' or, for the first time in twenty-five years, 'I think a world war is possible.' He ought not to respond to Stéphane's hope and hers in that disillusioned way. He ought to say what he thought. The progress of the world did concern him. He had thought as she did when he was confronted with Nathalie's love-affair, and had badgered her to help their daughter; faced with Stéphane's enthusiasm, he abdicated and abandoned him. He abandoned her too, leaving her alone to praise their son —she who knew nothing of such matters but who glimpsed in them the possibility of transcending set limits, of an answer to death on a scale other than that of physical love, for on the verge of his fiftieth year Marc was more shaken than ever by that ancient discovery, that short-lived triumph which responded only momentarily to the anguish of one's own death and not at all to the anguish of another's, yet was the only one which was truly felt. Marc was finishing where she had begun, and vice versa, and neither could accept the other's resignation. It was only because she loved him that Cécile would have liked to share in Stéphane's hope. She looked upon it as something strong enough to shatter personal limitations; she saw that it promised an advance that might compensate for erosion, she recognized sense in place of the absurd, and the taste of life. In this hope even a humble woman like her mother was vindicated—a child-bearer, launching the future all over again, giving life to Stéphane, and beyond Stéphane to other seekers, other finders in this world of men.

'Well, Pépette,' said Marc, 'I can hardly imagine you in Fidel Castro's paradise.'

She knew very well that she would not fit in there. For her it was too late. Yet in Stéphane she was there, nevertheless. She was ready to participate in the hope that had been able to make Stéphane dance, even if it meant giving up whatever she had found to love: her habits of mind, her beloved objects, the rhythm of her life, even the family graves—she was ready to let it all be swept away by the gust of great exalting hope.

But Marc said, 'The dreadful thing is the time, the immense amount of time it takes to get anything done. Always supposing that in the end anything is done. Delays, side-issues, blind alleys.'

'Nevertheless, Marc, there is progress.'

'When revolutions are finished the difficulties begin.'

'Still, Marc, there are more and more people in the world.'

'You can say that again.'

'More and more people who have the right to live.'

'And more and more who haven't, too. It gives you the shudders.'

She sensed that in the end ideology bogged down in bureaucracy just as love did in humdrum existence, and that in the final analysis materialism and neurasthenia were the reverse side of contentment, that man's only greatness was his need, that the Prince of Light and the Prince of the World would never end their battle, that everything was always to be done again and that the problem of life was unanswerable. But when love begins, what dreary wisdom is going to come and remind you that passion does not last for ever? In the same way, when hope is born again, even in a tiny country, even in a mind as young and ignorant as Stéphane's, who would dare assert that hope is vain?

'Still, Marc, Stéphane is right, don't you think?'

'Of course he's right. It's always on the cards that simpletons like him may end up achieving the impossible.'

They looked at each other, and a strange, melancholy smile lit their faces. 'I love you,' Cécile said. And for once she said it seriously.

He had gone with no ceremony or fuss; never again would he come back and live at home as he had done before; now he was dancing in an unknown land, her frustrated child, the indifferent student, the disappointed lover, the child his grandmother had preferred to all the others because of his disability and the only one who had not been present at her funeral. He was among strangers, people of all colours, who filled him, as he said, with a greater sense of friendship than he had ever felt for anyone. He understood the meaning of good and evil. He was fighting in the ranks of the Prince of Light. He was going to change the world. He had taken his mother at her word. He had gone.

So much the worse for her. He had red blood in his veins.

'He took hardly anything with him when he left.'

'I should have done the same at twenty,' said Marc.

'You did pretty well when you were twenty,' she said. And she added, 'Heavens, what an eventful year this is.'

Yet none of the events was all that remarkable.

9

Stéphane's room was empty for only one day. Cécile hardly had time to get it ready for her father's arrival.

The table was still piled with books and papers. The drawers were so stuffed that they would scarcely open. Cécile noticed Stéphane's diary in about ten fat notebooks, the eagerly-gathered honey of his short life, left lying about for curious eyes. She leafed through one of them and without reading it, looked at the close, unattractive writing that covered the pages from edge to edge. She shut it, put it on top of the others, made a parcel of them and put them away in a cupboard, as she had done with Emmanuel's letters. Then she stood motionless for a moment, with her hands in the air, for the backs of them were pierced through and through with that same feeling of undiluted pain that had sometimes woken her at night. The sensation was both intensely unpleasant and at the same time deadening; and it was familiar, although she had felt it only occasionally— after a nightmare, or sometimes very suddenly, without any dream that she could remember, so that she woke up because her hands were hurting. The whole of her being was pain, but it was a strange pain that spread in every direction, expelling all thought and then fading with the gentleness of a kiss. Now for the first time she was feeling it when she was awake.

She sorted Stéphane's winter clothes—he would not be wearing them this year. Which should be kept? Which given away? Which taken to the cleaners? She went through them all, with little doubtful movements of her head and hands. And to think the parents' house would have to be emptied too from attic to cellar of everything that had been piling up for fifty years. But we'll let at least the winter go by, she told herself. I shouldn't have the energy before that.

But you don't have to believe it, she said to herself a little later. And she went on getting the bedroom ready as though both her parents were coming to stay, and at the same time as though Stéphane were going to live in it again.

She opened the little cupboard in which her son kept the bottles he had used for his insect collection—ether for killing them, formol for preserving them, and all the other bottles that she was frightened of (poison perhaps?), now dried up or half full of dubious liquid and arranged in neat rows. A little snake had been coiled stiffly round a neon tube, like a bracelet. She pushed it gently with her forefinger, making it turn. Stéphane would find plenty of snakes in Cuba. But he was no longer interested in natural history.

When he had left in July, everything was in order, everything was as it always had been; everyone was pulling in different directions—Marc went to his office, the children went to their schools, the grandparents were expected. Every day she was aware of the family structure, with Marc and herself set firmly in the midst, flanked by the generations on either side. 'How everything has changed,' she murmured. Yet she could not bring herself to throw the old bottles away.

On the wall hung the glass cases that Stéphane had made in the carpentry class at the little school, a delightful place where they had sent him after his polio, and where the girls had gone too, later, so that there should be no jealousies. She could see her little Stéphane again, just as she had seen him one day from behind a pillar of the now demolished viaduct in the Boulevard Exelmans: she had hidden there to see how he behaved. In a long line on the opposite side-walk the children of the ninth class were going towards the Bois, all clinging to a rope to keep them together. He was walking with his head in the air, with that particular expression of innocence of his, not looking where he was going, pulled and pushed by the others; and he was the only one who limped. She saw him again, and again she felt that stab in her heart. Who would dare to say the past was dead?

And now her Stéphane was an instructor at the University of Cuba. 'Come and see me here, Mama,' he had written. 'Come and see for yourself the fire that is burning us, the romanticism of the present day.'

She remembered that day when she had tidied his torn-up essays. No more essays, and good riddance. Stéphane was a revolutionary now. Poor Stéphane, the ludicrous righter of wrongs. What was so dreadful about distance, and unbear-able in the vast distance of death, was people's weakness, so disproportionate to what they were trying to do and so clearly and nakedly revealed. 'Come and see for yourself the fire that is burning us . . .' I'll go, she thought. She did her best to picture her son, tanned, smiling and friendly, free, ready to give himself, moving through motley, colourful crowds, striding through towns, through landscapes; and she instinctively turned to her mother to tell her how big and strong he had grown—'Our Stéphane is an instructor at the University of Cuba, Maman, and he's going to explain everything to me; he's turned out all right, after all.'

It was the first time she had allowed herself to make a mistake like this, and it was soon over; for it is untrue to say that we take a long time to get used to the absence of the dead. On the contrary, as soon as their eyes have been closed life dispenses with them with a rock-like certainty.

Yet it is a certainty which we do not share. You don't have to believe it, she told herself again, for the impulse towards her mother had been very comforting.

We don't have to believe that babies no longer exist except in their photographs, that relatives are dead, childhood ended, grace disfigured, friends vanished, that those who taught us how to live have died without knowing how to die, and that our young will not come back to us. After all, a dog recognizes its master even though he be dead, and the night which floods into us is bright with our own flashes of enlightenment.

Papa was now no more than an hour and a half from Paris. Laura would be back very soon. Perhaps she would like to come to the station too. She would just have time if she had to be back at the lycée at two o'clock. Papa was travelling alone, going from one family to another, like an orphan, before being boarded out. Cécile waited for Laura.

She dusted the glass beneath which the butterflies, beetles, cicadas and dragonflies were ranged according to their kind and size, held by a pin in the middle. The gentle Stéphane could turn cruel enough when it was a question of system. She stacked the papers and reference books, and checked that the bed had been made up before the holidays, like all the others in the flat, against the family's return. Instead of Stéphane it was Papa who would lie here, and alone. If he did not like it in the old people's home they could keep him with them, now that Stéphane had gone. In the midst of the family, mingling with the other generations, he would stay in the full current of life. But if he preferred the home, then she would be able to move in there herself, have a desk of her own, cupboards, knickknacks. She would very much like to have a real bedroom.

And now she heard Laura's key in the lock and suddenly

she longed for living flesh, for kisses. Laura had come back, with her warm voice and her big arms.

'Darling Mama, isn't it too much work for you in here, all by yourself?' For Maria had vanished into the mysterious spaces of her native Spain. Laura's gaze took in the whole room, including the edge of the velvet bedspread caught up in the sheets. 'Grandpa will be comfortable here,' she said. 'Couldn't we keep him until Stéphane comes back?' Darling.

'We'll see,' said Cécile. 'We'll see how things go.'

'It would be so natural to keep him,' Laura went on. Between them they put the bedspread straight, and when it was done they sat down side by side.

'And how was the first day back at school?' asked Cécile.

'We have a drivelling idiot for philosophy.'

'There you go. The first day back and you're already starting to run down your teachers.'

'But it's a fact,' said Laura. 'Out of the six philosophy profs there's one who's senile and of course she's the one I get. You'll have to go and see the headmistress. I wasn't put down for that class at all. There must be some mistake.'

'Can't you see to it yourself?'

'Oh, you're grumpy!' said Laura.

Cécile moved away. 'Listen, I must get ready to go to the station and meet your grandfather. I can't have lunch with you. Cook your steak yourself. And there are boiled potatoes. You can have them the way you like, with butter. When you've done, will you peel the ones that are left, and I'll fry them for our lunch when I bring Grandpa back?'

'Isn't Nathalie coming home?'

'No; nor your father. Papa says he'll lunch at a restaurant until we've found another maid.'

'Let's hope we find one soon.'

'Yes, indeed,' said Cécile. And just as she was closing the

262

bathroom door she called to Laura, 'If it's too much for you, I'll peel the potatoes myself.'

But when she emerged she found Laura ready and waiting for her in the hall. 'I've had my lunch and got everything ready. I'm coming with you to meet Grandpa. I haven't another lesson until three this afternoon.'

So it was that Cécile was not alone when her father got out on to the platform, clutching his stick with one hand and in the other holding the ancient travelling bag that Maman had always carried.

10

'Shall we take the throughway?' Marc asked.

'If you like,' she said.

'I think it's quicker, really.'

'Let's take it then.'

It was only a thirty-mile stretch that had just been opened to traffic. They had driven that way coming down, taking Papa to the old people's home. It meant thirty miles of new road cut out of their old journey and it allowed them to by-pass the villages, the little towns, the countryside, a whole vast and beautiful landscape full of churches, châteaux, lanes, inns and houses they knew so well that they felt they had lived in them, a landscape full of a lost happiness —a late present that they had been able to give their parents when at last they had a car to drive them about.

'If Papa makes up his mind to stay in the old people's home it will be quicker to go and see him by car than by train, once the throughway is finished. If you count the time it takes to get to the station.'

Saulieu, Semur, Avallon, Vézelay. They had walked slowly on the rough sidewalks and steep cobbled street. They had craned their weary necks to look at the capitals. They had laughed together as they considered the menus. They had urged each other on—'Marc, do you still love snails?' At last they were giving themselves a little pleasure. They were giving it to others.

'I think I'll get a driving licence,' Papa used to say, 'and we'll treat ourselves to a small car.'

'My poor dear, you wouldn't get far. Don't invite bad luck,' said Maman. 'You let your children drive you about.'

'Do you realize we're no longer taking the same route for this journey?' Cécile said. 'There are changes already. Already it's no longer the same.'

Marc slowed down and stopped. 'You drive,' he said. 'I'm going to smoke.' They were at the end of a little tree-lined road. They could see the broad stretch that joined the throughway some miles ahead. 'ı their left was a dung-spattered, tree-shaded village, wherᵥ the doctor had been a family friend and his son a childhooᵥ companion. There was a good inn there, visible frᵒ⁻ ᵢ_ᵤ road, but its shutters were up and therᵉ ⁻ ᵤ notice saying that it was for sale. A little farther on, near the throughway, stood a big thatched roadhouse that offered instant grills cooked over a wood fire.

The shape of a town
Changes faster, alas, than a living heart.
She said it aloud: '*The shape of a town*
            Changes faster, alas, than a living heart.
When I was young I thought those lines very dreary—pompous and dreary. Now they quite haunt me.'

'Your father doesn't want to sell his house,' Marc said. 'Of course he would find it very hard to see it pulled down so soon. But I think he's wrong. They say that building is going to slow down. It may be a very long time before he has such a good offer again.'

Papa had waved goodbye, standing in front of the door of the old people's home until the car turned into the road at the end of the long drive. That was twenty-five miles back, and these were the first words that Marc and Cécile had spoken since.

'He mustn't sell it so quickly,' Cécile said. 'We don't know yet whether he may not feel like going back there in the spring. It's too early to know what he really wants to do.' She had put the last of the garden's rain-soaked dahlias in the boot of the car.

'He'll never go back and live in his own house,' said Marc. 'I'm absolutely convinced of that.'

'Who would ever have believed that such a habit-loving man as my father would sweep fifty years of his life away just like that?'

'You and your father are very much alike,' Marc said. 'Unless you can keep the lot you don't want any of it.'

'He didn't even want any of the photos,' Cécile said. 'He said his room would soon be as crowded as the house. Apart from his bed, he didn't want anything.'

They had changed places. Cécile put her hand on the gear-lever and paused. She could see her father, alone in front of the old people's home, waving goodbye. She could no longer hold back her tears. Marc was smoking. He lowered the window on his side and with his left hand he pressed Cécile's.

The house next door had been pulled down since Maman's death. The real estate agent had his eye on the fine corner site adjoining the one he had already bought. He had turned up at the house at almost the same time as the undertakers. They had put him out; he had written; and no sooner had Papa settled in the old people's home than he returned to the attack. They had repulsed him once more, but if Papa gave way, within a month there would be a building site there instead of the house in which the old people had lived for fifty years. It was said that the whole of the hill at Vrigny was being sold for enormous prices too, because there was a plan to establish a cement plant there that would distribute its white dust all over the village and the vine-yards and the cemetery in the open fields. It was said that

266

in a hundred years' time there would be no hills left round Vrigny.

Behind the little road they had just driven along still lay real country, with houses big enough to hold several generations at once, and lanes lined with trees where almost the only traffic now was carts.

'I don't think I can manage to drive,' Cécile said.

'Of course you can,' said Marc. And he kept his hand on his wife's until she said, 'I'm all right now.'

There was a slight traffic jam and a moment's hesitant waiting at the junction with the throughway, and then the car sped like an automaton through rolling country, woods and grassland at seventy or eighty miles an hour under the immense sky, without coming across a single house, a single man, a single beast or a single crossroads, sometimes passing another car, sometimes being passed with a swishing sound. It sped straight across that unpeopled countryside which called forth a strange remote affection, bearing a silent woman at the wheel, who watched the speedometer and from time to time lifted her foot from the accelerator to bring the needle below eighty, and beside her a man who smoked and said nothing either; they were both pale and their eyes were fixed upon the green of the fields, the gold of the woods, the grey of the sky and the succession of curves and straight lines that appeared before their unseeing gaze; they were obeying the motion of their machine rather than governing it; slowing down, stopping reluctantly to throw two coins into the bag at the checkpoint and light up the green light, and off again along an ancient road towards the spires of the next town, which fortunately could not be bypassed.

To their surprise they found nobody in the flat. And Laura had not even written them one of her usual little notes.

Cécile discovered that the children had bought nothing either for dinner or for the next day. It was Sunday. She had not the energy to go out again and find shops—God knows where—that might still be open. Their daughters could not have cared less. All right. Those girls could have dinner wherever they damn well liked and pay for it out of their pocket-money. There were still two eggs in the refrigerator and a little soup and some rusks. It was enough for Marc's dinner. All she wanted to do was to go to bed. She reflected that her father would already have had his meal and that his first long evening by himself was now beginning. His place at the flat was empty, cruelly free of his weakness that they did not know how to protect.

'Where do you think the girls are?' Marc asked.

'Out enjoying themselves,' Cécile said.

But Marc was worried. 'I'm surprised Laura at least isn't here. And you say they haven't done the shopping?'

'They probably went to bed late last night and got up late this morning. Or else each thought the other had done it.'

'It's not very kind,' Marc said.

But this desertion neither vexed nor worried her. What she saw was a big, comfortable room, devoid of curtains or carpet, with strip-lighting, and broad corridors with the white-clad nuns passing back and forth and the wavering, ghostly figures of the inhabitants of the home. Papa would sleep in his own bed, surrounded by a few books, a few photographs and a few knick-knacks hastily assembled there despite him. Night had fallen on the old house a mile away. Maman's spectacles were still on the sideboard, her clothes hung side by side in her wardrobe; but Papa had unhooked her bag from the coat peg and had taken the family papers and the jewel-box with him—'You two will look into all this a little later, one day when you're passing.' François had sent the piano off to Bordeaux for his daughter. Cécile had taken two little chairs to Paris. The parents' double bed had left their room. There were now a few gaps in the house, but Cécile had covered them with other things, so that everything still looked in order. The discoloured patches on the wallpaper did not show: it was not yet really the end. Papa watched the nuns; he had never seen so many starched coifs all at once. He was respectful, timid—'Are they going to let me stay?'—bowing low, conciliating, so conciliating. 'I think I shall settle down. I shall settle down quite easily.' 'They serve meals in your room. I prefer that. I shall be a bit lonely, but then I should be lonely at home too.' A very old woman came up to them. 'What time is it? Is the gentleman going away already? He was such a good neighbour.' A nun led her off, laughing with her as though they were children in the same class, and saying, 'Why, you can see he's only just come!' Embarrassed, they looked away. 'There are a few invalids on my floor,' Papa said. 'But the people higher up seem quite fit. They walk about all over the place. I had a chat with a very nice man; he was an orchestral conductor, but he's as deaf as a post.' Papa laughed. 'We had one of those absurd conversations, neither understanding the other. But perhaps we'll take a walk together one of these days.' Papa waved goodbye, standing in front of the old people's home.

Stéphane's room was empty. Cécile could no longer tell what was missing—her child, or her father, or some weakness, some burden that had been beyond her strength, or love. The room was awaiting some as yet unknown completion.

Marc telephoned the children's friends. 'They don't happen to be with you, do they?' No one had seen them.

Everything completely changed from one generation to

another. How could Papa adapt himself to the rhythm of Paris, to the rhythm of this family with its telephone calls in the middle of meals and in the middle of the night, its comings and goings, its turbulence, its wild notion of time, and everyone doing just what he liked? And how could they adapt themselves to Papa's rhythm?

Marc kept on telephoning. 'Oh, stop it, Marc. This isn't the first time we've found nobody at home.'

Marc grunted.

'If you like we'll have dinner right away, we'll eat the eggs, and then I'll go to bed.'

'You'll be able to move into Stéphane's room now,' Marc said. 'You'll be happier there.'

'Yes, perhaps. Certainly, if the room stays empty I'll take it over. But tonight I'm going to sleep in my den again. I haven't put sheets back on the bed—all I did was to take Papa's off.'

'You must move in tomorrow,' Marc said.

'Yes, tomorrow, perhaps. You don't mind eating rusks?'

Marc looked glum. 'I suppose I'll have to if there's no bread.'

'Would you like to go out and get some?'

'No.'

'I haven't the energy either.'

It was while she was waiting for the eggs to boil that the telephone rang. Suddenly uneasy, Cécile rushed into the nearest bedroom—Nathalie's. But Marc had already taken the call in his. In their respective receivers, each heard Laura's calm voice asking whether they had got back all right and whether things had gone well with Grandpa. Behind this calm they sensed some disaster, and they asked as one: 'What's happened? Where are you both? Tell us quickly, Laura.'

And Laura said, 'It's nothing serious. I can tell you right

away it's nothing serious.' But Laura could not go on because she was crying, and at the other end of the line Marc gave a kind of a shuddering cry like a wounded animal, just as he had done that morning when Cécile called him to show that Stéphane could not stand up and he had realized that something dreadful had happened, before he had even seen Stéphane. Laura could not reply: she just kept repeating 'It's nothing, it's nothing.'

'Nathalie?' they asked.

'She's here—she's all right.' But there was nothing more to be heard—only sobs. Then another voice, quite calm, that said, 'Hallo? This is Alain. Don't be alarmed. Everything is all right now. But we had rather a scare this morning. Nathalie took too many sleeping pills last night and she couldn't wake up. Laura phoned your doctor, but he wasn't there, so she phoned me. Luckily I was at home and I came round at once: I managed to take Nathalie to the Pitié hospital—I know everybody there. She's come round now, and she's awake. But they're going to keep her in tonight to examine her. If you'd like to come . . .'

'We're coming,' they said. 'We're coming immediately.'

'Laura will wait for you at the entrance and show you the way. I have to go home now,' Alain said.

They did not get as far as the garage. A taxi was going by just as they came into the street. 'The Pitié hospital,' said Marc. 'Quick.' Then, as the cab moved off, 'Did you know Nathalie took sleeping pills?'

'No,' said Cécile. 'As far as I know she doesn't.'

'Has something happened between her and Jo?'

'I just don't know.'

The taxi was driving fast. 'Oh!' cried Cécile, 'I forgot to turn off the gas. We must go back.'

'No,' said Marc. 'No. Never mind.'

'But what if the water boils over and puts it out?'

'Is it full on?'

'Only enough to keep the water simmering.'

'Then it won't boil over,' said Marc. 'Don't let's waste any more time.'

'I'm frightened,' said Cécile.

'Don't be frightened: Alain and Laura told us the truth. She's out of danger now, if indeed there ever was any.'

But the water had boiled over and put out the gas. The gas was escaping: the kitchen windows were shut. The gas was filling the whole flat. It was seeping into the rest of the building. The taxi drove on at full speed, as they had asked. Someone rang the door-bell and the whole building exploded. Cécile had lost control. She had given way. It was too difficult. She had had to look after too many people at once. Nathalie had been taken off to hospital unconscious that very morning. She had not taken those sleeping pills to make her sleep. That was nonsense. She had wanted to die. Once Laura had left them too and run away, and they had not noticed anything amiss. Nathalie had been so sad she had wanted to die. They had been giving all their attention to Papa these days. They had forgotten the others. The gas was escaping in the flat. The taxi drove on. Everything came to an end, disintegrated, blew up. It was really too difficult. A family was really too difficult.

'But,' said Marc, 'if she meant to do something stupid, for whatever reason, how we have failed!'

Failed.

They were already driving along by the river. Too late to turn back. What a failure, what a failure.

'We must keep the taxi and send Laura back right away and tell her not to turn the light on as she goes in.'

Marc's hand was still there on the seat. Nothing was left but Marc's hand, Marc's hand, Marc's hand.

The taxi drew up. The hospital forecourt was dark. There

was a dark form by one of the pillars. It was Laura waiting for them: she kissed them, comforted them—'It's all right, it's all right.'

'Can you wait a minute?' Cécile asked the taxi-driver. 'To take our daughter home?'

The driver looked surly. 'One minute, not more.'

'What happened, Laura? Tell us quickly.'

Laura hesitated. 'Well, it wasn't quite as Alain said. This morning I got up very late. And Nathalie told me to have breakfast without her—she didn't want to get up today— she was feeling blue—she was worn out. I left her in peace. But while I was washing she came into the bathroom and said, "I'm dying." She was dreadfully pale, and she could scarcely stand. She told me to listen to her heart. It was awful, the way it thumped. She said, "Call the doctor. Tell him I've taken some pills." I phoned but there was only the answering service. When I went to tell Nathalie she couldn't speak any more. So I rang Alain. He asked me what she had taken but I didn't know, so he said, "I'll be round at once," and when he saw her he brought her straight here—we managed to get her downstairs between us. Now they all say there's no danger. She can talk now. I'll take you to her.'

'Do you know if anything happened between her and Jo?' asked Marc.

'No,' said Laura. 'I don't know.'

'You must go home at once,' said Cécile. 'I've left the gas alight under a saucepan of water. I'm worried. I'm afraid the water may have boiled over and put it out and the gas will be escaping. You must go straight to the kitchen without putting the lights on anywhere, anywhere, do you hear, not even in the hall. You must see whether the gas is still alight, and if it's out you must turn it off at once and open the window as wide as it'll go. Listen carefully, Laura, it's very important—you must open the window as wide as it'll go and then open all the other windows; wait a little before you turn on the light, and breathe the air from outside. Do just what I say, or the whole building may blow up.'

'Did Alain say anything else?' asked Marc.

'No. You'd never believe how kind he has been. He stayed with Nathalie and me the whole time. When he left he said to me, "I'll come back and see Nathalie tomorrow if she'd like me to. If not, I shan't. But tell her I'd do anything for her, remember—anything at all." ' Laura was crying again.

'Take us to her now,' said Cécile. 'And then go straight home. I'm terrified of that gas.'

'She's coming back right away,' Marc told the taxi-driver. 'Right away.'

They went along corridors and through a big darkened ward where dim lights showed several rows of beds, with sheeted bodies that moved like a swell as they stirred with their night-time breathing and harsh gasps. In a kind of recess next to a corridor a man and a woman sat watching on either side of a pillar bed where a tiny face lay on the pillow. Child? Old man? Corpse?

'She's in the third ward,' Laura whispered.

They tiptoed on through the dimness, the moist atmosphere and the breathing. Among these suffering bodies they tiptoed as fast as they could towards the one that belonged to them. 'She's right at the end,' Laura said again, when they reached the third ward.

A bed had been added, outside the row and almost touching the wall, and there, by the light of a nearby lamp, they saw their daughter. She lay with her hair as lank as if she had been drowned, her misty eyes sunken, two great patches of shadow on her shrunken face, and her wild look. Their gaze enveloped her. She looked at them from a great way off and said nothing. For a moment they stood there

274

motionless at the foot of the bed, a little withdrawn from it, guilty, guilty, guilty, while Laura leant over her sister in a motherly way and said, 'Here are the parents, you see. I have to go home, Nathalie darling. But you can sleep now— the doctor says everything will be all right. I'll come and see you tomorrow after my morning classes. And Alain says he'll come too, if you'd like him to. Shall I phone and tell him to come?'

Nathalie only moved her head: no, she did not want Alain to come. A little way off there was a screen round a bed. Six feet from their child, someone was in the act of dying.

In their turn they kissed her. She was still cold and their kisses did not reach her. 'What on earth made you do such a thing?' Marc asked, and once more he shuddered from head to foot.

She was not wholly back from the edge of death: she still had its remoteness, its reproachful look.

There was a moaning somewhere in the ward, and from another direction a flood of meaningless words answered it. Then the breathing, the snores and the night sounds took over again.

'Was there a reason for it?' asked Cécile.

'Yes, there was,' Nathalie breathed, and although she did not make the slightest movement the reproach that emanated from her overwhelmed them. She added, 'I really thought I was going to die.'

All this took perhaps a minute. For the space of a minute they looked mutely at this child of theirs who was rejecting them and who still bore the trace of death on her face. 'I really thought I was going to die.' The words went round and round in Cécile's mind, arousing a vague surprise, doubt and questioning: what was it that didn't ring true? And all at once Cécile realized that their daughter had not meant to kill herself. It had only been a woman's trouble—a fear so great that anything is worth trying to get away from it. It was life, the terrible life of women. It was only life.

'You must go now, Laura,' she said.

Laura kissed Nathalie again. 'There, my darling. Now you are going to sleep and tomorrow you'll be home with all of us.'

Laura must surely know what the trouble was. Today a girl of seventeen kept her head in such circumstances. She knew how to behave with the right kind of affection and struck just the right note. A girl of seventeen was a help to her mother, and an example.

Cécile went as far as the door of the ward with Laura. This was not death; it was only life. They would cope with the situation; take the necessary decisions, do something, get Nathalie out of this. Thank God, it was only life. She could hardly wait to tell Marc. 'Above all, don't switch on the light as you go in. Don't forget, Laura. Oh, perhaps I had better come back with you.'

But Laura said, 'No, I won't forget. Why on earth should I? You stay with Nathalie a while.'

And Cécile knew that Laura would go on behaving admirably. 'Did she really call for me?'

'Why, of course she did, Mama. You stay with her. I won't forget—I won't switch on the light as I go in.'

Behind her Cécile could feel the grey ocean of the ward—a sea into which she was going to dive to save Nathalie. For a moment longer she looked intently at her youngest child's anxious, worn face. She saw her strength, her intelligence and her maturity. She drank her in with her eyes. 'Goodbye, darling. I don't know when we'll be back but don't worry. Go to sleep. Everything will be all right. We'll get Nathalie out of this.'

She saw childhood reappear in Laura's eyes; she saw the

276

child's relief—Mother has come home, Mother isn't cross, Mother will know what to do. She stroked Laura's cheek. 'You were very clever to phone Alain. How lucky he was there. You did exactly the right thing.'

Marc had found a chair. He was sitting with bowed head, holding Nathalie's hand in both his. He stood up when Cécile came back. 'Here,' he said, 'sit down.' Then he leant over the bed, sorrowfully kissing his daughter's hand before letting it go. Cécile could not manage to catch his eye to convey what she knew. An extraordinary energy had returned to her, an energy that was not unlike a kind of rapture. 'How do you feel now?' she asked Nathalie.

'I'm still afraid,' she said. 'It seems to me that my heart's no longer beating. Do please see the doctor.' She spoke without making the slightest movement, still as though she were speaking from some other plane where she was imprisoned, rigid with horror, weightless. And indeed they ought to see the doctor and make sure that the danger was over.

'Don't be afraid,' they said. 'Alain has assured us that everything is all right. Alain wouldn't have left you if it hadn't been. You know Alain wouldn't have left you.' She nodded vaguely. 'But we'll go and see the doctor and then we'll come straight back. We'll go this minute. Don't worry. We'll come back.'

Once again they tiptoed through the dimness and the sound of breathing. Cécile stopped. 'You go ahead, Marc. I'll catch you up.'

She went back to Nathalie, and this time at last she managed to take hold of her, to seize her firmly and to wrench her out of this frozen state. 'Why isn't Jo here?' she asked.

'He's on tour in Japan.'

'Does he know?' asked Cécile.

'No,' said Nathalie.

Marc was far away at the end of the ward, disappearing into the corridor. Behind the screen a couple of paces from Nathalie death made no sound. But suffering, sleeplessness and disturbed dreams filled the ward with a low general murmur. If anxiety and grief were not keeping him awake Papa was sleeping in the old people's home. Laura was going into the flat and remembering that she was not to switch on the light. 'Don't forget, Laura.' Deep night was covering the cemetery at Vrigny. Nathalie's forlorn body relaxed in her mother's arms.

'What did you take?' asked Cécile.

'Some pills.'

'What pills?'

Nathalie mentioned a name that meant nothing to her mother.

'Who told you about them?'

'A girl.'

'And all they did was to make you feel like death?'

'Yes,' said Nathalie.

'Couldn't you have told me about it first? Couldn't you have talked to me?' But Nathalie still looked at her mother from a great way off, only with a somewhat puzzled expression. 'Are you even quite certain?' Nathalie nodded again. Cécile gently rocked this fragile, almost inanimate body, which held another eager, stubborn life. 'Don't worry,' she said. 'Everything will work out all right.' Her hands were already reaching out for this child of youth, as lovely as freedom itself. 'We'll talk it over together, don't worry. We'll do whatever you like. You'll be the one to decide. And whatever you decide will be all right. It's life, thank God, it's only life.'

The shadow of a smile appeared on Nathalie's face. 'You're not too cross, Mama?'

'Oh, darling.'

'You go and see the doctor too. Ask him whether those pills have done any damage. I shouldn't like to have a monster, you see,' she ended in a whisper.

That was something Cécile knew about. 'Oh, no,' she said. 'You really don't have to worry. When these things don't succeed there are never any ill effects.' She paused, then went on firmly, 'No ill effects as regards the child.'

She saw that well-known flash light up and disappear in Nathalie's eyes. 'You're quite sure?'

'Quite sure. Can I leave you now?'

Nathalie nodded. 'But you'll come back?' she said.

Cécile caught up with Marc in the hall. He was waiting for the sister to deal with the admission of a young woman whose beautiful, smiling face was all that could be seen above the blanket as she lay on the stretcher on the ground. The sister grew impatient. 'It's urgent. We'll see to the formalities later. Take her up to the operating-theatre. At once, I tell you.' The young woman opened her eyes and cast a look of familiarity at her surroundings. They carried her away.

'Lord help us,' said the sister, 'ten times a day we have this sort of thing.'

'Even nowadays?' asked Cécile.

The sister shrugged. 'Oh dear me yes, even nowadays. More than ever. I don't know what they're thinking about.' Then she looked at Marc and Cécile. 'What can I do for you?'

'We are Mademoiselle Verdier's parents,' said Marc. 'A girl who was admitted today, about one o'clock.'

'Just a moment,' said the sister. A police car swept into the forecourt and a stretcher was brought out. 'An emergency,' said the sister into the telephone. 'Hurry up. Yes, at once.' They carried the injured man away. The sister came back. 'Yes?' she said.

'She's the girl who had taken an overdose of sleeping pills,' Marc said, stumbling over his words a little.

The sister paused a moment before answering, 'Oh yes. But she's quite all right now.'

'Even so, we'd like to see the doctor,' Marc said.

'The house-physician? Well, he's busy just now.' She made a gesture that meant *you saw for yourselves, didn't you?* and went on, 'If you don't mind waiting. But it may be a long time.' She left them to go and sort a heap of papers, dropping her task from time to time to speak on the telephone.

Marc lit a cigarette. 'It wasn't a suicide attempt, you know,' said Cécile.

Marc's cigarette paused in mid-air. 'How do you know? Did she tell you something?'

'She's pregnant.'

Marc went on smoking. 'Are you sure?' he asked after a while.

'Yes,' said Cécile.

'But . . .' said Marc. Then he stopped.

'But what?'

'Is that why she tried to kill herself?'

'She didn't try to kill herself. She has never tried to kill herself.'

Marc remained silent for another moment, then he said heavily, 'So it was an abortion attempt?'

'Oh,' said Cécile, 'that's a very big word. As I see it, all she meant to do was to convince herself that she wasn't pregnant.'

'You have put it beautifully,' said Marc. Then he added, 'In that case, I don't see why there's no young man with her at this moment. It's not us she needs: it's a man.'

'Alain was here all day,' said Cécile. And as she said it a terrifying idea came into her mind. Suppose Alain was the father of this child? Suppose there had been some dreadful quarrel between Jo and Nathalie and Nathalie had thrown herself at Alain to put an end to it and start another life for herself? Suppose she had been so stupid, so wrong, as to do that . . .

'You don't mean Alain might be . . .'

'That's what I'm wondering about, all of a sudden.'

'No,' said Marc. 'Alain would have stayed with her. He would have waited for us. Alain knows how to face up to his own responsibilities.'

'Yes,' Cécile said. 'You're right. Alain would have waited for us.'

'Where's the other fellow?'

'In Japan, it seems. He knows nothing about it.'

Marc nodded, threw away his cigarette and said, 'In any case, whichever it is, Alain or Jo, or whoever, or both of them, I'd rather have it this way. I'd rather have anything than that.' He looked at Cécile with his defenceless eyes. 'Wouldn't you?' he asked.

'Yes,' she said. 'Anything rather than that. But still, I'd rather it were Jo.'

The sister came and asked whether they would like to wait in her office. They accepted, and while she was typing, sorting papers and telephoning, they did not speak. At last, when Cécile was beginning to wonder whether she ought to go back to Nathalie, who might be getting anxious, the sister said that the doctor was coming. Already they could hear him crossing the forecourt when Marc asked, 'What was the result?'

'Nothing,' said Cécile. 'These drugs never work, as you know.'

Marc nodded, with the expression of one who did in fact know.

The house-physician quickly explained that Nathalie had not been in real danger—that the dose she had taken was not enough to be dangerous—and that the student who had brought her in had rather lost his head. They could go home with easy minds. They would keep their daughter in the hospital a day or two for examination, but there was no need for them to worry.

'And will she stay in that ward?' asked Marc.

'Yes,' said the doctor. 'There's no private room free.' And again he said, 'Just for a day or two.'

'Thank you, doctor,' they said. He was already moving off. He had maintained professional secrecy throughout. Cécile ran after him. 'There won't be any ill effects, will there? I can reassure her on that score?' The doctor stopped and looked at her. 'I mean, what she took won't hurt the child?'

'Oh,' said the doctor; then he added, 'Don't worry. She might just as well have taken aspirin.'

They were going in the direction of the ward again when the sister called, 'Where are you off to now?'

'We are going to say goodbye to her.'

She hesitated. 'Well, all right, but don't stay long. At this time of night it disturbs the ward, you see. And the patients complain.'

Nathalie's eyes were still open, but their expression was less vague. 'Well?' she said.

'Relax. It's going to be quite all right. Perfectly all right.' The three of them formed an island in the midst of sleep and death and there was a curious gaiety in their little group.

'Really? You're not hiding anything from me?'

'Of course not,' they said. 'Nothing. Nothing at all. Do

you think we'd leave you here like this if we were worried about you?'

'I can't help being afraid.'

'Don't be. The doctor told us quite definitely that there would be no ill effects of any kind, none whatsoever.'

'None whatsoever,' Marc repeated firmly.

'Go to sleep, darling, rest, don't keep thinking about things. We'll talk it all over together—we'll make up our minds together. Whatever you decide will be right. We'll help you. Go to sleep now. Put everything out of your mind. Everything will be all right. Don't be afraid. We'll talk it over tomorrow.'

They were ashamed of whispering there in the darkness, amid the groaning and the sleep of all these people who were alone, really ill, given over to their nightmares and their distress. How many beds in each ward? Forty? Sixty? For that night they would have to leave their child in the midst of this suffering community into which she had flung herself. And the idea did not altogether displease them.

'Would you like us to bring you anything tomorrow?'

'Some oranges,' said Nathalie.

They left her. On tiptoe once again they made their way through the sickly gloom that enveloped their daughter; but already they no longer belonged to it. They were returning to the light, to the side where life goes on.

'It's a catastrophe, none the less,' they said when they were outside. And in the taxi: 'Whether they marry or not, how are they going to manage to bring up this child?'

'We shall have to help them.'

'We certainly will.'

'But compared to what might have happened . . .'

'Let's wait for Jo to come back.'

'They're the ones to decide. It's up to them to make up their minds.'

They were tired: all they wanted was to g to sleep.
'Still,' Marc said after a pause, 'she might havᴼ
you, rather than to a friend. Or haven't things really
changed?'

'You heard what the nurse said,' Cécile answered. She
rubbed her forehead and her eyes, and went on, 'It's not
the sort of thing a girl tells her mother. Not yet. There's
nothing to be done about it.'

Everything was shifting and sliding in her mind. The old
order in which she had been brought up was cracking:
perhaps it was not so much an ethical system as mere
orderliness; but for the moment the most conspicuous
aspect of this want of order was less the freedom of women
than their everlasting tragedy.

'Still,' she said, 'at least the whole thing is based on love.
At least she and Jo love each other.'

'And if she wants an abortion,' said Marc, 'shall we help
her?'

'She won't want one,' Cécile said.

Her hands were already reaching out for this child,
already protecting this marvellous baby that would be as
beautiful as Nathalie, and as Jo, and as Emmanuel, this
gifted child, this lily of the fields. But at the same time she
made a little movement as though to keep it at a distance.
It would be even better to go on with my translations and
give Nathalie the money, she thought. I can't undertake the
bringing up of this child. Nathalie can do what she likes.

'It's better that Maman should never have known about
this,' she said to herself later. 'Heavens, what an upset a
thing like this would have meant in my parents' home.'

How old was Maman at the beginning of the war? Fifty-
one, fifty-two? A few years older than she was at present.
Just when she ought to have been able to take things easy,
she found herself hemmed in by work again. She had con-

trived a way of transforming old sheets by putting sides to middle with a bit of lace. She took the outer skin off haricot beans, one by one, and crushed these to make cakes. And after that she had been quite unable to relinquish brooms, saucepans, knitting-needles. She had never recovered from that war which came upon her at a time when she was still young enough to have returned to her golden age. No one had been able to prevent her from being on the go; what is more, no one had ever seriously tried; all they had done was to weep over those beautiful dead hands, now at last folded and at rest.

A few more years, Cécile thought, and I shall go the same way if I don't watch out. Is there always something in families that happens at the critical moment and tightens the bonds again?

'All the same,' said Marc, 'I don't understand a young fellow getting a girl pregnant if he hasn't at least made up his mind to live with her.'

'That's the way they are these days,' said Cécile. And instantly she was angry with herself for this betrayal. 'But at least they do love each other,' she went on. 'Our two do love each other.'

'It's all very well kicking public opinion in the teeth,' said Marc. And shrugged.

'Let's wait and see what they decide to do.'

Laura was waiting for them at the flat. The gas had not leaked. Everything was as it should be. There were still flowers in the vases: there were still potted plants and bright gilding and carpets. Laura had turned down their beds for the night.

'Everything OK?' she asked.

'Yes, fine.'

'Did you see the doctor again?'

'Yes. He said there was absolutely no danger and never

had been. You go to bed, sweetheart. You've had a rough day too.'

'The eggs were boiled hard as rocks,' Laura said. 'I've got them ready and cut some bread and butter. I'm sure you haven't had any supper. And then I went to the Italian's. His shop was still open. I brought you some cheese and fruit. You haven't told me how Grandpa is.'

'He's all right,' said Cécile. 'He has a fine big room with a wonderful view over the park. The nuns are very kind. I think he'll like it there; I think he'll stay.'

Shadowy forms moved along the corridor of the old people's home, far, far away. 'You mustn't think that all this depresses me,' Papa had said. 'On the contrary: I tell myself that perhaps I shall not become as difficult as some of the people here and that the nuns are kind—they never send anyone away.' The nuns were cheerful, the park magnificent. Papa had always been given to thought and meditation and he would get used to being alone; Papa was proud; he was self-sufficient. In the chapel the nuns sang with truly angelic voices.

'Perhaps it isn't such a bad idea to go and end one's days in a place like that, far from any noise or fuss,' said Cécile. 'Maybe Grandpa's right. For two pins . . .'

There was Nathalie in the thick atmosphere of a public ward's suffering, the prisoner of her own body, Nathalie who had said, 'Life ought to be fun all the time.' Was Nathalie now no more than an abandoned pregnant girl? There at least things had changed. They would not make a great fuss about it. One way or another they would get Nathalie out of this.

There were three of them left, sitting round the brightly-lit table which Laura had laid for them with bread and butter and the hard-boiled eggs and fruit. They were hungry.

'That old people's home sounds pretty much Grandpa's style,' Laura said. 'But if Nathalie gets married and now that Stéphane's gone, there'll be plenty of room for him here if he doesn't like it.' She said this in her comfortable voice and they stroked her hands, which were still as chubby as a baby's: they saw her as they had seen her transformed a few hours ago, her face refined by anxiety and sorrow, her slightly tip-tilted nose duplicating the enchanting curve of her lip, her hair all over her forehead and ears, like leaves through which the freshness of her skin gleamed, and her huge clear eyes: she was so kind, so wholly understanding and so much an innocent girl, yet they could already sense in her a strong, comforting womanliness—the mother of the weak and the romantic—something the world could not yet do without.

'Do you think Nathalie will get married?' they asked her.

'Yes, I do.'

'To Jo?'

'Who else?'

'Then perhaps they may want Stéphane's room for a while,' said Marc. 'Until Stéphane comes back, if that would suit them. In that way Nathalie could finish her course in peace.'

'Anyway,' said Cécile, 'nothing is going to stop me going to see Stéphane in Cuba this spring.'

Marc looked flabbergasted. 'But you never even mentioned such a trip. I don't know that this is quite the moment for it.'

'Oh,' Cécile said, 'if I wait until it's quite the moment . . . I want to see the United States before I die. And Cuba. This spring, while Stéphane's still there. While there is no war.'